COLD WINTER SUN

TONY J FORDER

Book 2 in the Mike Lynch Action-Adventure Series

Copyright © 2021 Tony Forder

The right of Tony Forder to be identified as the Author of the Work has been asserted by him in accordance Copyright, Designs and Patents Act 1988.

First published in 2018 by Bloodhound Books
This version published in 2021 by Spare Nib Books

Apart from any use permitted under UK copyright law, this publication may only be reproduced, stored, or transmitted, in any form, or by any means, with prior permission in writing of the publisher or, in the case of reprographic production, in accordance with the terms of licences issued by the Copyright Licensing Agency.
All characters in this publication are fictitious and any resemblance to real persons, living or dead, is purely coincidental.

tonyjforder.com
tony@tonyjforder.com

Original version Published by Bloodhound Books in 2018. Publication withdrawn in 2020.

Also by Tony J Forder

The DI Bliss Series
Bad to the Bone
The Scent of Guilt
If Fear Wins
The Reach of Shadows
The Death of Justice
Endless Silent Scream
Slow Slicing
Bliss Uncovered (prequel novella)

Standalone
Fifteen Coffins
Degrees of Darkness

Previously Published Mike Lynch Series
Scream Blue Murder

To my readers – with much thanks.

FORWARD

When the rights to a previously published book are returned, you have to make a few decisions. Firstly, do you want to publish it yourself? Secondly, if so, do you want to make changes to it?

The answer to the first came easily: absolutely. As for the second question, that was a little more difficult to answer. I've learned a lot since I first wrote this book, and hopefully I'm a better writer than I was then. But I had to consider the danger that I might lose its essence and edit out the better parts – yes, that really is a thing! So, having initially believed I would set about this book with the red pen, I decided to make only minor improvements, leaving the vast majority exactly as originally published.

I loved writing this book. In particular I enjoyed the freedom to 'purple-up' my prose at times, and to simply write to entertain. Ultimately, I felt the only way I could remain true to that was by keeping it largely as I originally wrote it, other than the obligatory edit and proofread.

Tony
March 2021

PROLOGUE

The man with the shiny blue suit and the red Senco nail gun circled his prey like a shark sensing a floundering seal in the water. He took his time, casual strides echoing on the cold, tiled floor.

'Tell me,' he said to the man squirming in the wooden chair in the centre of the room.

The man looked up at him but remained mute. Sweat dripped from his high hairline. His face was bloodied, already starting to balloon and darken and pucker. One eye was severely bloodshot, little white showing through the ugly inflammation. Both of his ankles were taped to separate chair legs. The adhesive tugged at stray hairs, but that was the least of his problems. He couldn't reach down to adjust the tape because his wrists were nailed to his knees. The man's skin glistened with sweat, and a thick mixture of blood, mucus and tears dripped slowly from his chin onto his lap. He had cried out when the nails went in; howls resulting from both the agonising pain of the moment, and the overwhelming fear of what was to come. But there was no point in continuing with his yowls of misery. No one was going to hear him, no matter how loud his shrieks, no matter how severe the suffering.

The abattoir had stood idle for the better part of three years. Windows boarded up with treated wood or corrugated sheets of iron allowed little light to spill into the main areas where twenty men had once worked. In the centre of these vast rooms, steel hooks caked in dried blood still hung from the ceiling like macabre pendants, swaying menacingly whenever the building settled on its foundations or a stray breeze cut through gaps around the doors and windows. The scuttling of inquisitive creatures caused mournful echoes in the gloom, and the dense shadows seemed to retreat at the sound.

Although the old abattoir itself was now nothing more than a bleak and empty shell, and the man in the shiny suit had need of neither secrecy nor quiet in this secluded location, he nonetheless chose to use the basement. There he had his own workbench of planed hardwood and stainless steel, as well as a narrow table upon which the tools of his trade sat gleaming beneath a bank of lights powered by a small generator. The work that he carried out there was often noisy, always satisfyingly messy, and he had discovered the basement to be perfect for both. Its cavernous rooms allowed for the most delightful echoes, while its slick tiled floor and drainage facilities made cleaning up afterwards a relatively simple affair.

In the heart of the desert, alongside a dried-up creek that had once claimed almost as many lives as it had vehicles, nestled the old Harrold buildings, in which the man with the nail gun had carried out some of his very best work. Across the uninspiring terrain, the desolate site could be seen from several miles away and from all directions; an unobstructed view of a dark smudge on a grey landscape. Its inactivity was a stark and unwelcome reminder of more prosperous days, yet in time people would come to realise that it had been busy after all.

'Tell me,' Nail Gun said again. His movements were languid, his manner calm and unhurried. He was a patient man who enjoyed his work.

'Tell you what?!' the man in the chair screamed at him this time, throwing his head back and rocking from side to side. 'I don't understand what you want of me.'

Nail Gun stopped walking. He peered down at his captive, and the corners of his mouth curled upwards. 'Tell me,' he said.

The man in the chair shook his head, sweat flying from his damp hair, pink ribbons of spittle from his lips. 'You keep saying those two words. This is not fucking *Marathon Man*. If you tell me what you want me to tell you, then I'll tell you what you want to know.'

Nail Gun glanced across the room at a small, bony man standing back in the shadows, wielding a ballpein hammer as if it were an extension of his arm. His suit was equally shiny, only grey and ill-fitting.

'*Marathon Man*?' Nail Gun said, arching his eyebrows.

'Lawrence Olivier film, boss,' Ballpein said. 'Nazi war criminals. He tortures a bloke asking only "Is it safe?"'

'Is it safe? Is what safe?'

'Exactly, boss.'

'Ah, I see. So, how?'

'How what?'

'How does he torture the man?'

'Teeth, boss.'

'Interesting,' Nail Gun said. He regarded the man with the nails through his wrists and knees the way a sculptor might study a rough block of marble. 'I've never done teeth before. You could be my first customer. No charge.'

The bloodied man closed his eyes and wept, shoulders heaving. He was a big specimen, now shrunken by all he had endured. 'Look, all you have to do is ask the question properly. Fully, so that I understand what it is you want from me.'

Nail Gun nodded, pursing his lips. Glanced across at Ballpein. 'Hear that? I'm being taught interrogation techniques by a man who couldn't avoid having nails driven into his body this afternoon.'

Ballpein nodded and shrugged expansively.

'Tell me,' Nail Gun said again, his eyes drilling into those of the man in the chair.

'Tell you what, though? Tell you what?! I don't fucking understand why you won't just say what it is you want to know!'

Nail Gun took a step closer and leaned in, holding the Senco tool like a pistol and aiming it directly between the other man's fevered eyes. Nail Gun flashed a predatory smile moments before he spoke.

'Tell me… everything.'

ONE

Standing by my canvas billet on the dome-like crest of a rise, I gazed out across the silver waters of Lochs Burifa' and Long which were both now pockmarked by falling snow. From this same vantage point I could often not only see as far as Dunnet Head, but also way beyond into the thrashing sea. It's the furthest north you can go on mainland Britain without hitting water, and there were crisp, clear days when I was able to stare out across the foaming water at the Orkney Islands some six miles away.

Today was not one of those days.

The snow was falling like scattered confetti upon an already white landscape which for days now had formed frozen and compacted layers. It was light and fluffy, but it was dense and would not melt in the air. Prior to the snowstorms blowing in, the moorlands had been thick with heather and scrub, though fighting a daily battle with the harsh elements. Over the past few days I had hiked for miles through hollows and over rises, exercised until my body could take no more punishment, but I had also taken every opportunity to breathe in the frigid air and repair my mind. There were better seasons in which to visit a place of such natural beauty, but I had chosen this one deliberately.

Over a number of years during which my life did not go according to plan, I had allowed myself to grow both weak and soft, and I believed I needed the mental and physical challenge of surviving out here for as long as I could find food. That particular task had become increasingly difficult over the past forty-eight hours, and as I gazed out of my tent at the thickening white wall falling upon the hoary landscape, I realised that from now on it would probably be impossible.

The bleak Highland terrain I gazed upon had its own beauty in the depths of winter. The monochrome world I now inhabited, that perhaps now also inhabited me to some extent, was stark and impenetrable. My canvas would shield me from the worst of the elements, clothing protect me from the bone-numbing chill of it, and melted snow provide my liquid intake. But no animals strayed these parts when the ice, snow, and strong winds set in, which left the sea as my only remaining source of food. Of course, I could walk the few miles to the closest village and purchase whatever I needed, but that pretty much defeated the object.

Which is? I asked myself for the hundredth time since my arrival. What exactly was the object of all this? Of removing myself from the daily grind and surviving like a recluse in such disagreeable conditions. Was this a further test of my character following the events of those few days back in the summer? Perhaps a way of examining the limits of my endurance. Was it conceivably a way to help sculpt the new version of myself? Or maybe it was a simple matter of seeking the kind of isolation that brought with it a level of mental clarity that could not be achieved in any other way.

Same old questions.

Same lack of answers.

I lowered my gaze, the snow on the ground a blank canvas for my thoughts. I became so lost in them that I almost failed to hear my phone ringing. The signal up here was patchy at best, but I had it connected to a satellite module. Every day I switched the device on for exactly an hour, so as not to drain the battery too quickly. Even so, I was about to ignore the call and switch the phone off when I remembered I had not spoken to my daughter in a week. I took the device from my pocket, smiling when I saw her name on the screen.

'Hiya, kiddo,' I said brightly, despite my sombre mood caused by a sudden adrenaline purge. 'Sorry I haven't been–'

'Mike, it's me. Donna.'

'Donna? What's wrong? Is Wendy okay?'

'Yes, she's fine. This is not about her.'

I exhaled a sigh of relief and saw my breath swarm and coil in the air before being snatched away by a gust of wind that took it back over my head and behind me. I was puzzled as to why my ex-wife was calling, but it didn't matter so long as Wendy was all right.

'Good,' I said, putting a hand to my chest even though she could not see me. 'I can cancel the coronary, then. So what's up, Donna?'

The line went quiet for a moment. It crackled and fizzed a couple of times before she spoke again.

'Mike, there's a problem.'

I felt ice in my veins once more. 'Donna, are you sure Wendy is okay?'

'Yes, she's good, Mike. Honestly.'

'And you? Is this about you, Donna? Are you ill, or something?'

'No, nothing like that. I'm sorry to be calling you, Mike. And now that I am, I'm actually second-guessing myself. Perhaps I shouldn't bother you with this. It's really not your problem after all.'

I heard something in her voice that demanded my full attention. Since we had separated, and subsequently divorced, my ex-wife had asked me for nothing. Literally not a single thing. I paid child support, and from time to time sent Wendy extra money for things she wanted. But Donna had always steered clear of requesting either cash or favours from me. I got the sense this was going to be something consequential.

'Donna, don't worry about whose problem it is. If it was important enough for you to pick up the phone, then it's important enough for you to tell me about it.'

'Yes, of course. Thanks, Mike.'

'No problem. Go on.'

'I have a favour to ask. A pretty big one, actually.'

A severe gust of wind blew in off the sea and found its way across the undulations and hollows, shifting snow along its path and tainting the air with salt particles. I brushed it off my face with a gloved hand.

Donna's words echoed inside my head. 'Fire away,' I told her. 'Don't hold back.'

'You may regret saying that, Mike. Once you hear what it is.'

I felt my eyebrows converge. It was unlike my ex-wife to be so uncertain of herself. Donna was a powerful force of nature, a determined character who spoke her mind and was rarely backwards in coming forwards. I wondered if she might be having problems in her marriage, then immediately dismissed the idea as laughable. I'm the last person she would discuss something as intimate as that with.

Realising the silence had stretched out too long, and that she was waiting for a final confirmation of my interest, I said, 'Donna, you're starting to worry me. Just tell me what it is. We'll deal with any fallout later.'

She cleared her throat. 'It's probably nothing, but Drew is going out of his mind at the moment, as is his sister. Sheryl's son, Vern, is missing. He went away on a two-week vacation, but that was three weeks ago and he hasn't been heard from since. I feel so helpless, Mike, and for reasons even I don't begin to understand, I said I would talk to you and ask if you had any ideas.'

Now I understood her reticence. Drew was Donna's second husband. I didn't know a great deal about him other than the fact he ran a software company and was considered wealthy even by Los Angeles standards. Up until now I hadn't even known he had a sister, let alone a nephew. I brushed aside any unease I might have had about the source of Donna's concern, and instead considered the implications of what she had told me.

'So it's a full week since he should have returned?' I said.

'Yes. He left late on the Friday evening, and should have been back a fortnight later on the Saturday.'

'So it's also Saturday today?'

There was a slight pause. I could imagine her face creasing with unease when she spoke next. 'Mike, where are you? You haven't spoken to Wendy this week, and you don't even seem to know what day it is? Are you okay?'

'I'm fine. I'm camping. The days got away from me is all.'

There was no need to elaborate on the exacting environment I had chosen to go camping in. I thought about what she had told me. A week was a long time to be AWOL. And if Donna was reduced to contacting me, that suggested she was not getting a lot of help from the authorities out there.

'I take it the police are not overly interested in Vern's absence.'

'Not really,' Donna said. 'He's twenty-four. The fact that a man his age has not returned home after a two-week vacation is not regarded as a priority for law enforcement. They did some basic checks, but we felt they were just going through the motions.'

'What about his employers?'

'Drew *is* his employer.'

'Okay. Tell me why you are convinced something is wrong. Wrong enough to call me. This sort of thing is out of character for Vern, I take it.'

'Completely. He's not the type to do something like this, especially without calling. He would not do that to Sheryl for one thing.'

That was debatable for a twenty-four-year-old, I thought. At that age young men tended to follow something other than their head or their heart. Still, to neither contact family nor return to work without informing his employer did suggest something out of the ordinary might have occurred. I always felt that a lot could go wrong very quickly out in the US where guns are so readily available and alcohol is so cheap.

'So what exactly do you know?' I asked her. 'Explain things to me in a little more detail, Donna.'

'Vern went on a tour of Nevada. At least, that's what he told us he was doing. We know he made it up to Vegas and checked out two days later. The hotel he was staying at told us that much. The idea was for him to camp after that. He didn't provide any of us with an itinerary, and we don't think he was going to use registered camping grounds.'

'So he was just going to pitch a tent in the desert where and when he felt like it.'

'That's as much as we knew, yes.'

'Is Drew an experienced camper?'

'Yes. Woods and mountains, usually. He disappears into the San Gabriels and Lake Arrowhead a couple of times a year. We're not sure if he's done a desert before, but he is used to making his own way outdoors.'

I let that filter. Woods and mountains threw up different creatures and animals to the desert, but there would be less immediate danger from the terrain where he was now. As for the people you might encounter... that was a different matter entirely. A thought occurred to me. 'Did he take his own vehicle or rent one?'

'The police asked that same question. I think they were hoping he rented a vehicle with a GPS tracker on it. But no, he took his own Kia minivan.'

I'd been hoping for the same thing. 'And there's no sign of that?'

'None, no.'

'How about his mobile? Were the police able to trace that?'

'His cell? I doubt they took it that far. It's a lot of work, apparently. So they told us, anyhow. Much harder than they make it look on TV.'

I thought that was most likely true. I also thought beyond law enforcement. 'Have you spoken with a private investigator?' I asked.

There was a slight hesitation before Donna admitted they had. 'Drew spoke with someone yesterday. They also said it would take a while to obtain any phone records. They are at least looking into it, which is more than the police seemed willing to do.'

I scratched my head, felt the chill wind bite into my flesh once again now that I had my hood down. 'Look,' I said. 'I'll have a think about it and get back to you. You seem to have covered all the bases. Your PI will hopefully investigate much more thoroughly than the police did.'

'Oh. Okay, Mike.' Her voice had become soft. I could hear the unspoken anguish in that tone. Would recognise it anywhere.

'What are you looking for here, Donna?' I asked. 'What did you have in mind before you picked up the phone to call me?'

'I suppose I'm not sure, really. Just to bounce it off you. See if you could think of anything we hadn't yet done.'

'You used Wendy's phone. Is that so's you'd know I would answer right away?'

'Yes.'

I understood then how desperate she must have been. 'You reported it, so you have the disappearance at least logged in the system. You have a PI who will follow up. I'm not sure what else you can realistically do, given that, from what you've told me, the trail effectively went cold more than a fortnight ago.'

'I suppose. It's just… you tend to think the worst in these circumstances. You end up having to put your faith in people you don't know, and that makes you anxious.'

'You mean you, or you and your husband both?'

'I guess I mean both of us. Drew doesn't know which way to turn right now. He's frustrated. He feels impotent, and I know he believes Vern is in trouble. I feel the same way. It's hard to explain, but something is not right, Mike.'

I took a breath. Pulled my hood back up to try and trap whatever body heat I was expelling. I thought I could still detect something in Donna's voice. Not anything she had said, more an unspoken request. I considered what that might mean, how it might play out and develop. There didn't seem a lot going for it, with far more unknown than known. Yet I also understood how distressed my ex must be if she was asking for my help. Even if she had not actually uttered those precise words.

The snow was falling harder now. I enjoyed what it did to the land, and the cold air invigorated me. The winds were harsh and punishing, but even they had a way of making me reflect. My time here had been well spent, my mind healing while my body did the same. Donna's call had come at the right time. I was done here. It was time for a different challenge.

'I'll be there as soon as I can make it,' I told Donna.

'Are you sure, Mike?'

'Yes. I'm sure.'

When I was through with the arrangements I placed a call of my own.

'Terry,' I said. 'How do you fancy a road trip?'

TWO

We were met at Los Angeles International airport by my ex and my daughter. Terry and I stepped out glassy-eyed and cramp-legged into the crowded arrivals hall, each of us lugging a hefty Bergen backpack in addition to our carry-on bags. Wendy came rushing towards me, her face wreathed in smiles. She threw herself at me like an Exocet missile and almost cut me in half as her body slammed into mine and we embraced in one mighty hug.

It had been eighteen months since I had seen her, and it felt so good to hold my little girl in my arms again that I did not want to ever let go. My daughter was fourteen and fast becoming a woman other than inside my head, where she would forever remain the same child I taught to belch the alphabet and from whose bedroom I regularly chased scary monsters. My nose buried deep into Wendy's sun-bleached hair, I breathed her in as I had when she was a baby. I wanted to soak up all of her essence so that it could remain within me wherever I went. She had grown so much since the last time we were together, and was slender but with healthy musculature. I peered over her shoulder, blinking away tears of unrestrained joy. Standing to one side, I noticed Donna was looking a little sheepish, her own smile forced and strained. When Wendy finally withdrew her arms from around my neck, I took a step back and made introductions.

'Wendy, Donna, this is my good friend Terry Cochran. Terry and I served in the Royal Marines together, and he also saved my life last summer.'

'And Mike saved my life also,' he said. 'For the second time, I might add.'

Terry was not overly tall, but cut a striking figure all the same. His hair was dark, short, and spiky in that unkempt kind of way that didn't seem to matter. He had shaved off the full bushy beard I had become familiar with, and in its place had some designer stubble going on. I had ribbed him about it on several occasions during our flight, and in return he found a way to drive an elbow into me every time he got up to visit the toilet. He looked about ten years younger without the beard, but no less robust. I had no idea how much he weighed, but I imagined ninety-nine per cent of it was muscle. His skin was the kind of nut brown that could only come from decades exposed to the sun.

Wendy surprised us all by jumping forward to give Terry a warm hug of welcome. 'Thank you for helping my dad,' she said, stepping back from the embrace. 'He told me all about it. I'll never forget what you did for him.'

'You're both very welcome,' Terry told her, clearly touched and also slightly embarrassed, I imagined, by the show of affection from my daughter.

Donna stepped forward to shake his hand. 'Thank you for coming, Terry. We met once before if you remember?'

'We did. At the hospital.'

I had forgotten all about that meeting. It was after I was wounded at Umm Qasr in Iraq in March 2003, less than a month after Wendy was born. I was flown to Germany for surgery and then back home two weeks later. Wounded in the same firefight,

Terry had returned via the same route and was sitting with me in my room at the Queen Elizabeth Hospital in Birmingham on the first day Donna visited me. It was hard to imagine ever forgetting that precious moment when I laid eyes on my daughter for the first time, as she lay cocooned in a lace shawl, pink cotton hat protecting her delicate head. I guess I had simply whitewashed my friend from that memory.

Wendy held my hand about as tight as she could as we navigated our way through the terminal and into the multi-storey car park, where we eventually piled into Donna's Chevy Tahoe. Having my daughter insist on sitting with me in the back was a thrill, though it left Terry to ride shotgun with my ex. We all made a commitment not to discuss our reason for being there until we'd reached Donna's home, so we chatted about the flight and other meaningless drivel.

The drive north from the airport along the I-405, following on to North Sepulveda Boulevard through to Bel Air in the foothills of the Santa Monica mountains, took little more than an hour in Donna's SUV. It was a warm and sunny day for the time of year, and everything around us seemed to glisten beneath an ice-blue sky. The blanket of smog that usually hung over the city like a brown stain that could not be erased, seemed to have been temporarily brushed aside in order to better welcome us. The roads were jammed, cars swooped in and out of lanes with alarming regularity, passing on either side of us. Though it was slow going, at least the traffic flowed reasonably smoothly. We made decent progress.

The grey stone and clapboard house painted a Wedgewood blue was part of a gated community, and for the first time I saw the opulent lifestyle my daughter had been enjoying for the past few years. As we drew up outside a triple garage, I had to acknowledge the small part of me that was envious. Yet I also recognised how tremendously fortunate Wendy was to be growing up in a place like this. I could not begrudge my daughter any of it.

She and I had spent the past ninety minutes catching up, and I could hardly escape her enthusiasm for the way her life was going. The one dark cloud had been those few days over the previous summer, during which both the Los Angeles police department and the FBI had been virtually encamped at the house waiting for me to contact Wendy. At that time I was supposedly on the run after murdering a gangster and abducting a young woman and a child. Which was another topic off the table until we were settled.

Drew and Donna had not listened to my assertions that Terry and I would be fine at a local motel. Drew had paid for our flights – to our surprise and delight we had been given first class seats – and offered me and Terry two of the house's five bedrooms. It was sixty hours since the phone call, and still I didn't know how I felt about staying in the home in which my ex-wife now lived with her second husband. And our daughter. On the one hand it meant I got to spend more time with Wendy, for which I was grateful. On the other, I would be forced to occupy some time with a man I had never met, but who was shacked up with the woman I still loved. It was the place where love and pain collide, and pain remained the overriding feeling.

Wendy could not wait to show me around. The interior was all cream walls, brown stone flooring with underfloor heating, dark wood, and a minimalist feel that I took to immediately. Spacious and cool, this was a home in which you could breathe and grow. Wendy's bedroom was about the size of our old barracks house in Plymouth, and from her private balcony she had a breath-taking view of the ocean glimmering away in the distance between the mountain ridges. Directly beneath the balcony was an oval pool whose blue illuminations had just flickered into life in the gathering gloom. We joined Donna and Terry out on the lower decking where they sat already nursing a sweating bottle of beer each amongst the jacarandas and palms, fuchsias and crane flowers. I reached for a third bottle on the table, whilst a cola had been poured for Wendy. Ice cubes bobbed and crackled in her glass.

'You two getting along okay?' I asked.

Terry looked up at me and nodded. 'Famously,' he replied.

'Terry has been filling me in on some of what happened over the summer.'

I nodded awkwardly and put away half my beer in a couple of swallows. I smiled then, and raised the bottle. 'I couldn't have had one of these back then. If I'd had one I would not have stopped drinking for the rest of the night. Or the following day.'

Wendy had clung on to my arm when we sat down, now she hugged it tighter still. 'That was so scary, Dad,' she said. She wore purple jeans and a plain white polo shirt, a pair of Vans sneakers taking pride of place on her feet. Her face lost its smile for the first time since she and Donna had met us at arrivals. 'The police and FBI said such horrible things about you. I thought they were going to hunt you down and shoot you like they do over here.'

'But you knew I was innocent and you stuck up for me, right?' My smile grew broader, as I recalled Donna telling me after it was all over how Wendy had shouted at anyone who dared suggest I might be guilty of murder and abduction.

Nodding, Wendy said, 'I knew they were wrong. I knew you must be trying to help that woman and little girl, not hurt them.'

I kissed the top of my daughter's head. I didn't want to dwell upon what might have been. What I had right here and now in my arms was all that mattered. 'Thank you, kiddo. That means the world to me.'

'It's just a shame that woman died in the end.'

I glanced across at Terry and raised an eyebrow. 'She did so rescuing Charlie, though. She did a very brave thing that night.'

'I still don't know everything that happened,' Wendy said, peering up at me with her large, brown, soulful eyes. 'Only what you told me when you called. Everything was still so confused and messed up at the time.'

I looked over at Donna, who shrugged and nodded. I gave my daughter the highlights – or lowlights. On a particularly bad day back in July of the previous year, I had witnessed a man being shot and killed in a lay-by. Because I couldn't reach my own car I ended up taking the victim's in order to get away, only to discover his daughter and her nanny lying in the rear footwells. A short while later I also discovered that the victim was a big deal in organised crime, and had been murdered by a serving officer with the National Crime Agency. I sought the help of an ex-colleague, who was shot and killed when she drove from London to Wiltshire to meet me, and then had to rely on another ex-colleague – Terry Cochran – to help us evade capture. By this time I was being hunted by the police, the gangster's brother and, as we were to later discover, a mysterious armed unit intent on killing us all. Three battles later, and with Terry now too injured to continue and the young child snatched from us, I had to ignore my own wounds and work with the nanny and the gangster's brother to both get the girl back and bring down our adversaries.

It transpired that the nanny had been the primary target all along, having worked for and been the lover of a man seeking titles and power, whose past included selling arms to the Taliban. The repercussions for Terry and me were minor, although his off-the-grid life had been exposed. I still felt bad about that, and I figured that had been one reason for my penitence up in the Scottish Highlands.

'How many times were you shot?' Wendy asked, interested in the gruesome aspect of the story as any teenager would be.

'Twice. Neither was bad enough to put me out of action. Terry got the worst of it.'

Wendy nodded solemnly. I thought she was perhaps reflecting on what might have been. The extra squeeze she gave me indicated I was correct.

'So what do you do with yourself now, Terry?' Donna asked.

Terry shrugged. 'This and that,' he said. He drained his beer and wiped his lips.

'Ah. Sorry, I should have known better than to ask.'

'No, it's fine. It's just… hard to quantify is all.'

I chuckled. Working private security black ops was impossible to fully explain in most company at the best of times.

'How about you, Mike?' Donna said, turning her laser-like focus on me. 'How is your business going?'

I set my bottle down and spread my hands. 'Let's just say I won't be floating it on the stock market any day soon. My appetite for the banal no longer exists. In truth, I was probably wrong to think it ever really had.'

'What you went through last year would have made anyone reflect on their life.'

'It did that, all right. It came at too high a cost, though. For some. On the other hand, I suppose I found myself again. I'm not cut out for the humdrum, it would appear.'

Donna laughed. 'I could have told you that.'

'Yeah, but you weren't around to do so.'

The words were out of my mouth before they had even scanned through the filter in my brain. I saw a flicker of hurt pass across Donna's face.

'I'm sorry,' I said. 'I didn't mean that the way it came out. All I meant was, you would probably have talked me out of what I was trying to do, which is why I didn't tell you before launching myself into it. You weren't there, so I didn't have to run it by you.

I forgot that you always give the best advice, whereas I simply suck at it.'

It was a good save, and Donna smiled and lost tension from her shoulders.

'If you're at a loose end you could always come over here to live,' Wendy said, giving me a hard squeeze around the midriff.

'Well, it's not quite as simple as that, kiddo. But I'm here now, so let's make the most of that.'

'How long are you staying, Dad?'

I glanced across at Donna. 'To a degree that depends on what Terry and I discover when we go looking for Vern. But I'll also find time to spend with you, sweetheart. I promise you that.'

I was still feeling guilty at not having flown over to see Wendy following all that had happened during the summer. We had spoken – often – but despite knowing full well that Wendy so desperately wanted to spend time with me, until now I had made my excuses not to travel. It was never a question of my not wanting to be with my daughter. If it were down to me I would be with her every day of my life. The simple truth was, I had struggled mentally to deal with everything that took place. The emotional wounds lasted far longer than the physical ones.

The mood having turned distinctly sober, we all looked up as the door leading from the kitchen onto the patio slid back. One or two photos that Wendy had sent me included Drew Mason, so I recognised the man now joining us. He was tall, lean, tanned and fit-looking. His suit looked as if it cost as much as my entire wardrobe. He smiled a greeting, but there were rings of neglect beneath his eyes, and his face was pinched with concern.

Introductions were made. Hands shaken. Drew joined us for a drink while Donna got some food going. I let her husband unwind a little before asking, 'Any updates while we were in the air?'

He sipped some bourbon and savoured the smoky flavour before responding. 'Nothing so far. The investigators I hired are supposed to be the best in the business, but the way they tell it the trail went cold in Vegas and has stayed that way since.'

'That needn't necessarily be a bad thing,' I said, attempting to offer a grain of comfort, though it was the very opposite of what I believed. 'I forgot to ask Donna, but does Vern have a girlfriend?'

'He did have a while back. Nice kid. She hadn't heard from him in a month or so. Certainly several weeks before he left LA. Theirs was always a vague relationship, so I wasn't surprised by that.'

'How about a previous girl? Any issues there for us to look into?'

Drew drained his glass and poured another. 'No. Elle headed out to the East Coast. University. Neither thought a long-distance relationship would work out. It was an entirely amicable split.'

'And nothing has popped up on social media?' Terry asked.

Donna had slipped back out onto the deck, wiping her hands on a dishcloth. 'I've checked everything I can think of,' she said. 'I even joined Instagram. Vern is not really one for posting aimless photos of himself, and one of the reasons he went camping was to get away from that sort of thing.'

'So no posts or updates since when..? Leaving home?' Terry leaned forward as he spoke. I could tell this bothered him.

'No. Not a thing.'

I looked at Donna properly for the first time since LAX. Her previously long, wavy auburn hair had given way to a sharp, stylish cut that feathered back and tapered into the neck. A jagged fringe hung down almost over one eye. Curved in all the right places, she looked a lot healthier these days, a decent tan replacing her previous pale skin. Expensive-looking clothes completed the picture of a modern middle-aged woman in her absolute prime.

I wouldn't say there was yearning in my gaze, but there certainly was a whole lot of regret.

After one more round of drinks we ate indoors as a chill settled into the wind that blew down the canyon. The background noise to our discussion had come from children's laughter as they played in a pool somewhere close by. The palms and pink oleanders created a decent buffer on the boundary of the property, leaving us with a view down into the heart of LA. As the night settled in, the city lights danced and twinkled like stars in the sky, while ribbons of white and red revealed the passage of traffic on the freeways.

We chatted aimlessly over dinner. From the dining room we moved into the lavish living area, two sides of which were bordered by glass. We started to relax in seats that swallowed us up, but I was drained, and Terry also seemed to be flagging. We both cut the night short, looking for an early start the following morning. Having no further news about Vern to consider didn't seem like a bad thing, but we hoped that would change soon.

By morning it had.

But not in a good way.

THREE

Donna woke me before dawn. It felt almost surreal, me lying there beneath a thin cotton sheet wearing only my boxers, my ex-wife standing bare-legged beside the bed with a short robe wrapped around her and tied in a bow at the waist. Nothing but that same old distance between us. Despite the hour, Donna looked beautiful, her bed-head and puffy eyes only adding to the cuteness factor. I sat up slowly, still feeling the previous night's beers in my blood, trying to blink some sense back into my life.

In a voice both urgent and distraught, Donna told me that Drew had minutes earlier been contacted by a police department in New Mexico, who informed him that his nephew's vehicle had been located in the middle of nowhere somewhere on the road to Amarillo. I resisted saying anything lame about somebody having finally found directions to that place, and instead focussed on the look of fear and concern on the face of the first and only love of my life. It was not a time for joking. It was a time for getting serious.

I wiped a hand across my mouth. 'Give me ten minutes,' I said. 'I'll join you both in the kitchen.'

I was better than my word, making it downstairs in half that time.

'He's more than 750 miles and two whole states away from where he should be,' Drew said, after taking a tall padded stool at the breakfast bar next to Donna and putting away half a mug of fresh black coffee in a couple of gulps. 'That simply makes no sense to me.'

I drank the coffee that had been placed in front of me. Black, no sugar. It was unbelievably tasty. I ignored the toasted English muffins on the plate in the centre of the long and wide bar. Having to look on in mute agony as the woman I still loved comforted another man, disturbed me more than I cared to think about. I had no business feeling that way anymore, but in my head you are what you are, and you have to deal with that in your own way. I dealt with it by pumping them both for answers.

'Do either of you know anybody down that way?' I asked.

They both shook their heads.

'How about business, Drew?'

'No, nothing in New Mexico at all. Phoenix, Arizona would be the closest, but that's still six hundred miles give or take.' It was obvious to me that the news he had learned that morning had crushed his resolve, and he was now distracted.

I looked between him and Donna. 'So neither of you can think of a single reason why Vern would head to New Mexico?'

'Not one,' Drew insisted. 'Especially not when he told us he was headed into northern Nevada, and we know he made it as far as Vegas.'

'Do you?' Terry asked at that point.

'What do you mean?' Donna asked, turning from her husband. Her hand remained folded around his.

Terry was already at the breakfast bar by the time I got there, spreading boysenberry jelly on two halves of muffin. He seemed rested and in good spirits, recovering better than I had from all the travelling. He cleared his throat before speaking.

'You know that his hotel room was used. You know that his credit card was used, both to check in and for meals. Do you know for certain that it was Vern who did the using?'

Now both appeared uncertain. Drew leaned forward, taking another hit from his soup bowl of a mug. 'I think I see what you mean. I suppose we never thought to question it.'

'So the police have not reviewed security footage in order to confirm that it was your nephew who used his credit card in Las Vegas?'

'Not that I am aware of, no.'

'Me neither,' Donna said, shaking her head. 'I'm pretty sure they would not have gone that far.'

I gave that some thought. We had no verification that it was Vern who checked into his hotel in Vegas, and all we knew now was that his vehicle had turned up in New Mexico. I could not decide what I thought it all meant, only that I didn't think it could be anything positive.

'Will you head over there for us?' Drew asked.

'To New Mexico?' I glanced across at Terry. He shrugged. That told me everything.

I nodded at Drew and Donna. 'I had anticipated us needing to drive up to Vegas, but in the absence of anything of substance perhaps we'll get lucky following the vehicle. In which case, Drew, you get your investigators to obtain whatever relevant security camera footage might be out there. Looks like Terry and I are on the move again.'

I made light of it, but the finding of Vern's vehicle was a major break. When searching for someone or something you needed markers, almost like milestones. You had to know you were getting somewhere, and where it would lead. We did not have Vern or even any sight of him to go on, so his SUV was the next best thing. It was both a starting point and an end zone for us, and I felt sure that it would be crucial in discovering Vern's whereabouts. Whether that would turn out to be in Nevada or New Mexico I could not be certain.

Having expected the hassle of finding two seats on a flight out of LAX, I was thrilled when Drew arranged for us to use his company jet instead. I'm easily pleased by shiny objects, but riding in luxury is way better than the alternative no matter who you are or what you are used to. The Lear jet was hangered at nearby Van Nuys airport in the San Fernando Valley, and we were assured that it would be made available to us as and when we needed it for the duration of our search. Buoyed by the news, Terry and I started making plans of our own. I went about it with a smile on my face, but remained thoughtful. Amidst all the excitement a brand new day had delivered us, I could not stop myself from thinking of the night before.

Before turning in, we had discussed Vern's disappearance in a little more depth, obtaining as much information as we could in preparation for what was to follow. After dinner when we spread out around the vast living area abutting the open-plan kitchen, Wendy and I sat together on a wide and soft sofa. I let her do most of the talking, which she did with enthusiasm and admirable candour. It was clear that she loved her life, and was growing into it more as the months rolled by. She enjoyed surfing, and was getting a feel for track sports. Her studies were going well, and she had a private tutor for chemistry. It hurt to hear, but I wanted only the best for her, so I nodded and smiled in all the right places and as the time passed and the city lights became more abundant, I grew close to my daughter once again.

A sharp, intelligent mind lay behind her natural good looks, and my little girl was developing into a fine young lady. Inevitably we drifted back to the events of the previous summer. I realised she was concerned that I had come so close to being killed, but with my safety ensured, Wendy had clearly then been hurt by my apparent unwillingness to fly across the Atlantic to see her.

'It was never that,' I assured her, holding Wendy close and enjoying the feel of her soft, warm hair against my cheek. 'Never about you. Kiddo, you have to understand that your old man was a wreck back then. You remember how on the night it all began I told you I was having a shit day in a week of shit days in a month of shit weeks?'

Wendy giggled. 'Yeah, but you say that a lot, Dad.'

'Well, this time I wasn't exaggerating. I was desperately trying to remain sober when all I could see was my whole life falling apart. What I went through in those few days was horrendous, and I was also responsible for the loss of my closest friend. If I had come to you in the aftermath of that, you would have seen a broken man devoid of any redeeming features.'

Wendy's eyes filled and her lips began to tremble. I smiled and wiped a tear away from her cheek, touched my finger to her mouth, shaking my head.

'Sweetheart, the least of it was the recovery from my own wounds, but I had to factor that in as well. I've been on the battlefield, so I know what PTSD is. I have to admit that there was some of that going on in my head as well. The truth is, Wend, I didn't want you to see me like that. But I also had nothing to offer you emotionally. I was an empty vessel. And I'm sorry. Sorrier than you will ever know. But that was the old me. I promise you I'm stronger now. Closer to the man I always wanted to be. And you and me, well, we have no secrets anymore. And an awful lot of catching up to do. Always keep in mind that I love you, and that there hasn't been a moment since you were born when I didn't.'

We had both gone to bed feeling better at having aired our views, and I guess we both understood each other a little better for it. As we stood in the kitchen the following morning, my mind was drawn back to that conversation irrespective of what might be happening out in New Mexico. Eventually I would separate that aspect of my life from the one I was about to encounter, setting it aside in a compartment all of its own. But not quite yet. I was not ready to immerse myself, and felt I did not need to until we were on the road.

After our early morning coffee and update from Drew, and with dawn still a pale light bleeding in over the mountain tops, I borrowed Donna's SUV and drove myself and Terry out to Pasadena where we met up with an old combat friend of his. An army ranger in his day, Steve Henderson now ran a shooting range and sold weapons to those who firmly believed in their constitutional right to bear arms. Those we took from him were not off the shelf, they bore no registration marks, and were provided at cost price from a stash he kept locked away in an outbuilding alongside the range. We hoped they would not be needed, but out here we had to be prepared for any eventuality and could no longer rely on Terry's multiple caches of arms in the UK.

'You two starting a war on your own?' Henderson enquired as we carefully packed everything into deep, black holdalls.

'I certainly hope not,' Terry replied with an easy grin.

'We probably won't even get off a round,' I said. 'But better to have them and not need them, than need them and not have them.'

'Amen to that,' Henderson said as we slammed closed the tailgate on the vehicle. 'But good luck to you both if your need becomes deed.'

By the time we got back to the house, Wendy had left for school and Drew had gone to work. Donna drove us out to Van

Nuys and dropped us off a short distance from the Lear, cool in the shadow of its own separate hangar. The place reeked of fuel and warm oil, and the sound was deafening as the plane's massive Pratt & Whitney engines went through a series of pre-flight tests.

Donna was quiet and a little teary-eyed as we said goodbye. Those little vulnerabilities amidst all the strength she showed, was one of her most endearing qualities. I had always loved that about her; the fact that once you were on the inside of her circle she allowed you to see both dimensions of her nature. Donna was neither complex nor enigmatic. She wore her concern like a shawl – something to ward off the chill, but equally something to shrug off when the time was right. I think the whole experience had got to her, and she was as confused as I was at the pair of us being in the same time zone again. That was about to change once more, so I held both her hands and told her what she wanted to hear.

FOUR

Sheriff Dwight Crozier stiffened as the Native American approached the black-and-white SUV. He knew Joe Kane well, and he was an impressive human being in so many ways, his physicality being only one of them. Crozier had known the man for the better part of ten years, and while they had never crossed swords as such, he was acutely aware of Kane's reputation as a man who never made a threat he could not carry through on.

Corona was little more than a scuff mark in the New Mexican desert dust. Around 150 people lived in the little town, and whilst it was by no means a wealthy burg, neither was it desperately poor. Its inhabitants mainly worked either construction or in the local school system, and were by and large decent people who enjoyed a lively social community. Unemployment was low, which helped a lot with the overall crime rate, and Crozier generally looked forward to his irregular visits to what was usually a pretty friendly place.

Today was different.

Today he sensed trouble brewing in much the same way he always seemed to know when a twister might be blowing through on a late spring evening, and he feared some of that trouble was coming his way right now.

Crozier swallowed, then used his tongue to remove a chunk of leftover breakfast burrito from between his back teeth. Every working day he started with a hearty breakfast from the same diner on I-54 just after the Ancho turnoff. To make himself feel better about being stuck in his ways, the sheriff skipped around the menu a lot. Today had been a choice between huevos rancheros and the rice and refried bean burrito. With towns spread so far apart he was taking a chance either way on a stomach that had served him well for almost fifty years.

He picked up his white Stetson hat from its travelling position on the passenger seat beside him, and exited his vehicle. After placing the hat upon his head, Crozier adjusted his gunbelt, whose worn leather creaked and groaned. If things were about to get confrontational and go south on him, he wanted to be upright and able to reach his weapon quickly and comfortably. The department issue Smith & Wesson was his only deterrent, visible or otherwise. A few years back the Albuquerque police department had been ordered not to carry personal weapons while on the job, and it had been fine by Crozier when that same instruction passed through sheriffs' offices in neighbouring counties. One handgun was more enough for him, and he was proud to have had nineteen years of service without firing his. Sure, he'd had to pull it on a few occasions, especially when dealing with rowdy drunks for whom a boot up the ass wasn't enough. There was also one occasion when a felon passing through San Patricio had held up a 7-Eleven store, but he had never been involved in a firefight and he hoped to retire with that record intact.

There was no cement sidewalk to step up onto, only a wide expanse of flattened dirt – pretty standard for Corona and other blink-you'll-miss-'em towns of a similar size and no account.

Crozier could therefore not bar the way as he would have done on a narrow strip of paving supplemented by buildings to one side, but he had a bit of bulk about him and he made sure that Joe Kane would have to deviate from his current path to avoid him.

'You waiting on me, Sheriff Crozier?' Kane said as he approached with a long, loping stride. Despite his stature, he had an almost graceful lupine gait about him. His arms swung freely, loose and powerful, fingers curled but not clenched into fists. The tone of voice he used did not indicate that the man was angry or troubled in any way. He always spoke in the same relaxed manner, even when beating a man down – according to scuttlebutt at least.

'That I am, Joe.'

Kane came to a halt less than a yard away from Crozier. Close enough to be intimidating.

'You're a long way from home, sheriff.'

'But not out of my jurisdiction. Not quite.'

'This about last night?' Kane asked. His voice was deep, booming on the bass notes.

'It is. You want to tell me your side of the story?'

The way Crozier heard it, Joe had entered the Main Street saloon in a highly agitated and charged state, hunting for someone as if that someone had trouble coming his way. An argument had subsequently broken out, during which a variety of threats had been made. Chiefly, that Kane would be back to slice and dice the Barrow twins at noon the following day.

This much had found its way to the sheriff via the saloon owner, Amber West, and that last detail had tickled Crozier. He could never understand why so much trouble was prearranged to kick off at either noon or midnight; not when there were so many other hours available to saints and sinners alike. Knowing the principal characters involved here, he regarded both the allegation and threat with the same small pinch of salt.

Todd and Teddy Barrow enjoyed basking in the somewhat dubious glow of being related to Clyde Barrow, the notorious Texan outlaw who had hooked up with Bonnie Parker to begin a reign of terror in the early 1930s. The sheriff knew the supposed relationship to be a complete myth, but the twins had been both dumb and trouble from an early age, and were no less so now that they were men in their late twenties. There was a Y in the day, so they would have been drunk when they argued with Joe Kane, and experience suggested they would have had no problem hurling racist insults at him. Neither man was known for their sensitivity in such matters. The Native American was a giant of a man, but the Barrow boys were more than a match in terms of physique. Equally, whilst Kane would undoubtedly have retaliated in no small measure, his supposed threat might well have been exaggerated.

Yet Kane was here. It was a few minutes shy of midday. The Barrows were in the saloon. An intervention was necessary.

'You know what happened, sheriff,' Kane said, his tone remaining flat and even. 'We exchanged insults – which, by the way, those two peckerheads started – but then they kicked in with the racist bullshit. I will turn a blind eye to most things, but not that. Not from any man. No idea why anyone would expect me to, either.'

Sensing a challenge in those final few words, Crozier flexed on the balls of his feet and said, 'I ain't got nothing against you defending yourself, Joe. You know me to be a squared away police officer in that respect. Leastways, I hope so. But, when I hear hooves I think horses, not zebras. So when cutting is mentioned, I think knives and not fists. I need to know what your intentions are inside that saloon bar, Joe.'

The big man stretched his lips into a thin smile. The leathery face crinkled and his wide flat nose sniffed the warm air. Crozier had no idea how old Kane was. Legend had it that this part of New Mexico had never known a time when Kane was not around, but that was as much a made-up tale as the Barrow boys being related to the legendary bank robber.

'I said something along those lines, sheriff. But only in reaction to one of those twins riling me with talk about scalping. Anger fuelled those threats, nothing more. I do not intend using a weapon of any sort in there.' He nodded at the bar entrance.

'You carrying a weapon, Joe?'

'Nope. If it comes to it, I aim to use my head, my elbows, fists and feet. Don't need no knife. Or tomahawk for that matter.'

Crozier scratched the back of his neck. It was hardly burning up under such an insignificant February midday sun, but he felt a thin film of perspiration there nonetheless. 'You know I can't let you in there, Joe. Can't allow you to enter the bar if you intend on fighting.'

'No reason for me to go in otherwise.'

'So don't go in.'

'But I drove all the way out here. Seems like a huge waste of time and gas if I don't finish what I started.'

'Still can't allow it, Joe.'

Kane's face clouded over, his eyes squinting now. 'They will think I am a coward if I do not show my face. It will shame me, and my people.'

'Oh, now don't give me all that nonsense. Shame you, maybe, but not your entire race. And look, if it means that much to you, I'll gladly step inside and tell them two morons that I put a halt to it, fearing for their lives.'

The two were silent for a few seconds. Nothing passed by on the deserted road beside them. Dwight felt the heavy weight of the Native American's cold, hard scrutiny. But then Kane nodded a couple of times and without a word, started to turn. Crozier called out to him to wait. The big man moved back to face him.

'You want to tell me why you went into the bar in the first place, Joe? This is not your typical hangout, that I do know.'

'Looking for someone.'

'You want to tell me who and why?'

'Nope.'

Crozier took a breath and blew it out his nostrils. 'Well, now come on, fellah. That's not playing the game. A man's gotta wonder. Especially a man who's also the local county sheriff. When you go looking for someone, that tells me that whoever it is will soon be in trouble. With you or your employer. Either way, that makes me a little uneasy.'

Kane heaved his massive shoulders. 'Looking for someone is not a crime.'

'Well, you're right about that, of course.' Dwight rested his hands on his belt. 'But what you do with them when you find them just might be.'

'Just want to talk.'

'Talk. Is that right?'

'Yep.'

'And what if your… talk doesn't go well. Doesn't go to plan. What then, Joe?'

'Maybe something, maybe nothing. Have to have the talk first to know.'

Crozier knew he would get nowhere with the man on this subject. He had to ask, had to do what he could, but Kane was about as tight-lipped as a person could be without actually having their mouth sewn shut.

'I hope I don't have to come looking for you,' he said, eyeing Kane closely.

'I hope not either, sheriff.'

Crozier waved him away with a flick of his fingers and a dip of the head. He watched the Apache from the Mescalero tribe walk away with that untroubled gait of his, then shook his head, removed his hat and stepped inside the bar.

FIVE

The wheels of our Lear touched down at Roswell International Air Center at precisely 12.46 New Mexico time on Tuesday afternoon, the day after Terry and I had flown into LAX. It was a relatively short hop by comparison to our journey over the Atlantic, but still I was feeling as if I was caught up in a cyclone, and my head was trying hard to acclimatise to more than the jump back and forth in time differences.

Seeing both Donna and Wendy again, spending some time with them, was a positive move my heart grasped and would not let go of quickly. That our time shared together had taken place in the home of another man, a man capable of providing the two women in my life with their every need, hooked spikes into that same heart and scrubbed it raw from the inside out. I begrudged neither of them a thing, and wanted only the very best for both of them. I had wasted my opportunity with Donna, and subsequently the chance to spend Wendy's formative years alongside her had also disappeared in a pall of smoke caused by the fire I lit beneath my marriage. Because I understood the process and the practicalities, and had come to accept them, did not mean it no longer hurt. The past few days had been a confusion of movement and discovery, and I had to admit that it had knocked me off my game.

I was in the moment now, though. A young man was missing, a young man who was part of my daughter's wider new family. I did not doubt that he was in some kind of trouble. All we could do now was hope to find him before it became the worst kind of trouble. If we managed to do that, my money was on us getting him back safely.

As promised, a Jeep Grand Cherokee was waiting for us at the airport in New Mexico. During the short flight in the Lear, Terry and I had discussed the best way forward, so by the time we stowed our kit away in the back of the Jeep and climbed aboard, our strategy was already formed. Despite knowing that by now Vern's minivan would have been towed to an FBI storage area and would probably be minutely examined by experts later that same day, I wanted to see where it had been found. Terry agreed that should be our starting point.

You think of New Mexico and you imagine baking heat, scorched earth, and fierce sunshine that beat down relentlessly until you were frazzled and cooked. I do, at least. None of that was in evidence as we headed east out of Roswell. The sky was low and a grey-blue colour that amounted to nothing much, though you could tell the sun was trying its best to burn through the cloud cover. It wasn't exactly cold, not for those of us used to UK weather, but there was dampness in the air that chilled through to the bone when the wind blew.

I thought the Fenlands back home could be flat and uninspiring countryside, but it had nothing on this place. The tawny plains were basically dirt pans with tufts of flora peppering the bleak landscape. At some point on the short drive we crossed the Pecos River, not that you'd know it without the sign to tell you; it looked more like an arroyo that had been arid for many years, with pockets of vegetation climbing their way out of the bed. If you blinked you would miss the miniscule town of Acme. We blew by a building called the Old Frazier Schoolhouse. It looked as if it might be important, though of course its history meant nothing to either of us. Highway 70 took us though Chaves County. We followed it in virtual silence. I felt a little laggy and out of sorts, and it's always hard to tell how Terry is feeling. His eyes were busy reading a position on his GPS device into which he had programmed coordinates, and eventually he pointed to our right.

'Just there by the telegraph poles,' he said, allowing me plenty of time to adjust.

I indicated, eased my foot off the accelerator, and bumped off the tarmac onto a dusty, dirt trail. Moments later we rattled over a single set of railway tracks that ran parallel to the highway. Ahead of us the dirt track seemed to peter out to nothing, leading nowhere in particular, to nothing we could see. To our left there was a small, flattened and bald dirt patch, upon which we could see a multitude of tyre imprints and swirls of footprints. I stopped the Jeep on the opposite side, and we stepped out. You could taste the desert dust in your mouth immediately, and the air smelled like baked soil. It was quiet. Other than the occasional hiss of tyres back on the highway, the afternoon was still and silent.

'Looks like the kind of place where you'd see tumbleweed rolling across the land,' Terry observed, squinting as he peered into the distance.

I nodded. 'And Wile E Coyote chasing that smug bastard Roadrunner.'

'Well, we did drive by Acme back there.'

I turned my head and gave him a hard stare.

'What?' He smiled and spread his hands.

'I can't believe you just made a pop culture reference.'

'That was pop culture about a hundred years ago, Mike.'

That made me laugh. He wasn't far wrong.

'So what do you make of this as a location?' I asked him.

Terry shook his head. 'Why would I stop here? Maybe to pull over after a long drive. Grab some rest or perhaps even some sleep. Take a piss? I doubt it, not unless it was an emergency. You can't exactly hide, and this close to the highway you're going to get noticed.'

'I can vouch for how dangerous that can be,' I said. All my troubles of the previous summer stemmed from my doing exactly as Terry had described.

'Yeah, but it doesn't look as if anyone came along and started shooting.' Terry's eyes met mine and an understanding passed between us. The bond of a shared history.

'Car trouble?' I suggested.

'Good point. We need to find that out. I wonder if the local cops or FBI agents even bothered to turn the engine over, check the gauges.'

'Other than that, maybe whoever was driving pulled off the road to meet with somebody.'

'You still thinking that maybe it wasn't Vern who drove down here from Vegas?' Terry asked.

'It's possible. There's a lot we still don't know, and we need to get into it fast.'

'I don't like what I'm seeing or hearing so far.'

'What d'you mean?' I asked him.

Terry shook his head, a look of frustration on his face. 'There's no sign or sight of him since he was in Vegas. Actually, since he left LA. Only use of his credit card. You put that together with his vehicle being dumped here, it doesn't look good for the kid.'

'So you don't think Vern drove out here, either?'

Terry was about to respond when he looked behind me and jerked his head. 'We've got company.'

The dusty Chevrolet with green paintwork faded by the sun followed our tracks as it bounced its way over the uneven surface towards us, pulling up opposite the Jeep. Two men climbed out, door hinges groaning and the Chevy's suspension complaining as it bobbed and settled. One of the men was short and wide, with a goatee whose colour did not match the apparent age of the man sporting it.

His companion was a Latino, taller, skinnier and younger, with sharp narrowed eyes and a gleaming bald dome. He was dressed all in black, and wore snakeskin boots.

'Have you got an anvil handy?' I whispered to Terry.

'Afternoon,' Goatee said, his gaze darting between us. 'I'm Detective Randall and this is my partner, Detective Garcia. What exactly are you two gentlemen doing out here today?'

Before I could respond, Terry said, 'Why, is this private property?'

Goatee fixed Terry with a hard stare for a second or two before responding. 'No, it's not. I still want to know why you two gentlemen are parked here.'

'And I want to see your badges before I answer.'

I glanced across at my friend, who stood a foot or so behind me, square on to the dynamic duo. Terry was not usually the kind of person to goad someone in such obvious fashion. I had to assume there was a good reason for his calm belligerence.

Goatee, a man with no discernible neck, slid a sidelong look at his partner, whose steady focus remained split between me and Terry. We were going to have to watch ourselves with that one.

'I take my badge out, I also take out my cuffs and gun,' Goatee said. He was ruffled, but he made a game attempt at keeping his voice neutral. His eyes darted back and forth, and he licked his lips a couple of times.

'I'm simply asking you to identify yourself, *Detective* Randall. As you are required to do if I make the request.'

'And I'm wondering why you're refusing to answer a simple question, buddy. That makes me suspicious. Making me suspicious is not good for either of you. So I will ask again: what are you two gents doing out here? At this precise location. At this precise moment.'

'Not answering your dumb fucking questions,' Terry replied with no noticeable change in the cadence of his voice.

'That's a sure way to get your ass arrested, my friend.'

'I'm not your friend.'

'Well, then that makes you my enemy. And my enemies don't tend to do well around here.'

Terry did not respond this time. A couple of seconds passed. By now we were all aiming glares at each other; our ocular version of a Mexican stand-off.

'Did our man with the tools send you guys?' Goatee asked, flapping his arms in the air. 'Did we get doubled up on a job here? The punk in the old abattoir gave up where the kid was headed, but it's our job, man.'

'I have no idea what you're talking about,' Terry replied. 'And nor do I care.'

Goatee moved his right hand towards the inside of his jacket.

'Don't!' Terry said, a harsh edge to his voice now. His own hands hung loosely by his side. He had sensed what these two men were long before I did. And they were no detectives.

The man with no neck froze. His companion did not. Terry's reaction was swift and mesmeric. He took two rapid steps forward, and as the Latino's hand came up clasping an ugly-looking switchblade, Terry chopped his left arm down to block the strike, stepped inside as his opponent followed through with the blade cutting only thin air, before delivering a thunderous blow with the inside of his fist to the man's temple. Snakeskin made a brief sound like a sigh, then crumpled to the ground in a heap, the impact sending up a cloud of dust. I had seen Terry use the side of his meaty fist before, often with devastating results for the recipient. My friend was a great believer in not risking broken knuckles if he could possibly help it.

Goatee reacted slowly. Too slowly. By the time he pulled his gun, I had moved in for my own strike. There was no finesse or martial art skill involved. I simply planted my left foot and used the other to kick him squarely in the balls. The sound he made was part cough, part scream. Neither emerged as even remotely human. He sank to his knees, all kinds of pain etched into the warped flesh of his face. He retched and vomited a little. Then he toppled forward, cupping his groin and moaning in a high-pitched keen.

Terry's man was out cold, a thin trail of blood leaking from his ear. I suspected its drum had been perforated by the club-like blow my friend had landed. Terry reached down, flipped open Snakeskin's jacket, and searched inside his pocket. He then checked the others, and the man's chino-style trousers. The knife appeared to be his only weapon. He carried no badge, and his wallet identified him as Ricardo Garcia, aged twenty-eight, from Reno, Nevada.

Goatee had not only lied about being a cop, he had also provided a false name. According to his driver's licence he was David Barclay, fifty, also from Reno. His Sig P226 lay on the floor inches from the man now writhing in agony. I scooped up the weapon, stuffed it into the waistband of my trousers, then flipped the guy over.

'What do you want with us?' I asked him. I shot a glance at Terry, who stood over Snakeskin, inspecting him like an entomologist might examine a new breed of bug.

'Fuck you!' Goatee spat through tight lips.

'Come on now, play fair.' I wagged a finger in front of his narrow piggy eyes. 'I could've shot you.'

Actually, our guns were still in a bag in the back of the Jeep, so that was not strictly true. But he wasn't to know that.

Goatee groaned and winced, hands still cupped around his groin. 'I fucking wish you had.'

I had to chuckle at that. 'What do you think, partner?' I said, looking over my shoulder at Terry.

'Kill them both. Leave them out here for the buzzards to pick at.'

'What do you say to that, Mr Barclay?' I said, turning my attention back to Goatee. 'You want to be buzzard food?'

I had no idea whether there was a buzzard within a hundred miles of us, and I doubted Terry did, either. But it sounded good.

Goatee said nothing, just stared at me with hate-filled eyes.

I took out the man's Sig. His eyes widened. I smiled, and smashed the weapon across the side of that dyed-black facial hair. His eyes rolled back, and he made no sound at all as he slumped onto the desert floor.

'Come on,' I said to Terry. 'Let's leave these two mutts and get the fuck out of here.'

We took time out for a quick sweep of their Chevy, but it told us nothing we didn't already know. In the boot – or trunk as they might call it – we found a shotgun and also a rifle broken down into its hold-all. We relieved them of these weapons, too. As we headed back towards Roswell, we both had some thinking to do.

'I don't know what to make of all this,' I said. The more I turned it over the less sense I found. 'Vern is supposed to be in

Nevada, but his car turns up in New Mexico. We turn up in New Mexico, and we're confronted by two men from Nevada. What does that suggest to you?'

'That we're on the right track,' Terry said.

'Yeah. But what does it all mean for Vern?'

Terry shook his head. 'Nothing good.'

I thought about that for a few moments, before nodding absently. Terry was right. Whatever had become of Vern, even if he was still alive, none of what we had discovered so far augured well for him.

SIX

When you wanted to speak with the Judge, you had to accept all the paranoid bullshit that went with that request. Having been thwarted in his attempts to deal with the men who had treated him so badly at the bar in Corona, Kane had called the man responsible for assigning the tracking job to him in the first place.

The gated home in Ruidoso stood on the very edge of the Mescalero reservation, located slightly within the southern lip of Lincoln County. Tucked deep within the woods, the property overlooked the canyon and beyond that the mountain range away in the distance. It was a secluded spot, with a lot of acreage between homes.

A great place in which to lose yourself.

Joe Kane made good time as he took the slick canyon roads before turning off onto the uneven gravel track that led the way to the Judge's place. Ornate steel gates guarded the entrance, but these were opened electronically after he pressed a buzzer and looked up into the overhanging security camera. The cabin was an architectural mish-mash of old and new, where rock and timber met steel and glass. There he had to suffer the indignity of three pat-downs and a pretty aggressive body search before he was allowed into the palatial home's recreation room, where the Judge held court. Whilst the home and the grounds were pretty enough, Kane considered the location itself to be a major disadvantage to the man who owned it, but it wouldn't do to let the Judge know that.

The man's real identity was Mangas Crow, and he came from a long line of Apache men who went by the same title. Mangas was a name for chiefs and warriors of the past, and so became dynastic within some families. Although various casino and hotel conglomerates celebrated other men as tribal elders within the Mescalero reservation, all leadership roads led directly to the man who over the years had simply become known as the Judge. No major decisions relevant to the tribe in this part of the state were made without first his counsel and then approval if that was required, and absolutely nothing of consequence occurred without his knowledge.

As Kane entered the room, the Judge was sitting before a massive widescreen TV, playing *Assassin's Creed* on an Xbox. He was sprawled out alongside a young girl who looked to be in her mid- to-late teens. The girl wore a flimsy nightshirt and very little else. One leg was tucked beneath her on a massive leather sofa that threatened to swallow her whole, whilst the other rested across the Judge's lap. From the vulnerable pose, and the fact that the girl's foot was idly toying with the Judge's groin, Kane assumed she was not the man's daughter. Neither was the equally young girl who sat with her knees drawn up on the floor. If possible, she wore even less clothing. To Kane's mind the girls were thin and undernourished, and he suspected they were both high on something. He did not approve of young women from the tribe being used in such a way, but he kept these thoughts to himself.

One of the men who had patted Kane down leaned forward to say something into the Judge's left ear. Crow nodded, flicked an irritated hand in the air, then paused the game. The girl lying next to him whined, curled both legs up beneath her and slumped to one side as she started playing with her hair. The Judge slapped her backside, and the sharp sound cutting through the warm air inside the room suggested the smack had not been playful. With a yelp, the girl stood and ran barefooted up a flight of wooden stairs that seemed to float unsupported against the side of the house. The other girl stood and joined her in just as much of a hurry. It seemed to Kane that such behaviour was commonplace here inside Mangas Crow's property.

Without turning, the Judge indicated that his visitor should step forward. Kane did so. He kept his eyes respectfully low, though inside he seethed. It was not often that he had to kowtow to any man, and doing so stuck in his craw no matter how powerful the person expecting this show of reverence. It bothered Kane more than most, because Mangas Crow had not earned his authority amongst the local Apache community. He had bought his way in with money earned from oil, timber and casino resorts.

'You have news?' the Judge asked.

Crow was in his mid-fifties, face cracked and lined, greying hair worn long and tied with a multi-coloured band to form a tail. He was tall and powerful, but overweight due to his lavish and sedentary lifestyle. He looked like a retired American football linebacker. When out on the res he wore a great deal of denim, but when lounging around his house the Judge habitually wore a loose white cotton tunic and elasticated pants. Kane despised the man, but was happy to receive a healthy annual salary for providing certain services both within and without the tribal jurisdiction. Unfortunately, that occasionally entailed dealing with the man in person. When Kane spoke, he did so with feigned reverence.

'I believe the men we seek were here and that they were close by. I personally saw no sign of them, I only heard of it from others. But then their vehicle was found way on the other side of Roswell, and the police and FBI circled the wagons. My information is that the vehicle was empty when it was discovered. It would seem that the trail has once again gone cold.'

The Judge settled himself deeper into the sofa's cushioned seat. He let the moment hang out there long enough to become unsettling.

'Let me get this straight, Joe Kane. You asked to meet with me here to waste my time telling me about an empty car? A car you don't have in your possession, and never even saw. A car that may or may not have been driven by people who may or may not have been the ones we seek.'

'That is not why I came here to speak with you. You asked me for news, and that is all I have. For the moment. It is not why I came.'

'So why are you here?' The Judge turned an irritated scowl towards Kane.

Whether the man was desperate to get back to his game or the girl, Kane neither knew nor cared. He cleared his throat to settle his temper. 'I seek your indulgence and require your influence, Judge. Need your reach.'

'Would this have anything to do with the incident you were involved in last night? At the bar in Corona.'

'You know about that?'

'As you mentioned, I have reach. People tell me things.'

'I will deal with that in my own time. However, while I was there I recognised a man in that bar, a man I need to speak to.

Given the circumstances, on this occasion you may be able to find out where he lives a lot quicker than I can.'

'So you wish for me to do your job for you, Joe Kane.'

Kane kept a lid on his rising temper. He could hold his own in most company, but he was outgunned here. The pristine white walls would be scarred by his blood before he had a chance to make a strike of his own. He was no fool. He knew precisely what discretion was the better part of.

'Only those aspects to which I currently have no direct access,' he insisted. 'I have tracked these people before, I will do so again. I do not doubt that. This time, however, I suspect they have outside help. The man I seek may or may not lead me further, but until I ask him for myself I cannot know for certain.'

The Judge angled his head, considering. 'They are being helped, you say.'

'I believe so, yes.'

'To what end?'

'I do not know. Escape, I must assume.'

'Very well.' The man gave an almost imperceptible nod. 'Let me have the name and I will have the information for you within the hour. Keep your phone charged.'

Kane gave him the name, then added, 'Some of those roads I travel have no cell reception, Judge.'

'All the better reason to keep on the move, Joe Kane. Keep mobile. Keep talking to people. Before you leave, though… what do your instincts tell you?'

Kane did not need time to deliberate. 'That they remain close. For now.'

'And yet you also believe they are looking to escape.'

'I do. But I believe they have unfinished business here first.'

'You understand how important it is that these men be shown the error of their ways?'

'I do, Judge. Of course.'

'And that they must then be persuaded to visit with me at the scene of their crime?'

'You made that clear when you gave me the task.' Kane eyed the man warily, wondering why he was now raking over past conversations and decisions already made.

Crow nodded a couple of times, looking within himself. For a moment he looked lost, but with a blink he was back in the room, looking hard at Kane.

'I trusted you with this errand, Joe Kane. I thought by now you would have brought me answers. Brought me justice. Was I wrong to put my faith in you?'

'Judge, I tracked them all the way to Las Vegas. I flew up there and would have had them in reach had they not seemingly vanished off the face of the earth. It is hard to track men who leave no trace of themselves.'

'Perhaps this is the fault of the tracker.' Crow's eyes had become black pinpoints.

Kane felt the atmosphere in the room shift. He sensed rather than saw Crow's henchmen standing more alert, coiled now as if ready to act if he did. Even armed he would not live beyond taking two lives himself. Unarmed he would simply stare them down and hope to capture their spirits at some time in some place in the future.

'I apologise,' he said. 'I do not believe my work could have been bettered, no matter who you sent. My honour is at stake here, and I will not rest until these men lie at your feet begging for mercy. They were in the wind, then they were not, but now they ride the breeze once more. They can be found again, and I will be the one who finds them.'

The room was silent for a moment. Kane could hear the waterfall beyond the back garden of the house as it spilled into the river at the far reaches of the property, crashing against the boulders along its path. He had felt for some time that it was his destiny to die within the sound of running water, and hearing it now he decided he could be at peace with such an ending. He did not believe his time was over yet, however.

'Find them, Joe Kane.' The harsh edges had left the Judge's face. 'You and I have a history, and I wish you no ill. I am a patient man, but it stretches only so far. As does my loyalty. Find them before I have to send someone else after them. And if I have to do that, make sure you lose yourself along with your prey.'

As he drove back towards the desert plains, Kane felt his features increase their rigidity. His fury was tightly wound. After the Judge called him with the information he had requested, he knew where to look for answers. But there was a fire in his heart now that would burn for many days. A fire stoked not by fear, but by a raging determination.

SEVEN

When the call eventually came in from Drew, it was not everything I had hoped for. Not to begin with, at least. His investigators had drawn a blank when it came to checking out security feeds at the hotel. I was not at all surprised. The places that didn't give a damn about handing over something usually requiring a search warrant either recorded over their disks or did not record in the first place. Those who both recorded and retained daily footage refused to co-operate without a legal imperative.

'That's a shame,' I said, scratching my cheek and wondering where we might now find a lead. 'We're here in New Mexico because the vehicle is, but it would really have helped if we had been able to focus on Vern rather than his car.'

'You and Terry might have better luck being... persuasive,' Drew said then.

I smiled. Did he imagine we could simply walk into a hotel and put the squeeze on the management and security people? I thought about that for a moment, still holding onto that smile. *Hold on, why* don't *we simply walk in and put the squeeze on these arseholes?*

'We could make our way up there if things don't go well here,' I said without considering the very real difficulties involved in taking on such a task. I didn't like the idea much, but it was the only one I had. It essentially gave us one shot, and it was a long way to travel on a maybe. Then some tumbler clicked inside my head and activated a thought.

'Hold on a moment, Drew. You work with some pretty IT savvy people, right?'

'Yeah,' he replied. 'Some of the best brains in the business.'

'Any of them happen to be a hacker?'

'Potentially, many of them, I guess. It's part of their… wait a second… are you suggesting what I think you're suggesting?'

'If you think I'm suggesting you have someone hack into the servers at that hotel, then yes I am. They could achieve in minutes what would take us hours. Days even. At least one of your employees must be close enough to the edge that they can be nudged over with some hard cash as an inducement.'

Drew was quiet for a moment or two, then in a voice dripping with unease he said, 'Not an employee, as such. I don't think I'd risk approaching any of my staff with something as illegal as this. But perhaps someone we have had work for us as a freelancer. Her ethics are a little vague, morals virtually non-existent.'

'Excellent,' I said. 'Sounds like the ideal candidate. Put a little distance between you and your company as well. I like it.'

'I'm not sure if she will do it, nor if she can do so while leaving no breadcrumbs.'

'Only one way to find out, Drew. We're winging it here, and currently spending valuable hours in a place your nephew may never even have come to. Terry and I are going to give this place a good go for the rest of today and tomorrow, but it would help to be fighting on two fronts.'

'I understand that, Mike. But what if we can prove one way or another that Vern was or was not the man who checked into the hotel? How does that help you answer the question as to whether he then drove down to New Mexico?'

I heard understandable frustration in his question.

'It's a process of elimination, Drew. And some guesswork thrown in based on sound logic. See, if it was Vern who checked into the hotel, and the vehicle he parked in the hotel car park was the minivan, then we can regard that as a pretty positive sign. If it was not him, or it was him but not his car, then that's a real negative. That might suggest Vern never left Vegas at all. In point of fact, you would most likely have to question if he even made Vegas in the first place if he doesn't show up on that hotel security feed.'

'Now I'm really starting to worry all over again.'

'Nothing has changed, Drew. Not yet. Terry and I are here and I'm sure we'll start to make sense of this, but the facts remain as they were before. We can extrapolate from some basic information, but not from nothing. At the very least, the hotel feed would be a starting point and we could do with one.'

'I realise you're working with nothing, Mike. I wish I had more. Hopefully I can get you what you need.'

Drew sounded both concerned and angry. With the situation rather than us.

'If this were the alphabet,' I said to him, 'Terry and I would be at about M and we have no idea whether to plough on all the way to the end or to head back to the beginning. If your hacker can provide us with a positive ID from Vegas, then it gives us something to go on.'

'I guess it can't hurt to ask,' Drew finally conceded. He killed the call after promising to get back to me before the end of the day.

Terry and I were sitting in the Jeep, parked up behind a Whataburger. The cheeseburger and fries had been pretty good, if a little salty, and we washed our meals down with some serious quantities of Mountain Dew. We'd refuelled the pair of us, done the same for the Jeep a little earlier. We were good to go. Only we didn't have a clue which way to head.

We had all the windows down, trying to get a cross breeze going, and the sounds of the streets washed in all around us. Gurgling engines. Cracks like rifle shots as tyres hits rumble strips in the road. Chattering voices. Blaring horns. Laughter. Music. Anywheresville USA.

'I like this new you,' Terry said as he munched his way through some fries. 'This take-charge you. Reminds me of the Mike Lynch I fought alongside against the ragheads.'

I had to admit that I was feeling more like my old self these days. I had wallowed after being invalided out of the Marines. My trend was already downward when that happened, and I used it as an excuse to allow myself to get sucked in deeper. In the absence of the physical crutch I had once used, I found that a psychological one was equally good to lean on. At that time there was only room for me – no one else got a look in. That's why I didn't blame Donna for cutting out, though I still believed taking Wendy thousands of miles away from me was a little extreme. Maybe I deserved it. I did not believe Wendy had as well.

'You're still my tactical guru,' I told Terry. 'And my hit-man when it all gets tossed against the fan.'

He laughed at that, scrunching up the bag his food had come in. He sucked his teeth for a moment, before turning to me. He grew serious. 'It's good to be riding with you again, partner.'

'You too, Terry.'

It was. Over a number of years I had avoided contacting him because he felt indebted to me for saving his life on the battlefield, yet that debt felt like my own weight to carry and something I wanted to avoid calling in. Last summer he repaid the debt – and more. It made all the difference. I could now relax in his company, and it felt great to have someone alongside me who I could trust – and *had* trusted – with my life. When I looked at Terry, I knew the man would die for me if it ever came to it. There are not an awful lot of things in life more humbling.

'It's been a long time coming,' he said, his eyes back on the car park surveying our surroundings. 'But I always thought we'd have our moment again.'

'It took me long enough to find my way through the mess I created for myself.'

'That's a little harsh, Mike. Losing your parents and getting invalided out of a job you loved all in the same year would screw with anyone's head.'

It all seemed so long ago now, but I knew he was right. Fourteen years earlier, a thin sheet of black ice less than a mile from our front door, led to a tragic accident that cost the lives of my adopted parents. My birth mother had given me up for adoption shortly after I was born, having apparently never made a note of who my father was. It was a closed adoption, but I'd never had a single moment of desire to meet my biological parents. Losing the only ones I ever knew didn't alter that, but getting wounded two months later and then losing my posting four months afterwards due to that injury, almost broke me. None of which was any excuse for leaving my wife and child, even though that abandonment was purely on an emotional and psychological level.

'Donna gave me plenty of chances,' I said, reflecting on how tough my anger and depression had made her life with me. 'She put up with it for years waiting for me to turn it all around. So I understand what you mean, mate, but I *did* create that nightmare, and I *did* take far too long to come out of it. I'm thankful every day that it didn't cost me my relationship with my daughter as well as my wife.'

'Wendy is a great kid. You have no worries there. She loves you to bits, that much is obvious. And Donna has forgiven you.'

'She has? How would you know that?'

'I can see it her eyes when she looks at you, Mike. She came through it okay as well.'

I hoped he was right. I knew Donna and I were finished as a couple, but we were still parents to a beautiful, vibrant teenager who needed us both in her life.

Over our food, Terry had suggested we look into the police side of things rather than the FBI involvement. The Bureau were not the first to arrive on scene, and it had to have been a cruiser that first came upon Vern's vehicle. We had no contacts out here, therefore no traction. But Drew's PI firm might have a way in. I didn't like the idea of us having to liaise with them. Point of fact, I wanted to keep as far away from the other team as possible. I had to admit that I didn't have a better idea, though. Other than maybe one, which had occurred to me only moments before. I discussed it with Terry, and as usual it took him no time at all to weight it up and make a decision. On this occasion, it was a single nod in the affirmative.

Ten minutes later, using the prepaid mobile I'd purchased from a nearby store, I dialled the local PD number I had pulled up on the phone's browser. When the call was connected I told the woman on the other end of the line that I had information about the vehicle found out on Route 70 and needed to speak to whichever officers had discovered it abandoned. I gave the woman the registration number, too. I assumed I would not be put through to the officers in question, but I did hope for a name to crop up in conversation.

'That case has now been taken over by the FBI,' the woman said after a few moments which I assumed had been spent checking the computer records.

'Oh, yes I realise that,' I said. I lowered my voice until it became conspiratorial. 'Thing is, I'm a fellow police officer visiting the area from the UK. I may have vital information, and I would rather give that information to the two officers whose job it was to secure the scene. I don't know about you, but I hate it when the big shots breeze in and scoop up the best cases. So if we can keep this away from the Feebs until your guys have had a chance to check it out...'

I left it hanging there. She would either take the bait and cave, or build her defences more strongly.

'Yeah, I get where you're coming from, honey,' she said after a slight pause. 'So, that would be Officers Fraser and Clark.'

'That's great. Thank you for your help. Are they on duty right now?'

'They are, but they are out on patrol. They are due back at the department in a couple of hours, so you could try calling back then. Or, how about you give me your contact information and I'll have them call you right now or maybe even pay you a visit.'

I smiled to myself. The anti-FBI bait had been juicy and far too tasty not to snap up. 'That would be perfect. I'm actually on the road between hotels right now, so if you could ask them to call this number I'd be happy to speak to them.' I gave the mobile number, thanked the woman, and hung up.

'Nicely done,' Terry said, nodding approvingly. 'You are getting more devious by the day.'

'That's your influence.'

'If so, then I'm happy to be of service. You think they'll call?'

'Oh, they'll call. They won't be able to help themselves.'

'So, what then?'

I grinned. 'You ever held two Roswell police officers at gunpoint before?'

EIGHT

Isaac Priest was a mean drunk because he was a mean man even without alcohol slopping around in his bloodstream. He was the kind of man who kicked stray dogs and cursed at the elderly who held him up waiting in line at the Walmart checkout counter when they pulled out a wad of coupons. A man whose face was twisted into a permanent sneer, and whose friends could be counted on the fingers of a single mitten. The liquor served only to fuel all of his numerous petty resentments, and when his words dried up he was not averse to letting his powerful fists do all of the shouting and hollering for him. Priest was banned from the three bars closest to where he lived, which is why he had been in the Corona Main Street saloon on the night Joe Kane ran into the twin peaks of the Barrow boys.

Kane knew all about the man. Still two years shy of fifty, Priest had nothing else to do and nowhere better to be when there was a bar open somewhere nearby. Not that his life had always been so meaningless, or his head so fucked up with anger and bitterness. He had poured concrete to earn a living for the better part of fifteen years, but blew two cervical discs and a patella in a hard collision playing football for his company team. He lost his job one month later, his wife of twenty years one year after that, and all of his friends somewhere in between. Living off part pension and part disability, and with insurance taking care of most of his medical needs, Priest had long since decided to take on his liver in a fight to the death, armed with booze and an unhealthy reluctance to stop drinking it.

No sane bartender took the keys to Priest's truck away from him, irrespective of how many beers and Wild Turkey chasers Priest had got himself on the outside of. Not unless they were looking for a beat down. Which was why, on Tuesday evening at a little after five, Kane knew that Priest would drive himself home on largely empty roads from the bar he'd been frequenting for the past few weeks. Travelling roads with a history of making corpses out of drunk drivers, Kane wished Priest a safe journey and hoped he would not fall foul of Sheriff Crozier along the way.

When Priest yanked open the door to his elderly, rust-bucket of a motorhome, switched on the dim lights, and laid eyes on the Native American from the night before sitting there in the Lay-Z-Boy recliner as bold as brass, Priest grinned and bunched his fingers into fists as tight as the arthritis in his knuckles would allow.

'You got some fucking cojones on you, Tonto,' Priest said, squaring his shoulders and staggering towards Kane. 'But I guarantee you'll weep like a fucking baby when I kick your balls so hard they'll need to Heimlich you to free 'em.'

Kane shifted faster than any man his size had a right to move. As Priest stepped in and swung a right-handed haymaker, Kane came out of the chair as if propelled by more than something physical. He dipped low and swayed sideways, the punch missing him by inches. In retaliation, Kane stamped down hard on Priest's shin, letting his boot scrape along the bone. Priest let out a cry that was all moist air from his lungs, the breath sucked away by a pain so intense it was as if a jolt of electricity had shot through his leg. Blinded by tears that flowed from both eyes, Priest never saw the head-butt that followed. He would have felt it though. Felt the cartilage in his nose crumple like a too-wet concrete that never got a chance to set properly, tasted the warm and cloying blood as it splashed down his mouth and chin. And then the pain again, just like before, only transferred from his lower leg to the centre of his face.

Priest's attempts to hold both his shin and his destroyed nose, whilst still computing the agonising pain, as a fresh welling of tears blinded him, were utterly useless. He didn't need either the hard slam to the gut or the uppercut to the chin that sent his world hurtling into darkness to know that he was done even before he'd got started. But Kane wondered if the man's final thought before slipping fully into unconsciousness was to wonder whether he would ever wake up again.

Kane heaved the big slab of meat that was Priest into the recliner and waited. He kept watch on Isaac Priest's eyes as they first flickered, then became thin wounds in his face, before finally opening fully. The man blinked several times, before fixing his gaze on Kane, who now sat in a chair opposite. Despite the beating he had received, Priest would undoubtedly have come barrelling out of that chair in a mad rush for vengeance had the man who'd handed out that punishment not been sitting there with a large hunting knife in his hand.

'Welcome back,' Kane said, no hint of triumph in his voice. 'I urge you not to try anything stupid. I could skin you with this blade and you would not even notice until you stood up to leave and shed it behind you like a snake.'

Priest swallowed hard. Anger flared in his eyes. 'I need to take a piss,' he managed to say through a jaw that must have felt like it was on fire.

'If you really have to, do it where you sit. If all you want is the gun you keep taped behind the toilet bowl, don't bother. I will leave it with you when I go, but for now it stays out of your reach.'

The drunk hung his head and exhaled heavily, a wheeze in his chest leaking out like a punctured air line. 'The fuck you want with me?' he said. His voice was deep but undemanding given his circumstances.

'Information.'

'You coulda asked. You coulda knocked on my fuckin' door an' just asked.'

Kane made a dismissive gesture with the hand not holding the knife. 'You would have told me where to go. We would have had words. Blows would have been exchanged. Ultimately we would have ended up right where we are now, but my way we got here quicker and less painfully for one of us.'

Priest jerked his head up. He glared at Kane and shook his head. 'You know you're gonna have to kill me, right?'

'Are you saying you won't give me what I came here for?'

'No. That's not what I'm saying. You ask, I'll answer. Like I woulda done if you'd only asked in the first place. But you didn't. Instead you beat me, humiliated me. So when we're done, you leave without ending me and I won't rest until I've drained every last drop of blood from the gash I'm gonna open up in your throat.'

'So you're what… going to hunt me down?'

'You bet your ass I am.'

'You do know I'm Native American, right? Indian.'

'You ain't exactly in disguise, Tonto.'

'And you're going to hunt *me*?'

'Yeah. Damn right! Cause I'm a fucking Marine!'

'Well, hoo-ra for you, Mr Priest. And you *were* a Marine. A lifetime and about fifty pounds ago. I will always be Native

American, and no "paleface" is going to get the drop on me. So, enough with the macho bullshit and let's get on with this.'

'Fire away, you red motherfucker!'

Kane smiled and edged forward on his seat. He toyed with the knife, twirling it between his fingers. He noted Priest's eyes straying to it, perhaps attracted by the gleam from the razor-edged carbon steel blade. The man behaved like a cat drawn to a glimmer of reflected light.

'Two nights ago you were in the Main Street bar in Corona,' Kane said.

'I was, yeah. And your fight is with those Barrow twins, so why are you dicking around with me?'

'I hope to meet with them again if time allows. Fate will decide that, not me. For now, you will have to do because you have the same information as them.'

'Which is?'

'While you were in the bar, two strangers entered. They asked questions. I want to know two things. First, when I show you a photo I want to know if it's of one of the two men from that night. Second, I want to know what they asked.'

Priest laughed through his obvious discomfort, his big chest heaving. He coughed a couple of times before replying. 'They asked what all those dumb fucks ask. They wanted to know where the crash site was. They got told about five different places, then they were impolitely invited to get the hell outta there.'

Kane maintained eye contact. He saw nothing to suggest the man was telling lies. The answer was as suspected, and counted for very little in the grander scheme of things. The most important clarification he sought was the identity of one of the two men. From the breast pocket of his raw cotton shirt he withdrew a passport-sized photograph. Taking care to ensure the hunting knife remained by his side, Kane stood and took a couple of steps closer to the man leaking alcohol fumes. He held the snapshot out in front of him.

'Was this one of the two guys?' he asked.

Priest squinted at it. Took a few seconds. Then shook his head. 'Can't say for sure. Could be, but I only got a look at one of the fellahs. This ain't him. Might be the other one, but like I say, I don't know for certain one way or the other.'

'Look again. Think harder.'

Instead, the man stared up at him. The flesh around his face was puffing up, and was already the kind of red that looked as if it radiated heat. Blood continued to trickle from one of his nostrils, the liquid slick against the dried smears. His once muscular arms, faded ink indistinct beneath the tan and matted hair, hung uselessly by his side. *A big man gone to seed is a sorry sight,* Kane thought.

Priest said, 'Don't matter how long I look or how hard I think. Ain't gonna change nothin'. You want me to lie, I'll say whatever the fuck you want me to say. You want the truth, then the truth is I don't know for sure.'

None of that was what Kane wanted to hear. He didn't deal in possibilities, and neither did the Judge. Kane was a man unused to being given the run-around by professionals, so having these amateurs cause him so many problems was becoming personal. He tucked the photo back into his pocket and moved away towards the door.

'If you want to come looking for me because of the beating I gave you,' Kane said, peering back over his shoulder at Priest, 'I will be around. Would be better for us both if you did not. But I will understand if I see you coming.'

'Oh, you won't see me until I'm sticking a gun in your ribs.'

Kane smiled. 'A word of advice. Do not be undone by pride. Better men than you have lost their lives on that score.'

Priest scowled and nodded. 'I guess we'll see.'

'I guess we will. I will say goodbye, then. For now.'

Priest nodded again.

Kane paused in the doorway. He looked around at the inside of the motorhome, which was cramped and dirty and unkempt. The place looked as if it had never felt the suck of a hoover or the touch of a dusting cloth. It smelled of sour breath, sour sweat, and a sour disposition.

'You like living like this?' he asked.

'What's it to you?' Priest said, his top lip a surly curve.

Kane shrugged. 'Nothing. Just don't understand it is all. I live alone, but I take pride. In my possessions. In myself. I wonder where yours got lost along the way. I kinda feel sorry for you.'

'Fuck you, Sitting Bull!'

Kane let out a low chuckle. 'You do know he beat Custer, don't you? You dumb fuck.'

'Yeah.' Priest nodded, his eyes blazing like wildfires on the edge of darkness. 'I also know he was gunned down by one of his own. Just like you're gonna be, man. Just like you.'

'What do you know about me?' Kane asked, interested in the dipso all over again.

Priest cackled, his big chest rising and falling like bellows. 'Enough to figure the Judge is gonna carve you up like a Thanksgiving turkey. Yeah, I know who you are, man. I know you work for that sonofabitch. That man sure loves to put his own kind in the ground.'

Kane stood there for a moment contemplating. He did not like the fact that this lowlife white man knew so much about affairs that should have remained within the reservation. Nor that he seemed well informed as to the true nature of Mangas Crow.

'You sure you do not recognise the man in the photo?' he asked

His swift change of tack was deliberate. Kane searched Priest's eyes for a tell-tale flicker of recognition, but all he saw there was a hateful glower.

'I told you all I have to tell you.' His head tilted a little then, and his eyebrows and the vertical line in the centre of his forehead came together to form a W. 'Except for one thing, I guess. Something that might interest you.'

'And what's that?'

'It's gonna cost you.'

'How much?'

'Fifty.' Priest's tongue snaked out, wetting his lips.

'I could beat it out of you.'

'You could. But it'd be easier just to hand over the cash. I can take a beating.'

'Make it thirty.'

Priest held out a hand, palm upward.

Kane shook his head. 'You talk first, then you get paid if I think it's worth it.'

'You'll stiff me.'

'That is a chance you will have to take.'

Priest growled and jabbed a finger at him. 'You keep talking about two men. Only, there was three of them.'

Kane paused, glanced down at his feet. Back up again. It didn't sound like bullshit, but this was news to him. 'You positive about that? Way I heard it, only two strangers came into the bar that night.'

'Sure, that's right enough. But when they left I got up to take a piss. I could see out through the window and I watched them walk to the car, get inside, and pull away. Thing is, neither of them got behind the wheel.'

Three men.

Kane caught his breath and considered that. Since his search had begun, one had become two, and now it seemed that the two had picked up a third somewhere along the way. Unless this piece of human garbage was lying to him. He nodded once, turned to leave.

'Hey! How about my damn thirty bucks?' Priest called out, heat in his tone.

Kane waved a hand in the air but this time did not look back. 'Always trust your instincts, Priest. Consider yourself stiffed.'

NINE

We chose a spot close to access points onto Highways 70 and 285. That way, if it all went to shit we'd be on a fast drive out of there within minutes. I parked up outside a desolate-looking industrial plant enveloped by a chain-link fence. From the number of steel tubes that were stacked up in piles dotted around the site, I guessed they either manufactured them at one point, or had used them for oil, gas or water distribution. It was hard to tell. Patches of hardcore lay like grey place mats in the dirt where once buildings must have stood. All that was left were a handful of doorless brick sheds, whose contents had long since been stripped away. A couple of forklift trucks stood idle, rusted, cables bubbling out of their inner tubing. Thick dust covered every surface, suggesting the plant had closed years back and had simply been left to its own devices while its acreage grew in value.

Other than the proximity to the highways, the spot had one other distinct advantage: you could see vehicles approaching for miles around.

'Dust spiral,' Terry said in my ear. 'At roughly your eight o'clock. Coming hard.'

I turned to look back over my shoulder. It took a couple of seconds to adjust my vision, but I finally spotted it. A tiny, dark speck with a cone of desert dust billowing behind it like a parachute.

'You think they got lucky with their approach given the way we're facing, or do they have eyes in the sky?'

'I wouldn't bet against it.'

I took a breath. Squinted at the vehicle coming our way. 'We should've gone with your idea, Terry. I've had doubts about this plan of mine ever since we got here.'

'Don't second guess yourself now, Mike. Each strategy had its pros and cons.'

'Yeah. Your way would've at least made them feel comfortable from the outset.'

Terry had suggested we meet with the cops in a crowded shopping mall or busy diner, somewhere with plenty of people around to lessen the possibility of gunplay if things did not go the way we intended. These cops were not going to like what we had to say, or the way we were going to have to say it, and one way or another it was going to draw a reaction.

'Don't sweat it, Mike. Their level of comfort will change the moment we tell them why they're really here. If we were back in town and had to run for it, we'd be caught up in a snarl of traffic, or running through crowded streets more familiar to the cops than us. At least this way we have a chance to escape and nobody around us gets hurt.'

'Unless the spy in the sky is there, in which case they track us. Plus, this location must have sent up all kinds of distress flares in the minds of those cops.'

'You ready for this?' Terry asked.

I took a breath. Let it out slowly. 'As I'll ever be. What's to worry about? All we're doing is inviting two armed officers way out here so's we can pull weapons on them. What could possibly go wrong?'

It had initially felt like the right thing to do. Lure them out to the edge of town, away from the general population, with escape routes close by. Now it felt as if I were a fly sitting in a web of my own making, and had brought a friend along to be the second course. I watched in the rear-view as the dark speck and cloud of dust gradually transformed into a police cruiser.

Officers Fraser and Clark, I presumed.

'I have them, Terry. You see anything else out there? Anything at all?'

'Nothing,' he said. 'Not on the ground, nor in the air either.'

'Which doesn't mean they aren't there.'

'True.'

'So we call it now. Stay or go?'

'I say we hang around.'

I had to smile. There was no way Terry was ever going to choose to run. The weight of it fell on me.

'You stay put,' I said. 'I'm going to get out and greet our RPD friends.'

I walked around to the rear of the Jeep and leaned back against it, making sure I showed them my empty hands. The rear door was unlocked and left slightly ajar. One swift flip up and my hand would be on an H&K assault rifle. Plus I now had a Sig tucked into the back of my cargo trousers. As the cruiser slowed its progress there was no further conversation required. Terry and I had no need to discuss our intentions. In a two-on-two situation our code was simple – whoever drove had the driver, the passenger took the passenger. If there were more than two people in the vehicle, then we played it by ear.

The cruiser pulled up short, leaving a dozen or so yards between it and the Jeep. This triggered another alarm inside my head, though it was the smart thing to do on their part. Two uniformed cops emerged from inside the black-and-white Dodge Charger. Both wore midnight blue jackets over grey and black shirts. All kinds of paraphernalia hung on their utility belts, but my eyes were drawn to their 9 mm S&W handguns. First thing I noted was their holsters flapping. Both had paused with their doors open, and now I knew why.

The two cops were unstrapped and ready for action.

Which meant they were suspicious.

Which in turn meant Terry and I were in all kinds of trouble.

The cops approached with understandable caution. The driver was a big man, white with slicked back fair hair and sideburns much longer than anyone ever needed. His partner was a smaller, wider black cop whose bulges of hard muscle made him look as if steroids were on his five-a-day list. The passenger wore sunglasses despite the fading light. I did not like being unable to see the man's eyes.

'Officers Fraser and Clark, right?' I said.

'Yes, sir,' Sideburns responded. I heard a hitch in his voice that told me his adrenaline was pumping hard. 'I'm Fraser, this here is Officer Clark. You have some information for us, Detective Reeves?'

William Reeves was the name of one of the four Newcastle-based detectives who grilled me following the events of the previous summer. I needed to use a name that would stand up to a cursory check, hoping the detective sergeant hadn't quit the service since. This was another potential hurdle in my fifty-fifty strategy. The choice was to either give them my real name so that I could show them ID if asked, but which would throw up nothing if the cops looked into my supposed service with the police, or a fake name which would check out okay but one I would not be able to back up with any identification. Becoming a fake cop was a no-brainer; these two were not going to be lured all the way out into the middle of nowhere by a civilian. Still, it had been a risk.

I knew right there and then that it had been a bad play on my part. The whole shebang, from location to use of name to the initial crazy notion of holding these two serving cops at gunpoint and doing so until they fed us the details we were looking for. As for what I had been thinking, I had no idea. But why on earth had Terry gone along with it? The master strategist.

I made my play anyway.

'To be honest, it's the other way around, officers.'

Fraser and Clark risked a sidelong glance at each other before turning their full attention back to me. 'Say again,' Clark said.

'I misled you. When I spoke to you earlier, I needed your attention. I thought you would be interested in beating the FBI to the punch. Now, please don't be alarmed because this is in no way a set-up. All I want from you is information.'

Clark's hand movement gave him away. It went immediately to his weapon. He did not draw the gun, but he was poised to. Fraser was a rock, albeit a clearly troubled one. 'You have some identification you can show me, sir?' he asked.

I shook my head. 'No, officer. I deliberately left my passport, driving licence and credit cards elsewhere. I admit I am not Detective Reeves, but I'm not one of the bad guys, either.'

Fraser nodded. He licked his lips while he chewed that over. 'Sir, you are dangerously close to becoming a threat to both myself and my partner here. That's a risk I don't think you want to take. I don't know what game you are playing, but I do think the best place to discuss matters further is back at our station house.'

'That's not going to happen. We need to talk, but we need to do it here and now.'

My gaze dropped from Fraser's eyes to Clark's twitching right hand. He looked to be the younger, less experienced of the two cops, and my guess was he would react first. I wasn't overly bothered by that, because I knew Terry would have his man. Fraser was the detonation switch here. If he decided to act, then the situation could easily get out of control. There could be four dead bodies lying here within seconds. I decided to ease the tension by showing my hand.

'Officers, I realise what this looks like. I've ambushed you and that must seem like a real threat to you. I assure you now that it is not. You have nothing to fear from us.'

Both cops peered beyond me towards the Jeep. 'Us?' they said in unison.

I nodded. 'Oh, my own partner is not in the Jeep. But he does have you in his sights.'

Terry had secreted himself inside the abandoned site behind a stack of dust-laden pipes. He was less than twenty yards away. We had been communicating on a two-way bug for the past thirty minutes.

'Really?' Fraser said, glancing around, a smile of doubt touching his lips. I knew he thought that I was playing him.

I nodded. 'Really.'

Less than a second later, a large red dot appeared on Officer Clark's forehead. It switched to Fraser's then back again. Kept on that way for a few seconds, until both of them became aware of what was happening. While they were busy being shocked by the trap, I eased out my Sig and held it on Fraser. The red dot stopped switching and held firm on Clark's face.

This was the point of highest anxiety.

These two proud cops would not like being taken for mugs, and having weapons pulled on them was akin to waving a red flag at a bull. This still had plenty of room to go sideways. I felt the adrenaline kick in like a sparking electricity circuit, but my gun hand remained steady.

'I know you'd like nothing better than to rip my guts out right now,' I said. 'But you two officers know better than most how necessary it is control a situation. That's all we're doing here. Managing the scene while you answer a few questions for us.'

'You're gonna drop us anyway,' Clark said, his face tight with fury. 'You get your answers, you'll put us both down like dogs.'

I thought I would try for the truth, let that fall where it may.

'No, see that's where you're wrong. Me and my friend here, all we want to do is find somebody who is currently missing. Someone whose vehicle you pulled off Highway 70 to check out this morning because it was left abandoned out there. Now, I know the FBI swarmed all over that scene once you called it in, but before they did, before they tossed you off your own case, you had some time with it. Free and clear time, just the two of you. You don't strike me as a couple of cops who would sit on your hands waiting. All I need to know is what you found. Your impressions. Anything you can tell me that will help.'

'What do you want with her?' Fraser asked, his gaze becoming venomous.

'What do I want with who?' For a moment I wondered if he was referring to the Kia, the way some men do think of cars as female.

'The woman who owns the vehicle. You say you want to find her. For all we know, it could be to kill her, abduct her.'

I smiled. Fraser was testing me. I admired the nerve of his play. 'Officer Fraser, given you two ran the plates and then called in to your HQ because of the red flag on that licence number, you know as well as I do that car belongs to Vern Jackson. Not a girl. Fair play to you for testing me out, but we're beyond that now. As for Vern, we don't know him at all, but we do know his family and they want him back. That's why we'd like to know more about the car and the scene when you first rolled up on it.'

'You think this is helping?' Clark said.

Anger and lost pride screamed loudest in his quiet voice. His fingers remained twitching by his side. He was edgy. Had a lid on it for now, but I wondered how long that might last. I did not want to put these cops through the indignity of having their service weapons taken from them. However, I saw now that it wouldn't be too long before that was no longer contained. I did know someone who would control it, but I also had no doubt that Terry would blow this cop away if it went bad here. So I had to turn to the one other person capable of reeling the nervous cop in.

'Officer Fraser. I look at you and I see a man who doesn't much like the situation he finds himself in, but is prepared to bite down on it. I think you believe what I'm telling you, and that you will also believe me when I tell you that when we're done here you two will be fine. Officer Clark there, however, has other ideas. All the way through he's been thinking of the best time to remove his weapon. Not whether to, but the best time to. That's a danger this situation simply does not need. Now, as a gesture of good faith I'm going to slip my own weapon away. In return, how about you ask your partner there to strap his holster.'

Fraser went ahead without any hesitation.

'Officer Clark. Re-strap your holster and keep your hand well away from your firearm. Trust me, there's no need. It's clear to me that these men are not amateurs, and professionals would not kill us for no good reason. Pulling your weapon at this point only gets us both dead. I get the feeling that as soon as they get what they came here for these two will be on their way.'

'But, sir, I–'

'This is one of those big decision days, Clark.' Fraser turned to face his partner. 'Better to be pissed and alive, than glorious and dead.'

I could not have said it better myself. Still I had no idea which way this might go. My chest was rising and falling as the swell of panic rushed over me. It took a few more seconds, but the pumped-up officer finally complied with our wishes. Fraser did the same, and I respected him for that.

'What exactly are you looking for here?' Fraser asked, eyes only for me now as the desert breeze blew fine billows of dust around us.

'You found the minivan. What did you bag and tag?'

'Nothing. FBI wanted their own people on it.'

I wondered why the Bureau were investing so much time and effort in this. Drew and Donna only wanted to know where their nephew was.

'Okay. So what did you find while you had time alone with it? And I know you searched it. No way you could resist, right?'

Fraser nodded. 'Coupla overnight bags. Nothing out of the ordinary. I heard one of the agents talking about sending a photo of the contents to the kid's mother.'

'That was it?'

He looked up at me, checking me out more closely. 'You expecting something else?'

I shook my head. 'I'm expecting everything and nothing. So, that's what you found. Anything you didn't find? Anything unusual about the scene?'

The cop regarded me as if he had a newfound respect. 'Anything I didn't find, huh? You and your partner out there really cops?'

'No. Military. At least, once upon a time.'

'I did my own tours, man.' The first semblance of a smile passed across his lips. 'Maybe that's why I got that you two were the real deal.'

'We are. We didn't draw you here to hurt you. Neither of us want it this way and I feel bad that we had to do this at all. It won't go down that way, least not from us.'

I saw something glint in his eyes, sensed him reach a decision. 'It was a little too clean for my liking,' he said. 'You travel several hundred miles, your vehicle collects a certain amount of trash on the interior as well as exterior dust and grime. Not the Kia. I got the impression that whatever had accumulated was removed, which meant what they left us was deliberate on their part. There were also a couple of maps lying on the ground by the open driver's door. They looked out of place to me. As if perhaps when the rest of the garbage was tossed, the maps were kept and laid out on the floor to get them noticed.'

Maps.

I chewed that over. From Drew and his PIs I knew the minivan had no GPS, but people these days often have some form of Sat-Nav app on their phone. I thought maybe the poor signal in these parts precluded that option. But if Vern was using maps, would he also be using indication markers? Like a cross through a chosen destination, or a circle. Maybe even a route highlighted with coloured marker pen. I looked hard at the two cops.

'Think about it,' I said. 'You saw the maps, but did you see any markings on them?'

Clark cut a look across at his more senior partner. Fraser gave a couple of nods.

'Corona,' he said.

'You mean, like the drink? The beer?'

'Sure,' Fraser said, nodding. 'It's the kind of place you could drive through while blinking and not even notice it.'

'And any other markings?' I prompted.

'Not that I noticed.'

I had to wonder if he had the balls to be hiding something from me. Likely. But he'd given me a town, somewhere to begin our search. Which was more than we had before. If we managed to drive away from here without firing a shot, then it would have been worth the risk after all.

The breeze picked up and the desert dust swirled and settled back down again. The air was dry and stuffy and tasted foul. The light was winking out, and I thought we had overstayed our welcome.

'Let's go,' I said.

I turned to face Terry who was now standing by the Jeep. None of us had seen or heard him coming. He held in his hand the laser scope from his rifle.

'The real deal was never on you,' he said. 'Either of you. Only the sighter.'

'That's true.' I nodded to confirm. It was important to me that the cops understood we had wished them no harm. 'But,' I said as I saw Clark's hand flexing once more. 'We do have one more partner in the game. He fixed his nest a long way out, so you're painted for him and you will never even hear his bullet coming if you make a move on us.'

'Who the fuck are you guys?' Fraser asked.

'Nobody. You never came out here, you never met us. You go about your business, we go about ours. That's all this needs to be if you keep your man Clark in check.'

'That might be a struggle,' Fraser admitted.

Terry was now back at the Jeep and behind the wheel, which was rumbling in the background. I stepped forward two paces, drew the Sig and blew out one of the rear tyres of the police SUV.

Clark's face grew all kinds of serious, and Fraser didn't look best pleased, either. 'The fuck you do that for?' he asked.

'Just to buy us some time. Anyhow, we're gone. Thanks for the tip.'

'Hey!' Fraser called after me. 'Tell me something.'

I turned. 'Would we have shot you?'

'Something like that, yeah.'

'Not unless absolutely necessary. Only if our lives depended on it. Like I said before, I hated doing this to you two, especially now that I see you are both honourable and professional men. But we were in a bind. We wanted information you had. That's all it was.'

Fraser seemed to chew that over.

'Now you tell me something,' I said. 'Out of interest, if we'd asked to meet you in a diner or mall, would you still have tried to pull your guns on us?'

'Absolutely. Like you said, you gotta take control. Crowded situation, I would've had my weapon out on you from the moment I saw you.'

That was good enough for me. As crazy as my plan seemed, it had been the right one after all. We got out of there. A mile into the highway, I tossed the burner. I had no idea if it could be traced, but it had served its purpose. The cops had provided us with our next move.

TEN

It didn't take us long to drive through Corona. The main road slicing through the dot of a town on Highway 54 took us past an auto sales that seemed to specialise in beaten-up old trucks with more gaping holes than metal, a budget motel in the process of being refurbished, a number of general stores, a bar, and a couple of fuel stations.

It was a curious mix. The relatively new sat shoulder to shoulder with the very old, fresh alongside shabby, in-use sandwiched between the abandoned, maintained abutting neglected. Some buildings looked as if the owners had simply given up hope and moved on, allowing their properties to become ramshackle, while others suggested the locals were at least attempting to regenerate the place. Red or sand-coloured brick buildings dominated Main Street, some of which looked unfinished, as if the developers had perhaps run out of finances part way through. Decay had set into others, stucco having fallen away to expose the brick framework beneath. I circled back a couple of times and navigated the side streets for a while. A Baptist church looked to be one of the few places in good order, sporting a fresh coat of white paint, which I guess spoke volumes for the people who lived in the town. Elsewhere, the dwellings and other structures we drove by reeked of neglect. Following our third drive-through I pulled the Jeep off the road about a mile outside Corona's perimeter. I kept the engine running and the heat on because it had turned cold outside.

It was the morning after the evening before, and I was more than a little anxious.

By the time we had left the two cops behind in Roswell, Terry and I decided it was too late in the evening to do anything about what we had been told. There was also a fair chance that Fraser and Clarke had requested a car or two sat on the place in case we showed up. Terry and I were both beat, so rather than getting a taste of Roswell's night life, we made our way back to the airport and crashed out on board the plane which was now sitting inside a shared hangar. A few of the seats reclined far enough back to make comfortable beds, and there were shower and other facilities on board. Neither of us wanted to go through the fuss and bother of booking into a hotel. The Lear provided us with everything we needed, and with the door closed we managed to keep out most of the fumes coming off the warm oil and aviation fuel.

We had picked up a takeaway pizza close to the airport and I was making my way through my third slice when I got a call from Donna. She told me they had received a mail from the FBI, with a couple of photographs attached. The photos revealed a hold-all, and spread out next to it lay some clothes and a washbag. The attire was male, the bag a soft brown leather.

'We showed the photos to Sheryl,' Donna said, her voice low and hugely dispirited. 'She's positive it all belongs to Vern. None of us knows quite what to make of it.'

I had to think about that some. 'It's useful information,' I told her. 'But it's neither a good nor bad sign. Don't fret about it too much.' I caught her up with our progress, omitting the fight with the men from Reno, and the part about pulling guns on a couple of Roswell PD cops. There was no point in worrying her unduly. I didn't tell her about Corona, either, only that we had a lead we were following up on in the morning. I didn't want to get ahead of ourselves or go into any detail at this stage. The mantra that the less you told people the less they could tell others remained true, even in these peculiar circumstances.

I was still waiting for a response from Drew about my hacker suggestion, but when I asked to speak to him Donna told me he had not yet arrived home from work. I asked her to remind him that he owed me a call. Before we were done, she handed her phone to Wendy.

'Hey, Dad.'

'Hiya, kiddo. How was school?'

'School. Mostly lame, but it's okay. I miss you.'

That felt so good to hear. Not too long ago I had a feeling that my daughter and I were drifting apart, but the simple act of being with her for even a few hours had convinced me that the gap between us was not so large after all. Miles, yes, but nothing we could not bridge.

'I miss you, too. I expect to be gone another few days, but I meant what I said last night, sweetheart. When this is over, you and I will spend some time together. Just the two of us.'

'Sure. I'd like that.'

'Hey, I thought about something when I was lying in bed. You remember when you were a little kid and you'd sneak into our room during the night?'

'Yeah. I'd snuggle down right in the middle of you and Mum.'

I laughed. 'I'm not sure about snuggle down, more like stretch out like a starfish and force us to the edges of the bed. But what really used to crack me up was that you'd scuttle in and bring one toy with you. Always the Disney one, Sebastian from *The Little Mermaid*. As soon as you realised we weren't throwing you out and back to your own bed, you'd go back and forth between the rooms fetching the rest of your stuffed menagerie. I can't count the number of times the night reverberated to the sound of your little feet padding in and out of our bedroom. Then we'd wake up the next day surrounded by all these glassy, beady eyes.'

Wendy had started out chuckling as I reminded her of this childhood ritual, but by the time I was finished she was howling with laughter. 'Sometimes you got cross with me and sent me away, but mostly you put up with it and let me stay.'

'Truth is, it was never a matter of putting up with it. I loved it. Loved the fact you wanted to be with us. Loved waking up to find you still there. We only ever sent you back on the odd occasion so as to remind you who the bosses were.'

'Somehow, I think I was always the boss in those days, Dad.'

'I think you're right, kiddo. I'm not sure that ever changed, actually.'

'It's cool that you remember all that. Love you, Dad.'

I felt a solid weight drop into my throat. If there were more wonderful words you could hear from your own child, I had yet to learn of them. 'I love you more,' I told her, understanding that I could never describe how powerful that emotion was.

After we had finished eating, Terry and I decided we would head to the place marked on the map first thing in the morning. At that point neither of us knew what to expect, nor what we might find. We just hadn't expected it to be more nothing. Which was pretty much what we had found.

'Well, I'm puzzled,' I said to Terry, as we sat in the Jeep on the side of the road. Corona lay behind us, a forgotten town undeserving of a red circle around it.

He nodded and stroked his chin. I could hear the harsh scuff of nails on beard stubble. 'What was so important about this place that they had to mark it off on the map?'

'You think the cop was bullshitting us? That he deliberately sent us to the quietest town in all of New Mexico out of pure spite?'

'Maybe. I didn't get that read from him, though.'

I shook my head. 'No, me neither.'

'But there's nothing here, Mike. No reason to come here deliberately, that's for sure.'

'Maybe the reason for the mark is not the place itself,' I suggested. 'Maybe it's about a person. What if it's simply a meeting place?'

Terry sighed. He made no reply. There was nothing to say, not without some hard facts to wrap our brains around. Now that we had laid eyes on the place and driven through it a few times, the question remained: if you were going to meet with someone, why Corona of all places?

Frustrated, I took out my mobile. I had no signal. I slammed my palm against the steering wheel and cursed. I swung the Jeep around and crawled slowly back in the direction of the town, checking the signal as I steered with one hand. The moment I had a couple of bars I edged back onto the dirt verge once more and pulled over. I used Google to look up Corona, adding 'NM' when all I got were links and images to the beer company. I jabbed on a link that looked intriguing, read the first couple of paragraphs on the web page that popped up, and then set the phone face down on my lap. I sat there staring out of the windscreen at the mountain ranges away in the distance to our right, the dilapidated beginnings of Corona peeking out from behind a slight curve on the road ahead. It was a stretch of wide blacktop that you'd blow through on your way to somewhere less dead, only now I knew it had a history.

'What's on your mind?' Terry asked, fixing me with those stone-dead eyes of his. 'I know that look, Mike. I've heard those gears in that big brain of yours squeal like that before.'

'Just a thought,' I said. 'Just a coincidence, perhaps. Maybe not.'

'Go on then. Spill.'

I shifted in my seat to face him. 'Okay. So as far as his family were aware, Vern was headed north from Las Vegas, intending to camp out in the desert. Now, I happen to know that you go in a certain direction from there and you end up passing close by Edwards Air Force base. Edwards is otherwise known as Area 51. That's a bit of a pilgrimage if you're a UFO nut.'

'So..?'

'So, were you aware that where we landed in the Lear was once the Walker Air Force base, which at one point was simply known as Roswell Air Force base?'

'And? Don't get me wrong, this is a fascinating story, Mike, but that *is* the name of the city where the airport is situated. Other than the fact that I now know it was once an Air Force base, I still don't understand what you're getting at.'

I raised my eyebrows. 'Come on, Terry. No need to be tetchy. I could tell you, but I'm trying to get it to dawn on you the way it did me. It might mean more that way. Don't think of it as a city, or the airport. Think of the name. You've heard the name Roswell before, I know you have. Then put that together with the old Air Force base.'

Terry looked hard at me. For a moment I thought I had angered him, but then I realised he was simply straining to think. A moment later I saw the flare of recognition in his eyes. I assumed it looked something like the one in mine a few minutes earlier.

'Okay, yes. Roswell, where that UFO supposedly crashed back in the fifties?'

'Close. It was actually in June or July 1947.'

'And what exactly does that have to do with Corona?'

'The UFO supposedly crashed on a ranch deep into the desert. Back then, Corona was the closest inhabited town to the crash site.' I jabbed a stiff finger at the dark smear ahead of us. 'This is where it was first reported.'

Terry puffed out his cheeks. 'So why do people call it the Roswell UFO crash site and not the Corona UFO crash site?'

'Because when it first came to the attention of the media, people didn't know the full story.' I read off my phone again before continuing. 'It was a while before the crash was even reported. A few weeks, apparently. Soon as it was, the Air Force was all over it like a vegan on tofu. Them and the men in dark suits. They closed the place down, took the debris back to the closest major city, and by the time the news leaked the name of Roswell became synonymous with the crash. It was only much later when the actual site was identified and revealed to the public.'

'Okay, so I see the thread you're drawing together here. Vern possibly went to Area 51, may have driven all the way down here to maybe take a look at the site, and then his vehicle was found the other side of Roswell. None of that explains why, nor if it was even Vern who made those trips. And it still doesn't tell us where he is now.'

'But it's something, right?'

Terry twisted his face. 'I'm not sure, Mike. I'm hearing a lot of speculation that may or may not involve Vern. If he was off on some UFO hunt, why would he not call home first?'

'I don't have all the answers, Terry. Perhaps he got excited and overwhelmed by it all. And yes, I am speculating. Speculation is all we have right now. But it would maybe explain why Corona was circled on the map.'

I was about to say more when I noticed a vehicle pull up behind us. It was a black-and-white SUV. Although we had swapped the Jeep's licence plate back for the original one, having stolen and used a plate from a shopping mall car park before our run-in with the cops, I wondered if our description had by now been put out on an all-points bulletin call. Fraser and Clarke might not have wanted to admit how easily they were taken down, so it was possible that they had kept our encounter to themselves as I had suggested they do. If not, there could be eyes on the roads looking for a silver Jeep with two men in the front seats. We were some way from Roswell, but the cruiser slipping in behind us gave me a bad feeling.

I checked out the cop in the door mirror. I saw then that I had been wrong. It was a sheriff's vehicle, and the man exiting the vehicle was a sheriff and not a police officer. He was getting on a bit. Late forties was my guess, though his bushy moustache was perhaps adding a few years. He hefted his gun belt a couple of times and placed a white Stetson hat on his head. The sheriff ambled across to the door on my side. He remained clipped, hand nowhere near his weapon. Did not appear to be expecting trouble. I buzzed the window down and raised a half-smile. Full beam worried people. Made it appear as if you had something to hide.

'Good morning, officer,' I said. 'Is there a problem?'

'Morning, young fellah,' he said in a low drawl. He ran a finger and thumb in opposite directions across his moustache. 'Name's Sheriff Dwight Crozier, and I was about to ask you the same thing.'

'No, no problem here, sheriff.'

'Uh-huh. Only I saw your vehicle on the side of the road and wondered right away why you'd be pulled over here when you got a small town up ahead you can stop at. Thought you might be having car problems.'

'No, we're fine thanks. We were just having a chat. Thought it best to pull off the road while we were doing so.'

The cop peered beyond me at Terry. Left his eyes there a few seconds while Terry stared ahead impassively. 'That an English accent I hear?' Crozier asked, his gaze dropping back on me.

'It is. Good ear. Americans often confuse it with Australian.'

'Me and the wife spent a month touring the UK back in…oh, 2009. You people have a rich history behind you, that's for sure.'

'Yep.' I nodded, smiled again. 'And an uncertain future.'

'Well, that goes for all of us I reckon.' The sheriff chuckled softly and took a quick peek in the back, saw nothing to trouble him. 'Where you folks headed today?'

I thought about the best thing to tell him. We were pointing back towards Roswell, but I did not want his mind going there in case it reminded him of something he might have heard on his radio earlier in the morning. Something popped into my head and I thought maybe we'd caught a break.

I pulled a 'you got me' face. 'I'm sure you get this all the time out here, sheriff. I was a little embarrassed to tell you why we pulled off the road, because we were actually talking about how we might find out where the crash site was. We didn't want to ask in town in case we looked foolish, so we've been driving around for a while trying to find signs for it. We thought it was on the outskirts of Corona, but we can't find a thing.'

I saw Crozier relax and knew that had done the trick. I'd noticed his senses were heightened, and even if he wasn't aware of an APB I did not want him to think of us later on. Assuming this was his patch, my guess was he fended off UFO thrill-seekers all the time.

'You boys are looking for the guided tour right? Follow the sign and we'll show you where it all took place, that sort of thing?' The sheriff gave a dry laugh. 'Well, first of all, I reckon the outskirts of a place means something different out here than it does to you back home. We judge distance a little differently. The homestead where they say the crash took place is not far off thirty miles from here, so you won't bump into it driving in and around Corona itself. And second, sorry to disappoint but the tours don't run anymore. The signs were taken down a coupla years back. New people own that land and they don't much like visitors trampling all over their property and someone else making money off the back of it.'

I gave it my best shot at appearing crestfallen. 'That's such a shame. We only drove out here for that.'

'You would,' Crozier said, nodding. 'Nothin' else here to see. You boys checked out the museum in Roswell? It's not much, but if you like that sort of thing you could visit on your way back to wherever you came from.'

I tried reading the cop's face. The latter part of what he'd said sounded to me as if he might be suggesting we get on our way. I smiled and nodded. 'Thanks for the tip. Seems like we had a wasted journey.'

The sheriff reached for the rim of his Stetson and tipped it a little. 'You take care now. Oh, and if you decide to ignore everything I just said and go off exploring anyway, let me tell you there's a whole lot of land out there, and you're more likely to find a nest of rattlers than you are a scrap of spaceship. It doesn't look like much, but it can be dangerous country for those who don't know it.'

'We weren't looking to salvage anything,' Terry said, leaning across slightly. It was the first time he'd engaged the sheriff. 'We're neither crazy, nor opportunists. We only wanted to check the place out is all. Tick something else off the old bucket list. If people offer tours to a place, you assume it's legitimate, right?'

'I guess so,' Crozier said. The way he regarded us suggested he might be re-evaluating. 'I didn't mean anything by what I said. We get a lot of folks out here wanting to dig the place up looking for something seventy years' worth of exploration and excavation hasn't already found. It's like it's regarded as buried treasure, or something.'

'Not our intention. But that's okay. No harm done.'

Crozier gave us a nod, rapped on the Jeep's roof a couple of times with his knuckles, and walked back to his car. He climbed in and sat there.

'I had to say something,' Terry said. 'He might've grown suspicious if I'd stayed silent the whole time.'

'You did the right thing,' I told him. 'He seemed to relax a little at that moment.'

'He's not in a hurry to drive off though, is he?'

I checked the rear-view. 'No. Let's go. I reckon he'll follow us a while.'

I was right. Crozier stuck to us for about ten miles, before indicating and taking a left turn. The moment he was out of sight I pulled off the road again. My phone was still on the same web page, and even though I'd lost my signal, the page remained visible in the phone's memory.

'We need the GPS device again,' I said to Terry. 'I'm not sure how accurate this is going to be, but I have some latitude and longitude coordinates here.'

Terry reached into the glove box and took out the locator. He plugged it into the cigarette holder, shaking his head and snorting. 'Are you serious, Mike?' he said. 'You really think Vern came here looking for a seventy-year-old crash site?'

I shrugged. 'Mate, I really have no idea. What I do know is that whoever was driving Vern's car probably left that map out to be found, and they probably also circled Corona for a reason, and from what we saw and what Sheriff Crozier just said, that crash site is the only noteworthy thing ever to have happened around here. What's more, did you catch the bit about the tours being stopped by a new owner? I don't know about you, but I'd really like to learn the reasons why.'

Terry shrugged. 'I suppose. What are you going to tell Drew and Donna?'

'Nothing. Not until there's something *to* tell.'

I read out the coordinates. Terry punched them in. 'According to this, it's in the middle of nowhere,' he said.

I rolled my eyes. 'It would be. Nowhere is what they seem to specialise in out here.'

I slipped the gears out of park and stepped on the accelerator.

ELEVEN

Appearing to float over a khaki foundation of sandy dirt, the plains were a curious patchwork of grass so bone dry it had turned the colour of hay, tawny tufts thrusting through the soil having somehow found the strength to fight off the lack of nourishment, and a heavy freckling of foliage and shrubs on the darker spectrum of green. It looked for all the world as if the land was trying to camouflage itself from predators. The horizon on both flanks of the highway rose up into sweeping hillsides which seemed to kiss a low sky the colour of glaziers' putty. Away in the distance, cattle lumbered around without a care in the world. The herds were a welcome reminder that we were not so far from civilisation as it may have appeared. As we pushed on into the desert, the colour of the terrain changed dramatically, so much so that I squinted ahead to see more clearly, scarcely believing what I was seeing.

'Is that snow?' I said, pointing out of the windscreen at the landscape ahead of us.

'I'm not sure what else it would be,' Terry responded. His lopsided grin implied familiarity with what I was thinking – that

I had flown over five thousand miles looking to get away from the stuff.

It was a fine dusting, but the low temperature suggested it would hang around for a while. Nothing was currently falling from the sky, but the thin layer of white looked so fresh and crisp my guess was that we had missed the flurry by minutes at most.

'Hopefully it'll stay ahead of us and keep the creatures in hiding beneath their rocks,' I said. 'I suspect we may have a bit of walking to do.'

'Or it'll cover them up just enough that we won't see the things until we tread on them.'

I glanced across at him. Shook my head. 'You're in a real negative frame of mind today, Terry. What's going on?'

'Nothing. I think we're wasting time, that's all. In my view this is a fool's errand. I'm sitting here beside you waiting for it to be over.'

'You have an equal say in this. You know that. If you felt strongly enough about it why didn't you say so before we even set out this morning?'

Terry took his eyes off the GPS reader. 'When we left the airport I had no idea what Corona might offer us. The place meant nothing to me. To either of us. At that point it may have held some promise. The moment I heard about the whole UFO thing, that was when we should have cut our losses. I did say so at the time if you remember.'

I shook my head. 'Not quite. You poured scorn all over it, that's for sure. But you didn't put up much of an argument over coming out here.'

'Mike,' he said, 'you were never going to listen to me. You see something in this whole UFO business that I don't. I came here with you, not the other way around. This is more your thing than mine, so I'm along for the ride. I'm in the shotgun seat, I'm your backup.'

Terry was partially right. I felt duty bound to lead, given he was here in the US at my behest. We were together right now because of my ex-wife. But he was wrong about one thing.

'Try not thinking about this as having anything to do with UFOs,' I said. 'I think there is something going on with the whole Nevada–New Mexico UFO trail, yes. But not UFOs themselves. I'm not saying that at all. I'm not even sure that's what Vern was up to, either. What I think may have happened is that he somehow got caught up in something connected with the whole UFO mythology. Maybe he discovered something. Maybe he was led here and stumbled onto something. Perhaps it's the old journalistic instinct in me, mate, and maybe I see conspiracies where none exist, but my spidey-senses tell me it has something to do with whoever bought the land and no longer wants tourists visiting the site.'

Terry appeared to consider that. It occurred to me that I perhaps ought to have explained myself better before we set out from Corona to locate the crash site. My head had been muddled at the time, processing the information and the suspicion that was creeping up on me. My thoughts could sometimes get away from me, but I reckoned the vicinity we were now in was somehow pivotal to Vern's disappearance.

'How about this for a suggestion,' I offered. 'If we turn up nothing concrete here, we split up for a day or so. You head on up to Vegas, see what you can dig out. I'll stay here and do the same. How does that sound?'

Terry smiled at me. 'Sounds like you have your thinking boots back on.'

I couldn't tell if that was a compliment or a sly dig, but I let it slide. After many years of friendship based on the odd telephone conversation, Terry had dropped everything the previous summer to help me out of a dangerous and life-threatening situation. In doing so he had given up his off-the-grid existence, had seen safe houses and arms caches exposed, and put himself not only in harm's way but also back into full view of those who wished to either use him for nefarious purposes or remove him altogether. Until he was wounded in a firefight, Terry had taken charge of both the situation and me when I needed it most. I emerged from the event a different man; perhaps more the man I had once been as opposed to a new man entirely. In doing so I had regained my confidence. Knowing Terry as well as I did, I felt he would not have gone along with any of this had he been convinced that we were headed in the wrong direction. Then again, he might be simply riding it out so as not to pop the fragile bubble of my self-esteem.

'Mate,' I said, keeping my eyes firmly on the road, 'I shouldn't have to tell you this, but if you see me on the wrong path, you need to let me know. Right?'

'Of course.'

'I mean it, Terry.' This time I glanced across to my right. 'Don't let me lead us both astray.'

'I won't. Don't worry about it.'

I nodded. If Terry was back to his usual conversational self, then there was not much wrong. He would see this out with me, then head off up to Vegas to do his own thing. I had to have faith that he knew when and how to draw the line as far as my taking charge was concerned.

'Take the next right,' Terry said then.

I did. We came up on it fast, and it wasn't much of a road, but at least it had a gravel surface, albeit a narrow and uneven strip that meandered across the land, announcing our presence with every crunching turn of the wheels. The Jeep paid no attention to the many potholes, although I had a couple of fights with the steering wheel along the way. The road – such as it was – curved left for a long time. I took it slowly, all the while looking out for any indication that the site was close by.

'Next right again,' Terry said.

This time we ran right out of road. Whatever trail there was had been created by the weight and regularity of vehicles flattening the surface across the rough terrain. I stopped for a moment, keeping my foot hard on the brake. I checked my phone but had no signal. Terry did the same, came up equally empty. This was no place to break an axle, especially with no reception for our phones. I released the brake and started taking greater care over our progress. It was slow going, but the further we could make it on four wheels the less hiking we would have to do.

'There used to be a sign back on the main highway,' I told Terry. 'According to the website I was reading, that was taken down, and now I suspect it was the new owners who did so. There was an old shed and a gutted-out truck left close by after a festival celebrating the fiftieth anniversary of the crash, plus a sign dedicating the ground as sacred, but rumour has it they are all gone as well. There may be something to look out for once we reach our destination, though. There were two red stone monoliths at the site, a bit like goalposts from hell. Could be they are still there.'

Terry reached into the back for his bag, and came up with a set of Newcon Optik binoculars. He proceeded to scour the countryside around us. I stared ahead intently at the trail surface much closer to us, searching for any dips or crevices that might make our passage too dangerous for the vehicle. A few minutes later, Terry took the binoculars from his eyes and said, 'Did you clock what I noticed at the highway turn off?'

I shook my head. I had been engrossed in looking for any remnants of the sign that once pointed the way to the crash site.

'I'm pretty sure it was a mobile phone mast. Had its own electricity feed, tall tower with plenty of directional antennae on top.'

That got me thinking. 'Did it look new?'

'Relatively. Didn't look old, that's for sure.'

'Could it have been for Wi-Fi rather than phone? Cable TV, maybe?'

'Perhaps.'

'If it was phone, then you have to ask why we still have no bars. That would suggest it's a private mast, perhaps installed by the new owners of the land.'

'We're still on public land as far as I can tell. I've not seen any signs warning us off.'

Terry was right. The land appeared to be open to all. We were still going which meant we'd not reached the crash site, so maybe we had yet to bump up against the boundary of the farmland.

'You have to wonder why, if they went to the trouble of installing a mast for Wi-Fi or cable TV, they didn't extend the cell service out here at the same time.'

'Might be an interesting thing to find out,' Terry said.

Right then was when I saw it. There was no fence, no gate, no noticeable difference between where we were and where we were heading. Apart from one thing. A sign. So new that no one had yet taken a pot-shot at it. It stood face-on, mounted on two sturdy metal posts buried deep into the ground. Black lettering on a white metal board.

PRIVATE PROPERTY
KEEP OUT
TRESPASSERS WILL BE SHOT

Apparently they didn't mess around with trivial matters such as arrest, trial, and prosecution out here. Shoot on sight appeared to be the way they addressed unwanted tourists. This again suggested to me that the new landowners were doing more than protecting their land from a few UFO nutjobs. I understood that it might be a major irritant having people traipsing all over your property making holes and maybe creating a garbage nuisance, but I also could not see why anyone would visit this area if it weren't for the UFO mythology.

Terry brought the binos back up to his face. Focussed beyond the sign, out across the prairie, where the vegetation was more lush. A couple of quiet minutes went by before he said, 'Got them. Two red standing stones.' He flicked a switch in the centre of the binos to activate the laser rangefinder and was now drawing a bead on one of the monoliths. The rangefinder was good for up to 4,000 yards.

'Just over two miles,' he said.

On this rough terrain, lugging our Bergen rucksacks and weapons, maybe an hour of solid hiking. A walk in the park compared to many a yomp we had taken part in, much of it in either sweltering daytime heat capable of sapping the fittest man's reservoir of energy, or the bitter cold of night that gnawed deep into your bones. Plenty of deadly creatures out there, too.

I took the binos from him and surveyed the plot. I saw no sign of habitation, nor the slightest movement or errant shadows. *We are on our own out here,* I thought. Or at least that was how it looked. I narrowed my gaze as I swept the view slowly from side to side, verifying my initial impressions.

'It's almost too quiet,' I said.

Terry grunted and threw open his door. 'Come on,' he said. 'Let's see if we can find some golden eggs at the end of this wild goose chase.'

'You think someone could be out there waiting for us?' I asked.

'Could be.'

'You think Vern is out there?'

'Might be.'

'Are we about to walk into trouble?'

Terry looked at me as if I had asked the dumbest question ever. 'I think there's every chance of that,' he said, and started walking.

I took a breath and moved off with him.

TWELVE

Fifty minutes later and we were wondering what all the fuss was about. Our march across the prairie had been uneventful. While Terry scouted the way ahead searching for any sign of life, my eyes were focussed on the ground about a dozen yards in front of us, looking for cracks or crevices that could possibly turn an ankle, or early-rising creatures that might react angrily to our presence. We made our way across country as a team, and it felt good to be doing it again.

The layer of snow had been much thinner here, and was pretty much gone now. The temperature had climbed a little since we'd set out from Corona, but the wind that ripped across the plains in staccato bursts carried with it a chill factor and minute grains of desert dust you could feel stinging your flesh. Our direct passage diverted here and there around impassably dense shrubs or outcroppings of boulders and rocks that looked too risky to climb, but Terry kept us on course with the aid of the binoculars, zeroing in on the twin towers of red stone. We reached our target without so much as a pause, and once there I felt a sense of anticlimax.

Other than the twin monoliths there was nothing different about this patch of land to any other we had traversed since leaving the Jeep. In places it looked recently disturbed, but that was it. I stood between the stone pillars and turned a full circle, surveying the undulant hillsides all around us. Nothing stirred that was not prompted by the breeze. I saw no structures, no fenced-off corrals, no mechanical objects of any description, nothing man-made whatsoever. Thousands of acres of land stretched out before us, yet not a single scrap of it gave any clue as to why this supposed crash site had been secreted away from the public.

I let go a long sigh of frustration. 'Sorry,' I said to Terry. I shook my head and spat onto the dirt at my feet. I took a bottle of water from my backpack and unscrewed the lid. 'You were right to question me on this. I just wasted an entire morning. A day, if you consider we still have to go all the way back again.'

'What were you expecting to find?' Terry asked as I took a few thirsty gulps from my bottle, no judgement in his voice.

'I'm not sure. Some kind of production, maybe. Meth. Drugs of some kind. Something that Vern might have inadvertently come across and been chased off the land over. I genuinely did not expect to find this… barren, inhospitable scrubland.'

The shot arrived a split second before we heard it.

Something cut the air between us, and a cloud of dirt erupted in a sandy-grey puff about five yards to our left. The snap of the supersonic rifle shot hit our ears right after. We must have both immediately sensed the direction from which the bullet had travelled, because the pair of us took a couple of steps across to shelter behind a standing red stone each.

'Did you see the flare?' Terry called out.

'No.'

'Me neither.'

I set my Bergen on the floor, unzipped the largest compartment and withdrew a short-stock AR-15 semi-automatic rifle, with a thirty-round magazine already in place and good to go. I knew Terry would be doing the same from behind the stone that now stood to my six o'clock. Just as I knew that he would use this opportunity to step in and take over the tactical aspect from hereon in.

'Fire a burst in the general direction on three,' he said, loud enough for me to hear but not forcefully enough for his voice to travel more than a few yards. 'I'll look for muzzle flashes if he returns fire.'

I set the stock against my shoulder and licked my lips. Set my feet, sliding them from side to side until they felt firmly dug in. I wasn't about to step out from cover, merely lean out and squeeze the trigger for a couple of seconds so as to attract attention. The one thing I did not want to do was to become unbalanced and stumble out into the open.

'Ready,' I said.

Terry counted off. On three I did my job. I ducked out and back in before anyone could possibly react and get off a shot of their own. My weapon was not supressed, so whoever had fired at us would hear it even if the volley of bullets went nowhere near them. In response I heard two loud snaps of gunfire, at which point Terry sent back half a magazine in three easy bursts. Safely tucked behind the monoliths, we waited for the echoes to fade away and the land around us to become still once more. It seemed to take an age before the sound of gunfire could no longer be heard.

'Whereabouts?' I asked Terry, keeping my voice low. On these plains, with a prevailing wind, I knew my voice could carry for some distance.

'A hundred yards or so. Roughly two o'clock.'

'That was a rifle, yes? And he missed us from that distance?'

Terry made no reply. Before he could – if he was even going to bother – a cry came from the gunman's approximate position high up on a rise, somewhere amidst a scattering of bushes and boulders leading up to a much steeper climb.

'Hey out there! I know you can hear me! Need some help here!'

The voice was weak and a little throaty.

'Yeah, what do you need?' Terry called out.

'I been shot.'

'That can happen when you fire on people without knowing what they've got for you in return.'

A few seconds ticked by before the voice came again. This time the guy sounded as if he might be in pain. 'Yeah. I guess I really didn't think it through. I coulda hit you if I wanted. One of you, at least. Didn't want to do that, though. I aimed to put one across your bows. I want you to know that.'

'He's bullshitting,' I said over my shoulder. 'Either of us steps out to go up there and he'll have us in his crosshairs.'

Terry's only response was silence.

'Whoever you are,' I yelled, 'you can forget it. We're not about to fall for that.'

'I… I understand. I shot first, so you have every right not to trust me. But I ain't trying to fool you. I'm shot and I'm too busy holding my goddamned leg together to use my rifle again.'

'That's easy enough to say. How do we know you won't take one of us down if we come over there?'

'I guess you don't. But right now I ain't even looking your way. I have my back jammed up against a boulder and I'm sitting here trying to keep from bleeding to death.'

Our voices bounced back and forwards off the rocks, a ghostly sibilant whisper in the air as they faded away to nothing. I felt as if I needed to keep him talking.

'Look at it our way. You could still be bluffing, looking to even up the odds. How about you throw out your rifle?'

'I could do that, sure. I can reach it if I need to. I toss it in the air back over my head I'm sure you'll see it fly, hear it clatter on the rocks behind me. But how you gonna know I ain't got another one?'

I nodded to myself. 'That's a good point. You see our dilemma?'

'I guess.'

I lowered my voice again. 'What d'you think, Terry? You want me to draw his fire again?'

Still nothing from behind me. I turned to look back at him, but the tall standing stone hid him well. I thought about it a little more. A man has a rifle he ought to be able to hit a person walking at a steady pace from a hundred yards away. The first shot had been in the general vicinity, but way off the mark if either of us had been the intended target. The other two hadn't made an impression anywhere near us. Perhaps the voice from across the way was genuine. Maybe the man really hadn't shot at us, only shot near us. And maybe he was leaking blood on New Mexico soil right now.

'Tell you what,' I shouted out. 'Toss your rifle anyway. That'd be a good start.'

Silence.

Terrific. Now neither of them were responding.

'Terry!' I hissed. I picked up a small rock and tossed it towards the foot of the monolith. It jumped and skittered along the floor. 'Hey, you fallen asleep back there?'

When his voice eventually came, it was loud and strong, and it originated from behind a rise of rocks and boulders about a hundred yards away at roughly the two o'clock position.

THIRTEEN

His name was Dale Everest. 'Like the mountain,' he told us, in case we weren't clear.

While Everest and I were calling out between us making arrangements for some half-arsed surrender and rescue attempt, Terry had as usual been getting the job done. Using the noise Everest and I were making as cover, and the time it took for the back-and-forth as a distraction, Terry had edged backwards from the red monolith, crabbed across to his right, before snaking his way around in a wide arc up and around the rocky hillside on which Everest had perched himself.

When Terry called out he told me to get the medical kit over there because the man he had shot was in trouble. Which I could see was true, the moment I came over the rise lugging two lots of kit and laid eyes on them both. The large calibre bullet had taken Everest an inch or two beneath the left hip, and had sliced a deep and messy gouge out of his flesh, leaving a bloody, pulpy groove of gore and torn tissue. It looked raw and painful as hell. I tried keeping the instinctual wince off my face, but failed miserably.

The man talked all the while as Terry administered first aid in his usual methodical field-treatment manner. Everest kept apologising for trying to scare us away by shooting, insisting that he would never have actually aimed his rifle in our direction.

'What the hell are you doing all the way out here anyway?' I asked. 'And why did you even want to scare us away? It's not as if there isn't enough land for us all.'

Everest looked up from the patching of his wound, fixing me with slits for eyes. He looked to be in his sixties. A tall, slender man with a fluffy white cloud of hair behind each ear, and a short beard of the same. His flesh was bronzed like a surfer's, with ribbons of hard, taut muscle running through it. He looked as fit as the dog the butcher's dog trained.

'I could ask you two boys the same thing,' he said, his voice cracked and dry. 'You sure ain't here for the scenery.'

I squinted at him. 'Hey, Dale. You shot first, so you get to answer first. Deal?'

After a moment or two he nodded. 'I thought you was a couple of saucer ghouls. I figured a shot coming your way would make you think twice about sticking around where you weren't wanted. That's usually all it takes.'

'You've shot at people before?'

'Shot *near* people. Sure.'

'Saucer ghouls?' Terry said, still intent on perfecting his bandaging skills.

Everest gave a nod. 'That's what we call these oddballs who come out here looking for scraps of UFO. They don't give a damn about the craft itself, nor the incident or the history of the place, only what kind of buck they might make if they find something to prove it was real.'

'So what are *you* here for? And why do you want to scare everyone else away?'

'I'm out here in protest.' He held his head upright and struck a pose of pride. 'I been coming out here ever since they closed the place down to the public. Something as unique an event as a UFO crashing to earth ought to be celebrated. At the very least acknowledged and made available to all of us. Instead, piece by piece they've taken it away. First the military turned their backs on their own men who made statements about the craft, then the men in suits made sure that everybody else involved was either bribed, beaten or humiliated into taking back their statements. You had all these experts talking about what was found, only for another bunch of experts to say how the others were all just plain wrong. Got so's the incident became something to mock, to sneer at others about. Through it all, though, there was the crash site itself for folk like me to come and visit.'

'Folk like you?' I said. 'Are you a believer, Dale?'

The man winced as Terry pulled the bandage tight, but he threw some spirit into the look he gave me. 'Damn straight I am. I wasn't born yet when it happened, but my daddy was and I'm here to tell you that Neil Everest was the most down-to-earth man God ever saw fit to put a breath into. Never missed a week at church, never told a lie in his entire life. If my daddy says he saw the craft then he saw the craft. If he said he held a piece of it in his hand and it was about as light as a feather, then I guarantee he held a piece of it in his hand and it was as light as a feather.'

I nodded, not quite knowing what to say. I glanced away from him for a moment and for the first time noticed a couple of items leaning up against a boulder about ten feet or so away. One was a satchel type bag that I guessed held some food and water amongst other supplies he might need out here. The other was a metal detector. I shook my head and turned back to Everest.

'So those who come out here hunting for relics are saucer ghouls,' I said. 'What does that make you, Dale? I see your detector over there.'

The old man glared back at me but said nothing at first. Moments later, his temper appeared to get the better of him. 'It ain't the same thing at all. Those… parasites are only here to find something they can make money out of.'

'And what are you looking for?'

'Same thing, different reason. I want proof. I want something I can put in the museum and stick it to all those know-it-alls who say people like me are messed up in the head.'

The way he said it sounded genuine. Maybe I'd misjudged him.

'Okay, you made your point. Just seems a little odd you coming out here to do that, even going so far as to fire off warning shots at strangers.'

He jerked his head, indicating the sloping path behind him. 'Take a look at what's over that ridge,' he said. He hissed through his teeth as Terry completed his work.

I moved past them both and made the short climb. It was tough going, and once again I had to admire Everest's energy and determination. As I stared down over the hill I saw for the first time a group of buildings. There were four mobile home type cabins, two of them joined together to form a double-wide. Behind them stood a line of portable toilets. Sitting around them were several vehicles and what looked like a tall oil well derrick. No people that I could see, but whatever the place was it looked to be in its infancy.

'Frackers,' Everest explained once I had scuttled back down the hillside. He was wincing badly, and had lost some colour from his face. 'This land ought to have been secured for the people as a monument to our history, and instead they sold it off to a bunch of frackers who only want to raid it and destroy it. Next thing you know we'll all have flames blasting out of our faucets, and poison in our drinking water.'

'Looks like they're doing their best to hide the fact, too.'

'Yeah. But I been filming them. They ain't started fracking yet, and if I get my way they won't ever get the chance to.'

Now the tearing down of anything remotely connected to the crash site made sense, as did the new technology at the side of the highway. Not the manufacturing and dispersal of drugs, as I had suspected, but greed in another form. A more legal one, albeit strongly opposed. I could not see how any of it had anything to do with Vern, though.

Meanwhile, Terry had finished administering his medical expertise and declared his patient good to go. 'That'll hold you for a while, Dale. The shell took a chunk out of you, but left nothing of itself behind as far as I can tell. Still, you've got yourself a large and ugly wound there, and you're going to need it checking out by a doctor. You'll need stitches and antibiotics to prevent the spread of infection.'

The old man cursed and threw his hands in the air. 'How in the hell am I going to get myself to hospital? I'm shot, damnit!'

Terry looked up at me. 'I guess we could take him.'

I did not like that idea. 'Dale, do you have anyone we could call on your behalf? Someone who could meet you back on the highway and take you the rest of the way to hospital?'

Everest raked his nails down one side of his cheek. 'I'm not sure. You shot me, why can't you take me?'

'See, the thing is, Dale, you're going to have to explain that you got shot and then the police will be called in. As I understand it, that's mandatory here. Now, given you fired first and ours were in retaliation, I think we'd be okay on that score. The problem for us is that we're not exactly supposed to have these weapons. So if we take you in, it creates a big problem for us. One we'd rather avoid if at all possible. Especially as you created the situation in the first place.'

'I guess there may be someone. In fact, it could work out quite well if the person I'm thinking of is available. You boys are gonna have to help me back out to where we can pick up a phone signal, though.'

'That we can do,' Terry told him, still on his haunches by the side of the old man. He patted one of his wiry arms. 'We'll get you back to our Jeep, drive you to the highway and then we'll find ourselves a signal. By the way, how did you get out here?'

'Truck,' Everest said. 'I parked it back a ways, on the other side of the valley there. Must've taken a different route in to you two boys.'

'Okay. I guess it'll be safe enough out here until you can get it back. Let's get this show on the road. Now, me and my friend here are going to get our things together, hook our backpacks on, then we're going to create a kind of human hammock with our hands and arms for you to sit in while we trace our way back to our vehicle. It's going to be slow going, Dale. Bumpy, too. I'm sorry to say, but it'll also be painful for you. We'll make sure we have plenty of rest and water breaks along the way. You up to that?'

The old man gave a twisted smile. 'Well, I'm more up to that than I am being left out here to die, so let's do it.'

I met my friend's gaze as he stood up straight. 'What did we get ourselves into this time?' I said, allowing myself a chuckle and a weary shake of the head.

His sardonic smile was all the reply I needed.

FOURTEEN

I WASN'T KEEN ON GOING back to Roswell, but the woman who drove out to collect Dale Everest convinced us that if we were looking for UFO aficionados, there was no better place in the entire world. Not even the Extraterrestrial Highway up in Nevada out near Area 51.

Sixty-year-old Delta Vigo was as lean and spry as a woman half her age. When I first saw her jump out of her truck I thought Everest had to have been wrong when he told us all about the woman and her father. But when she moved up close I could see all six decades in her eyes, though she moved with a fluidity and grace that belied at least three of them. I smiled when I noticed a bumper sticker on the truck that had on it an image of a cartoon figure holding a metal detector standing above the words 'I'd rather be dirt fishing'. I hoped she was in it for the same reason Everest was. There were also several eco-type stickers, and I assumed she felt the same way as Everest did about the fracking that would soon be going on out there.

The way Terry and I were told the story of their friendship, Delta's father, Jorges, was a sky watcher who added fuel to a young Dale Everest's fiery interest in UFOs. Jorges claimed to have been eighteen when the craft crash landed on the Foster homestead in June 1947. He also claimed to have seen it hurtling down to earth and skimming like a stone across the prairie. Said it sounded like dynamite going off every time the thing hit an outcrop of rocks and blasted through them. Everest and Vigo had stayed in touch down the years in between, and Dale sounded very pleased with himself when he announced Vigo's daughter as a life-long compadre.

'What in the hell have you done this time, Dale?' were the first words out of Vigo's mouth. She dipped her head in greeting at me and Terry as she strode by us to where Everest was lying stretched out on a bed of dry grass. We had parked up off the highway a little, keeping ourselves out of view of any passing police vehicles.

Vigo squatted down to check out the old man's wound. She turned her head to look back at us. 'Where did this old fool find another two younger fools to take up his cause?'

I smiled at her. 'Oh, we're not on his side, believe me. Your friend here took a shot at us while we were minding our own business.'

'I shot *near* you, damnit!' Everest growled. Talking set off his wet cough. 'Ain't the same thing at all.'

'You two saucer ghouls?' Vigo asked, fixing us with sharp, liquid eyes.

'No. Nothing of the kind.'

'You work for the new folk who bought up the old Foster ranch?'

'No. We're looking for someone. Now, he may well have been one of these saucer ghouls you mentioned. We're not really sure about that. But we do believe he came here. We think he may have been up at Area 51, then here, and maybe then in Roswell. That sound like these UFO nutjobs to you?'

'Nutjobs?' Vigo said with a groan as she helped Everest to his feet. She leaned the old man against her side, taking his arm in her hand. 'You ever have the privilege to meet my daddy, I suggest you keep that sort of talk to yourself. Old as he is now, he'll kick your ass for calling them nutjobs.'

'Sorry. I meant no offence.'

'Well, there was plenty taken. Look, I don't know you or your friend there from a hole in the ground. I'm not saying I believe in little green men and all, but something sure as shit came crashing to earth back then and it weren't no aircraft or weather balloon neither.'

'Grey men,' Everest said, correcting her. 'They'd be grey men if they was anything at all.'

'Whatever goddamned colour, Dale, what I'm trying to tell these fellahs here is that my daddy is no crank. He knows what he saw. And though maybe he don't know exactly what it was that came down, he sure as shit knows what it wasn't. Your daddy was the same way.'

Neither Terry nor I had it in us to argue. We helped Vigo ease Everest into the truck on the double-wide passenger seat. Got him comfortable and pulled the belt tight. When she closed the door on him, she turned back to us.

'You want, you boys can follow me into Roswell. That's the best hospital for this old fossil. I can tell you where to find your bunch of "nutjobs" – and believe me there are plenty of those, too.'

'Thank you,' Terry said. 'Listen, we need to be kept out of this shooting business if it's all the same to you. We'd have some explaining to do which we'd rather avoid. And Dale there would have to reveal why he fired on a couple of strangers for no good reason. We spoke to him about it and he's going to tell them he never saw the shooter, and can't recall precisely where it happened, either. He'll tell the doctor that he did his own bandaging, and the police that he must have been close enough to a cell signal that he didn't have to struggle too far before calling you. Now, are you going to be okay with that story?'

The woman looked between us, then nodded on a sigh. 'I reckon it was that coot's fault, and you did right by him afterwards. I hope you find whoever you're looking for, fellahs.'

'Thank you,' I said. 'Maybe you could give us a call, let us know how he's doing and maybe we can tell you both what we discover along the way.'

Vigo nodded. We swapped numbers.

'What were you expecting to find out here in the desert?' she asked.

'Trouble,' Terry said.

'And what do you think you'll find in Roswell?'

'More trouble.'

'That what you two boys do with your day? Go around looking for trouble?'

'We don't necessarily go looking for it,' I explained, giving her my best world-weary look. 'But it seems to have a habit of finding us.'

Vigo smiled as if she knew exactly what I meant. Then we said goodbye, climbed into the Jeep, and followed her back to the city.

FIFTEEN

THE BAR WAS FILLED with UFO-related items filling almost every inch of wall space. Vigo had given us the location of the bar, and the name of the person to ask for once we got there. Sure enough, we made our way there, bought ourselves a couple of beers and the bartender agreed to pass on our request. He made a call from the bar phone.

While we had been waiting for Al Chastain to arrive, Terry and I discussed what our approach to the meeting ought to be. He was all for sliding a couple of drinks across the table and showing the stranger Vern Jackson's photo before he had even picked up the first glass. I knew why. Terry thought we were wasting our time, and the sooner we had that confirmed the quicker we could both be on our way. I could tell he was fast losing patience with this line of investigation, and I could not entirely blame him.

My spin on things was different. It sounded to me as if this man we were about to meet with had a story to tell, a story he clearly enjoyed telling, a story that came with a reputation that endured beyond the confines of the bar. I reckoned that allowing him to tell his story might put him in a better frame of mind to answer our questions. Without even meeting the man, I got the distinct impression that whilst alcohol was the lubricating oil for the mechanism, the story was what opened up the spigot.

'Where's the harm in stroking his ego for a few minutes?' I asked. I appreciated my friend's position. We were being bounced around New Mexico, when all the time he was convinced that Vern's story was playing out to the north-west in Nevada. 'We give him twenty minutes to tell his tale. Ten minutes later we're out of here. I'm asking you for half an hour more, Terry.'

'It's your rodeo,' he said by way of a response.

I raised my eyebrows. 'Get you with the lingo. You're really trying to fit in, cowboy.'

His smile matched my own. 'I draw the line at chaps,' he said. 'Thirty minutes it is, Mike. Then I'm off to Vegas with or without you.'

Twenty minutes later an elderly man entered the saloon and made his way on unsteady legs across to the booth Terry and I had taken.

'You the two Brits who want to hear what really happened the night that UFO came down?' he asked.

'That's us,' I admitted.

Chastain slid into the seat alongside Terry and let out a hearty chuckle. 'Set me up with some Jim Beam, boys. Believe me, the truth ain't out there, it's in here.'

Chastain proved to be a charming old man. With his first Jim Beam knocked back in two thirsty swallows, he readily confirmed that a farmworker by the name of William Brazel had brought a pile of debris into Corona in the back of a pickup truck in the first week of July 1947. The area was rife with rumour that an airliner or fighter jet had come down a couple of weeks earlier, but since no one had found any wreckage, and no investigation had been carried out, it remained little more than barroom tattle until the moment Brazel showed a handful of Corona residents the pieces of metal he had with him.

That fired the starter pistol on what became known as the 'Roswell Incident'. No sooner had the USAF been contacted at the nearby Roswell base, than the military and defence agents swooped in to seal off the area and kill the entire story. Those who claimed to have seen alien figures strewn across the desert, and mysterious metal debris thin as paper that moved on its own and was as strong as steel, were dismissed as tellers of tall tales, seeking to gain either cash or notoriety or both. The story rumbled on and on, and the conspiracy theorists refused to be denied. Ultimately, the official version was that a weather balloon had snapped its moorings and had eventually landed up in that wide-open space thirty-odd miles outside Corona.

'Course, that ain't what happened at all,' Chastain said as he started in on his second shot. I watched the man slide it down smoothly, enjoying his enjoyment. For a man into his nineties he still had some tough meat on his bones and a good sharp mind, but rheumy eyes and a rattle in his bronchi suggested he had more bad days than good to look forward to.

'So you're saying it wasn't a weather balloon?' I said, urging him on, conscious of Terry's growing impatience.

'That's exactly what I'm saying. Wasn't no USAF jet fighter, neither.'

'Then what was it?'

'It was exactly what folk said it was. A UFO.'

I glanced across at Terry and frowned. I was confused. Delta Vigo had told us this man was a non-believer.

Chastain spotted our exchange of looks and cackled a wet-sounding laugh into his curled hand. 'No, I don't mean it was no spaceship manned by alien beings. Unidentified Flying Object. That's what a UFO is, yeah? So that's what this thing was – unidentified. Officially, anyhow. Now, the panic that set in when this craft came down led to all kind of mistakes being made by the military and department of defence agents in the first few days after the site was discovered. Story after story was leaked, but each had holes you could drive a tank through. Of course, they tried dismissing it as nothing more than a weather balloon having shot its moorings and come to ground, but that never sat right with the destructive force that put craters in the desert soil out there. So later they came around to "admitting" that it was part of a US experiment called Project Mogul, which was all wrapped up in the nuclear arms race and a desire to create aircraft that were lighter and faster and capable of going further than anything ever thought of before.'

'You seem to be implying that this was also bogus,' Terry said.

'That's because it was. Oh, the project itself was real enough. Mogul existed exactly like they told it. Just had nothing to do with that crash. Fact is, the craft was unidentified by the USA because it was a new Russian flying machine. A Russian aircraft so advanced that our own scientists and military personnel were scared rigid by it. Think about that for a moment. Better to have US citizens believe it was just about anything else other than what it actually was. In those days, not long after the Second World War, and just about slipping into the Cold War, there was not a snowball in hell's chance of our government owning up to the Russians having more advanced technology than us.'

'But it was manned, right?' I said, leaning across the table. I knew we were not there for this, but I was intrigued and still had time out of my allotted thirty minutes. 'That's where these so-called alien figures come into it.'

He nodded. 'The craft was small, scaled down from the real thing for testing purposes, and the Russians used only small men to crew the craft. Four of them in all. Tiny little fellahs they were.

I guess you'd call them midgets at the time, or dwarfs these days. The size of them, added to the type of flight suits they wore, plus the breathing apparatus, made people think they'd set eyes on alien beings. In a way, I guess they kinda had.'

'If you don't mind my asking,' Terry said. 'How do you know all this, Al?'

'Oh, I was there,' he said looking up. In those watery eyes of his I saw no obvious deception. 'I saw the wreckage, I saw the crew. You can find my name on the records to prove I was on base at the time. I was military police, and it was my job to help guard it all. Since I came out with my story – shamefully far too long after it all happened – there's been three attempts on my life. My own government tried to shut me up. Now that I'm old and crusty I guess they figure nobody is gonna believe me anyway. But there you have it. No great mystery after all.'

It was some story. I didn't know if I believed it or not, but I'd heard crazier things in my time. 'Thank you for telling us, Al. I appreciate it. We both do.'

'But it's not why you're here, huh?' The old man smiled at me and his eyes glistened.

I took out my phone, found Vern's photo and showed it to Chastain. 'We're looking for this man. It's important to us that we find him, and soon. We believe he may have been one of these UFO hunters, who came down here looking to confirm his own beliefs. We wondered if he had stopped by for a chat with you, Al.'

Chastain was already shaking his head. 'I can safely say that I have never knowingly laid eyes on this young man before in my life. Not in person, anyhow.'

I set my frown on him. 'What do you mean by that?'

He jabbed a finger at the screen on my phone. 'I seen him in another photo, on another phone.'

'You have? When was this, Al? Who showed it to you?'

He smiled at us. 'You got me at just the right time. A few days more, a few shots more, I might not have recalled the face. But I remember it well not only because I saw it just yesterday, but also because the pretty little thing that showed it to me was just about the most gorgeous creature I ever laid eyes on.'

SIXTEEN

The Days Inn, Roswell, stood on the corner of Highway 285 and West College Boulevard. On one side opposite was the New Mexico Military Institute, on the other a strip mall that featured a unit that sold and fitted tyres, a pub and eatery, and a large Starbucks. I sat in the Jeep out in the car lot directly facing the entrance to the Days Inn hotel on the other side of the highway, sipping my plain Americano. I stared through the windscreen as Terry came jogging across the road from the hotel, his face as inscrutable as ever.

As I looked at my friend I think I became more fond of him with every pace he took. Once again I had summoned him with a call out of the blue. Once again he had asked few question, and only then after agreeing to my proposal. This time it was overseas, unknown territory for us both. If that made any difference to the man, he never once showed it. If I excluded my ex-wife and daughter, Terry Cochran was not only my best friend, he was that by default because he was also my only friend. I was by far the more gregarious of us, but Terry was the kind of man who said so much without needing to speak. We seldom discussed our time in battlefronts together; no drunken, back-slapping tales of heroic deeds. Neither Terry nor I felt the need to reminisce on a regular basis in order to cement the bond between us. I treasured his friendship, and was certainly glad of his presence.

Earlier, back in the bar following his story and a third shot of bourbon, Chastain had provided us with a name, hotel and room number. Grace Bergstrom. Room thirty-five. From the bar it was a straight run east on the 70 and then north on the 285. It was evening by the time we got back in the Jeep, and we hit the local rush hour traffic. What was probably no more than a ten-minute drive at any other time of day took three times as long. That was okay by us – we had nowhere else to be. Not now that we had our first human lead.

Having avoided the traffic on his way across the highway, Terry jumped in beside me, the Jeep rocking as he settled into his seat. I handed him his cappuccino. 'She's not there,' he said. 'But she hasn't checked out, either. She also gave a false name to Chastain. Her real name is Chelsea van Dalen, at least according to her ID. I got the bloke on reception to give away the make and model of her car as well; I went for broke and asked him if she was still in the Kia, but he told me she'd had to rent a vehicle and he had arranged it for her. She's in a silver Ford Explorer.'

'Good man. You want to sight it or should I?'

'You go for it. I was wrong about this and you were right.'

'I don't know about that, mate. We may have found someone who maybe knows Vern. That's not exactly a resounding success for a day and a half of our time.'

He sipped some of his coffee before responding. 'It's more than we had, and a lot more than I thought we would ever get out of this particular line of investigation. We'll have more answers soon enough. I have a feeling this woman is crucial.'

'You think Vern is still alive?' I asked, the question having hung unasked between us for too long.

'I have no idea. I have no answer, and neither do you.'

'But what does your gut tell you?'

'I honestly don't know, Mike. The moment we find out why he's here, why he disappeared, then I'll have a better idea of what to expect. We both will.'

I nodded. 'I'm afraid for him.'

After a brief pause, Terry nodded as well. 'I am, too,' he said.

I retrieved the sniper scope from the kit bag behind Terry's seat. Held it to my eye and fingered in the correct focus. In a US city the night is never really dark, and even here on the northern outskirts we were illuminated by neon. The highway was wide, and although we would make the vehicle coming from a block away, there had to be plenty of them in these parts. This way, the moment we saw one I could get a close look at the driver through the scope. We were looking for a young woman. A gorgeous one, if Al Chastain were to be believed. That was good enough for me.

'I'm wondering what to say to Drew and Donna,' I said. 'I have to update them. What we have right now is something, but I wonder if it's enough to call it in.'

'Hey, you can also tell them we went UFO hunting, that we got shot at by a crazy old man who I ended up wounding in the crossfire, after which we dragged his sorry arse out of the desert and put him in the good hands of the youngest sexagenarian I've ever seen, and talked with a man who knows the absolute and final truth about the Roswell spacecraft crash incident.'

I laughed. 'Yeah, pretty boring I suppose, when you put it that way.'

'Wait it out,' Terry suggested. 'See how this plays. We could have a whole new story to tell once we've spoken to this woman.'

Nodding, I took out my phone anyway. 'Tell you what, I'll get an update from them instead.'

Drew had specifically asked me to use his phone when reporting back, so I called Donna's number and started things off casually with a few questions about Wendy. A couple of minutes in she asked me how things were going. I told her I'd be calling Drew within the next hour or two, hopefully with a strong lead.

'How goes it at your end?' I asked, throwing it out there.

'A little rough if I'm honest. The PI guys were getting nowhere. We had them working on the security feeds, but they seemed so disorganised that we had to let them go. Drew has another recommendation if you think you might need more eyes and ears.'

I was grateful for the thought. 'Let's put that on the back burner for now, see where we end up today. Did he get anywhere with his one-time IT colleague? He was going to ask her about gaining access to hotel feeds and then get back to me. I've not heard from him, though.'

'Oh, the hacker, you mean? Yes, Drew told me about that. The issue of legality concerned him, but decided it was a risk worth taking. Anyway, he got knocked back. He left a message but she hasn't returned his call. Drew was trying to think of another way around it before speaking to you again. He wanted something more positive to report. Ironically, Vern was so good he could probably have found himself.'

'If he wasn't completely off the grid. Let's hope that's not the case. Although Terry may be able to help us out there. He spent enough time under. Listen, to move things along I think Terry and I are going to split. He'll take Vegas while I remain here. We may speed things up that way.'

'Okay, Mike. Whatever you think best. We're in your hands. There was one thing, though.'

'Fire away.'

'Someone called Sheryl at home. Said his name was Fraser and that you'd know who he was.'

I tensed immediately. I had told the RPD cop that we were hunting for the owner of the minivan and knew the young man's family. In retrospect that may have been a mistake. 'What did he tell her?'

'Nothing. He asked Sheryl to pass on a message to the two men searching for her son. Said that he wished you both well, but that if he ran into you two again there would be a different outcome next time.'

I relaxed a little. It sounded as if the cops had not reported their run-in with me and Terry. Then I thought of something else. 'Donna, do you know if Fraser asked for our names?'

'I don't believe so. He didn't mention either of you by name, either. Sheryl said the guy was extremely vague.'

I blew out a long breath. We had taken a risk but it looked to have paid off.

That was pretty much it. I had barely killed the call when Terry raised a finger. 'Explorer,' he said. 'From our three o'clock.'

We were facing west, and the Ford was driving straight towards us from the north. I raised the scope, located the Explorer's windscreen. It rolled to a complete stop at the traffic lights.

'Female,' I said, my voice a virtual whisper. 'Black hair. Stunning. If she signals right and turns into the hotel entrance, I'm betting this is our girl.'

The light changed to green. The SUV pulled away, already in the right-hand lane. Its indicator came on. It turned into the entranceway leading to the Days Inn, Roswell.

SEVENTEEN

You could tell by the way she walked and the haunted look in her eyes that Chelsea van Dalen had a story to tell if you took the time to get to know her well enough. Beyond the natural perfection of her facial features, the young woman was a bit of a waif. Her movements were lissom, but this svelte creature we had found appeared weak and fragile to the point where you felt a harsh look might crush her as easy as a Christmas tree bauble.

Initially startled by our presence outside the door to her room, the young woman relaxed considerably the moment I explained who we were and what we were doing there. Terry and I were starving, so we managed to persuade her to join us in the eatery back across the road from the hotel. We ordered drinks and a side of nachos with cheese ahead of our main meals. To my surprise, our willing guest opted for a toppings-heavy burger with onion rings on the side. Once tucked away inside the pub-restaurant, and having introduced herself to us, Van Dalen opened up as if relieved to have someone to share her misfortune with.

She explained that she first met Jackson in a bar in the Gateway district of Las Vegas, close to the Stratosphere hotel and casino. She had arrived thirty minutes late for her date with boyfriend Bruce Kelper, and when she walked in he was playing pool with a man who gave his name as Vern Jackson. The three spent a couple of hours together before Vern headed out on his own. Later that night, he called and asked if the two of them would like to join him the following morning for a drive and a hike. Kelper readily agreed, and Van Dalen told us she tagged along willingly, though she recalled being a little disappointed that it wasn't going to be just her and her boyfriend spending time together that day.

'What's your relationship with this Kelper bloke?' I asked, enjoying a nice chilled bottle of lager and helping myself to a handful of nachos.

'We've been friends for a while. High school. Recently it started looking as if it could be more, but we're not quite there yet. Or, at least, we weren't until this past week. We're now an item, I guess.'

'And how do Jackson and Kelper know each other?'

'I didn't know at the time, but I've since learned that they met at a casino last year, and whenever they can find time they hook up in either Vegas or LA.'

There was more there, but I decided we could swing back around to it. 'So you two joined Vern for a drive and a hike. Where did he take you?'

Van Dalen revealed that, while the excursion had been Vern's suggestion, it was Kelper who chose the destination and drove them in his own truck. 'After a couple of hours of driving we hung a left onto a dirt road. It was not at all comfortable, but Bruce drives a four-by-four and after around twenty miles or so of bouncing along listening to our moans he finally pulled over and we all got out. The hike was brutal. It wasn't much more than a mile, but a lot of it was on loose shale and we climbed a thousand feet or more very quickly. Poor Vern was clearly suffering by the time we got to the summit of Tikaboo Peak. That was when I realised where we were and what we were looking down at in the valley below us.'

'Which was?' Terry asked.

'Tikaboo Valley. Which includes Area 51 out on Groom Lake.'

I couldn't help myself. I turned my head to look at Terry, and our eyes met. Although the possibility of Vern having gone there was my initial suggestion, it had been based on nothing more than supposition and knowing the base was in the general area when you headed north out of Vegas. I had no idea what his presence there meant, only that it had to be more significant than even I had initially suspected.

Except that I was almost entirely wrong.

'It was Kelper's decision to go up there, right?' Terry clarified with Van Dalen. 'Vern had no say in it?'

She shook her head. 'Neither of us knew where we were until we reached the peak and Bruce told us what we were seeing away in the distance. The base was still more than twenty-five miles away, so it was impossible to make anything out in the distant haze. He handed us some binoculars to use, told us to check out the base and all of the fencing and signs around it warning people to keep out.'

'Did he explain why he had chosen that hike? To me it sounds like a very long drive for a very short walk.'

I nodded. Terry had made a good point.

'I knew he was a bit of a UFO buff,' Van Dalen said. 'Just not how much until we reached that point. Bruce told us that there used to be another vantage point called Freedom Ridge, which the government scooped up in a land grab. Though at the time they still officially denied the existence of Area 51, clearly they were trying to keep sightseers away. They said it was a remote detachment of Edwards Air Force base, a place they called Homey Airport. But when they denied access to the ridge, that left the peak as pretty much the only place you can go and still see Area 51. Bruce told us he'd been up there many times, often at night. That he'd seen all kind of things going on there, including some weird-looking flying objects. Said he knew they were testing new aircraft out of there, but he seemed pretty convinced that not all of the developers or developments were human.'

'And how did you and Vern take that?' I asked.

She shrugged. Van Dalen wore a loose 'Flight of the Conchords' tee and cut-off shorts that revealed shapely, skinny legs. Costume jewellery in a variety of bright colours adorned her wrists and neck.

'I'm a free spirit. I have my mind open to all possibilities. I couldn't deny his beliefs, because I had no proof he was wrong.'

'And Vern?'

'His response was a little odd, to tell the truth. His head hadn't seemed to be in it at all. He'd been the one to suggest we go out, but it felt like he was less interested in where we were and what we did than in just being away from Vegas. Of course, I now know why.'

Our server arrived with the food. We requested some more drinks and waited until she'd cleared out before continuing.

'Chelsea, I think it's time you told us what's going on,' I said then. 'How is it that you ended up here in New Mexico? Why was Vern's car dumped on the side of the road? And I'd also like to know where Vern and Bruce are right now.'

Van Dalen finished her soda. Took a bite from her burger and popped a couple of fries into her mouth. A battle seemed to be raging inside her head. You could see her brow almost rippling as the various emotions tore through her. She took on a pained expression when she spoke next.

'When we left Tikaboo Peak we drove out to a spot on the road between Alamo and Rachel where the Black Mailbox used to be. Bruce told us it was really only a fun mailbox which visitors wrote on and was used to post letters to aliens, that sort of thing. Mainly it was a place where enthusiasts got together to hang out. Some asshole stole it – probably some dickwad from the government – and it was never replaced. People still meet there, though. So we were there, talking with a bunch of other people with an interest in UFOs, when the discussion turned to Roswell and the crash site. There was a lot of anger that the remnants of the fiftieth anniversary had been stripped away, tours stopped and visitors no longer made welcome. There was some enthusiasm for heading down there to protest later in the year when it turned warmer. By this time, Vern had become even more edgy. He was on alert every time a vehicle flew by.'

'So the three of you decided to go on the Roswell road trip,' Terry said.

She shook her head. 'Not right away, no. And in the end it never really happened the way we all discussed up there. It was just the three of us who took off together. And only then because of what happened later that day.'

'Which was?' Terry prompted.

'On our way back to Vegas, Vern said he thought we were being followed. Me and Bruce laughed it off, but then Bruce started wondering about a car which seemed to slow as we did and quicken to keep pace with us. It hung back at about the same distance for miles. So he spotted a place where we could pull over, and slipped onto the side of the road and stopped. As the car drew alongside, it slowed almost to a crawl. It was eerie, because the side windows were tinted and we couldn't see into it. But then it took off and we all laughed in relief. I think we convinced one another that it was either a government car checking us out having been to Area 51, or just someone headed in the same direction who slowed down to make sure we were okay.

'Anyhow, by the time we got back to the edge of Vegas we were all starving, so we stopped at a diner. When we came out afterwards the same car was there. Its engine was running, and as we entered the lot it drove past us and then took off again. We thought that was it, but when we got to the truck all of the tyres had been slashed.'

'Do you remember what the vehicle was?' I asked. 'The one that followed you, I mean.'

'Sure. Bruce mentioned it. Said it was an old Chevy. It was green and not in great condition.'

I looked at Terry once again. 'Garcia and Barclay.'

He nodded.

The two arseholes from the desert on the other side of town.

In between consuming her dinner and putting away her second Coke, Chelsea van Dalen spent the next twenty minutes telling us that, after a great deal of persuasion from Vern, she and Kelper joined him for the road trip. They got a cab to Vern's hotel, where he collected his things and his minivan. They then picked up her stuff from her apartment followed by a fleeting visit to Kelper's house. They got on the road and drove through the night. At various points during their journey, Vern revealed more about what was going on. In many ways it was a typical Las Vegas story. The one where a gambler obtains a line of credit and then cannot repay it, resulting in a couple of heavies paying them a visit.

'So Vern actually told you it was all about a gambling debt?' Terry asked.

I knew why he sought the clarification. Nothing in Vern Jackson's financials suggested he had any such debt, and there was no evidence either that he was the kind of gambler who might require a line of credit.

'Sure.' The willowy young woman nodded. She shoved her plate to one side and mopped her lips with a serviette. I thought she couldn't be more than twenty-two, maybe a year either side. She had the kind of confidence that came with being a natural beauty, yet at the same time it felt like a façade. An exterior behind which she hid away her true self. 'He told us that was why he'd wanted to get out of Vegas for a while.'

'Except, why did he then go back?'

She looked at Terry with a puzzled frown. 'What do you mean?'

'I mean, Vern claims to be in debt to a casino or maybe even a few, is being hounded by hired muscle who go so far as to follow him out of Vegas, yet still he returns.'

'Well, only to collect his things and his Kia.'

I shook my head this time, stepping in line with my friend's thinking.

'No, that's not quite accurate. That happened only after your friend's truck was vandalised. By then you were already back in the city. At the point at which you all stopped to eat, it doesn't seem to me that Vern had any intention of leaving Vegas for good.'

Van Dalen had to think about that for a while. I could see her eyes flicker and gleam in the low light as her mind turned it over.

'We did talk a lot about the Roswell journey, but you could be right,' she said eventually. 'And now that you mention it, I think that maybe he urged us to pack up some gear and join him more for our sake than his. I think the slashing of the tyres unnerved him, but looking back I'd say that was because we had now been dragged into his shit.'

'And what exactly was that shit, Chelsea? Because I'm not buying this gambling debt nonsense.'

At this point, she put a hand to her head and looked away from us for a few seconds. Clearly she was troubled at the thought of betraying a confidence. When she turned to us again, her eyes were sorrowful and moist.

'You asked me earlier why the Kia was dumped and where Vern was. What happened was that when we eventually found the site of the crash, we spotted two guys out on the plains who definitely were not there for the same reason as we were. Neither was dressed for a hike across the desert. They didn't see us, but we followed them because Bruce thought maybe it was the same guys who'd slashed his tyres. We didn't have to go far, because we spotted the car in the distance parked up right alongside the minivan. They hung around, but we waited them out. They eventually took off and we remained where we were a while longer before heading back to the minivan and doing the same. We found a different track about halfway back to the highway and decided to take that, thinking maybe they would be stopped on the side of the road somewhere further along. To be honest, none of us knew what we were doing. We were just scared.'

'So you got away,' Terry said. 'What happened next?'

'We'd booked into the hotel under my name, so we drove back here. We talked it over for a while, and Vern became convinced that they must have had a tracker on the minivan. He didn't believe it was possible for them to have followed us all the way from Vegas. That sounded credible to me and Bruce. He and Vern checked out the car, but they found nothing, and had no clue what they were even looking for. So we hatched a plan… of sorts. Bruce hired an SUV and drove out of town following Vern. The idea was for them to leave the car out in the desert, but also to try and make people think we were just on the UFO trail. Vern bought some maps and marked Corona on one of them. We thought that was cool because they gave Vern and Bruce shit when we stopped off at a bar in the town to ask directions to the crash site. I guess we thought it would be kinda funny for them to have others stopping by and doing the exact same thing.'

'So what happened after they got back?' I asked.

Van Dalen looked at me. Blinked away a couple of stray tears. 'Well, that's just it. They left here to do exactly what we'd planned. And that was the last time I saw either of them.'

EIGHTEEN

WELL THIS IS AWKWARD.
Their humiliation in the desert at the hands of the two Brits still needling both men, Barclay and Garcia had reported back to their boss and were instructed to head out to the Main Street saloon in Corona to talk to the owner. One snakeskin boot through the doorway of the bar, Garcia froze as his eyes swooped in on the jackets marked with the letters F, B, and I. The man and woman wearing them at a table in the centre of the bar turned their faces towards him and Barclay and they also went still. For a moment it was exactly how Garcia had always imagined it to be in one of those wild frontier western saloons when a stranger walks in and the whole place becomes so quiet you could hear a mouse fart. All that was missing was the final fading note from a honky-tonk piano.

He could not tell if there was any hint of recognition coming his way as he went through the possible permutations. Deciding that the pause was in itself enough to attract attention and maybe even a little suspicion, he turned his head to Barclay and hissed a warning.

'Keep cool, man. We gotta play it through now.'

Ignoring the two agents, Garcia strode across to the bar and caught the eye of the woman standing behind it.

'Two shots of tequila. Don Diego Gold if you have it,' he said, taking a stool at the end directly facing an elderly woman who looked as if her face was slowly melting. The woman's eyes were cast downward, her mouth hanging open. In front of her sat seven shot glasses, two of them still on the go.

Barclay eased onto a stool beside him and leaned across to whisper in his ear. 'What the fuck, Ricardo?! We should have turned around and got the hell outta here.'

Garcia dipped his head low and dropped his voice lower still. 'Yes, because that wouldn't have looked at all suspicious. Those two agents woulda followed us out and then who knows what might've happened. Take it easy, man. We sit, we drink, we leave. Unless they leave first. Otherwise we drive around and come back later to ask what we need to ask. Just keep your shit together.'

The barkeep pushed two drinks onto the bar top in front of them. 'You want me to run a tab?' she asked.

'No, thank you.' Garcia shook his head, smiling. The diamond in his left upper canine winked. 'Just getting rid of some of the desert dust from our dry mouths, then we'll be on our way.'

'That'll be fifteen bucks even. Where're you folks headed today?'

'Oh, just touring.' Garcia had no clue what lay in any direction other than the route they had taken in from Roswell. He pulled a thick wad of notes from his jacket pocket, peeled off a twenty, and handed it to the woman. She grabbed it up and her squint dared him to ask for change, clearly deciding the other five was her tip.

'Really? Touring, huh?' Leaning an elbow on the bar top, she raised an eyebrow. 'Not like there's much in the way of scenery out here. Less you like dirt and scrub and the occasional herd of cattle.'

'So we're discovering. The mountains never seem to get any closer, either. A poor choice on our behalf, perhaps.'

This was a drinker's bar. There was no pool table, no slot machines, no widescreen TV, and the music was so low it was barely audible. He thought he could make out John Cougar Mellencamp singing something about a couple by the name of Jack and Diane, but nobody here was about to break out into a line dance. Garcia figured the FBI pair would be tuned into the conversation. He could only assume they were here for the same reason he and Barcs were, only with very different motives and outcomes in mind. His senses were jumping, on high alert. He had to be careful what he said, while at the same time remaining aware of the attention the pair of them might be getting from the two agents. A thought hit him and he decided to feel it out.

He stretched across the bar and said in a soft and smooth voice, 'What's with the agents over there? Regulars here, are they?'

For that he received a dig from Barclay's elbow, but chose to ignore it.

The woman regarded him as if he were insane. 'Regulars? What do you think? All I know is something is going on around these parts lately, and we appear to be at the centre of it.'

'Really? Sounds intriguing.'

The barkeep stood upright and planted her hands on her hips. A good-looking woman worn down by life and all the excesses it offered. The few extra pounds she carried looked good on her though, and as she spoke again Garcia admired the way she returned his steady gaze.

'This town gets its fair share of hippies and crazies all out looking for any sign of UFOs, crashed or otherwise. But over time you learn to recognise them for what they are even before they reach the bar itself. This past weekend we get a coupla young men who ain't sending out the right signals. Then we get an Indian fellah looking for them. Earlier today we seen a Jeep prowling around, then later it's the government waltzing in and looking for information.' She paused, met Garcia's eyes. 'And now it's you two, I'm guessing.'

Other than the old woman at the far end, he had noted the other barflies. It was his job to maintain awareness at all times. The two guys hogging the middle were impossible to miss. They were big and tough-looking, meanness stamped all across their pudgy faces like a snarling tattoo. Another guy looked angry and spiteful enough it was probably best *to* ignore him completely, especially when it looked as if he had recently been on the wrong end of a beating and was itching to take it out on someone.

Garcia knew a bit about that.

The runt of the customer brood seemed to be in a world all of his own, standing there in his dark blue overalls and tugging on his baseball cap every few seconds. Two protruding front teeth overlapped his bottom lip, but you wouldn't bet against them being the only ones still in his gums, judging by the chipped edges and stains on them. Garcia could tell that everyone at the bar was eavesdropping despite trying real hard to seem as if they were doing otherwise. But now they all sucked in a breath at the same time. All waiting for him to answer the barkeep's statement.

He widened his smile. Hiked his shoulders. 'You got me. My friend and I are indeed looking for a man who we believe came this way. He might have passed through, or he could well have stopped to ask for directions. Either way, we are concerned for his safety, and wish to find out his whereabouts so that we can offer some comfort to his family.'

The woman stuck out her hand and fluttered the fingers. 'Show me. I'll tell you if I seen him and I'll tell you if it's the same guy everyone else is looking for.'

Garcia was alert to the movement from the table in the centre of the room. He sensed Barclay stiffen by his side, but held up a hand palm out to forestall any action his partner might be considering taking. Had the FBI not been in the saloon he would have taken out his phone and shown Vern Jackson's photo to the woman behind the bar. Now he thought it best to keep those details to himself.

'All I have is a description,' he said, feigning embarrassment. 'I know that's not very helpful, but it's all we have to go on right now.'

'Your friend camera shy, is he?'

'I don't recall saying he was a friend.'

As he spoke, the man and woman at the table got to their feet and moved steadily closer to the bar. Garcia steeled himself and hoped Barcs would keep his cool.

'I'd be very interested to hear that description for myself,' the male agent said.

Garcia switched his attention immediately, turning to his right. 'Would you now? And what does our private conversation have to do with you?'

'We'd like to know whether the man you're looking for is the same man we're looking for.'

'I very much doubt that.'

'Oh, I don't think doubt comes into it. Mr..?'

'Garcia. Agent..?'

'Wilson. *Special* Agent Wilson. My partner here is Special Agent Green.'

Garcia kept his eyes firmly on the male. 'Very well. To satisfy your curiosity and to move things along, I'll describe him for you. The man we are looking for is in his mid-fifties, two-hundred and fifty pound, drives a big old BMW. Oh, and he's black.'

The agent looked hard at him for a few beats. Nodded, seeming to reach a decision. 'You know what, sir, I have a feeling you made up that entire description right there on the spot. I also reckon you do have a photo somewhere about your person of the man you're really looking for. And to top it off, I'd bet my house on it being the very same man we came here to find.'

Swallowing down both fear and anger, Garcia drew in a deep breath. 'Agent Wilson,' he said. 'I realise you have a job to do, and that your job requires you to be naturally suspicious. I have encountered FBI agents before, and you are by no means unique. But I can assure you that the man I described is the man my partner and I have been searching for these past few days. A wife is missing her husband, a son his father. All we are doing is attempting to reunite them. It has nothing to do with your own search. So, if you don't mind, we would–'

'Whatever it is you're about to say, I do mind,' the agent said firmly. He moved half a step closer. 'Just so's we understand each other, there are two ways this can go from this point on. You either take out the photo or your phone on which you have the photo stored, show it to us and then tell us exactly why you are looking for this man, or we have to go to all the trouble of cuffing you both, taking you all the way back to Roswell, where we'll obtain the very same information from you anyhow.'

There was a loud snick sound. Garcia leaned closer, touching the point of the switchblade he had instantly produced to Agent Wilson's stomach, so that the man would feel its tip prod the skin beneath his gleaming white shirt.

'You forgot the third way,' Garcia whispered. 'Me and my partner kill you both and walk away without enduring any of that nonsense.'

By now Agent Green had pulled her own weapon and was pointing it two-handed directly at his head. He did not have to check back over his shoulder to know that Barclay would also have a hand on his own gun, ready to blow holes in anyone who got in their way. The conversation had gone sideways, but he was prepared for anything.

'I put my weight into this blade, Agent Wilson, you die a slow and painful death,' Garcia said.

'You do that and Agent Green here blows a hole in your face so big you could put a fist through it.'

'After which, my friend here will do the same thing to your colleague. He gets to drive away, you two each get to leave in a coffin.'

'How 'bout none of you do a damned thing other than put your dicks away and we try figuring this thing out.'

They all turned towards the voice, which echoed loud and clear around the bar. In the doorway stood Sheriff Crozier. He was holding a Remington pump-action shotgun in both hands and it was pointed in their general direction, but mostly at Garcia. His hands were steady and his voice firm.

Crozier shook his head, his Stetson puffed up tall and proud. 'Whatever you do,' he said. 'Don't make me squeeze the trigger. I ain't shot nobody in all my years on the job and I don't want to be starting with any of you. But know this – just because I ain't shot anybody before don't mean I can't or won't. Set your weapons aside, people. I got this now.'

NINETEEN

Joe Kane relied on more than either hard work or good fortune to help steer a way through life. His efforts were thorough and organised, carried out with fortitude and strength. Luck came in two flavours: the sweet taste of good and the sour tang of bad, and he rolled with whichever of the two came his way at any given moment. But then there were the spirit guides who assisted him whenever he needed it most, and their role in his destiny was the strongest of all.

When he was ten years old, Kane was sent into the woods by his parents, with only a pouch of water and some hallucinogenic mushrooms to eat. He was told by his mother that he could return home whenever he liked, but that if he did so without first having found his animal spirit, he may never find one in later life. He remembered his father sitting him down prior to his journey of self-discovery and insisting he must be observant at all times, looking for animals behaving out of the ordinary, and that he should do so with good grace and a positive mind if he did not want to invite in unwelcome and mischievous spirits in their place. It was both a ritual he had been eagerly anticipating, and a challenge he willingly accepted.

After four days, Kane stumbled back into the village. He was later told that he arrived in a trance-like state, but that having rested, and with a good supply of hot food and fresh water inside him, his strength returned as the effects of the mushrooms were flushed out of his system. The following day, he sat with his family and together they attempted to interpret the things he described as having witnessed.

At various stages during his time spent out in the woods, an eagle, a fox and a snake had called to him. On the very first day, he had climbed over a rock fall, which eventually led to a clearing on a vast plateau, and it was here that he had seen the shadow of an eagle glide across his path. On the second night as Kane sat before a crackling fire, a fox stole quietly into his sleeping area looking to pilfer food, and upon being confronted had simply sat on its haunches staring into his eyes. The animal's own eyes glowed like torches, and Kane read something in them he was unable to explain. But it was the snake sidewinding its way through the heat of the late-afternoon sun on the third day who had the loudest voice, and his father especially welcomed this.

'You will see into the hearts of men,' he told his son. 'This will always provide you with an advantage, a keen edge. All you have to do is listen carefully to its voice.'

His mother was joyous, as she believed that both the eagle and the fox had also touched his soul, and that although the snake would forever be his true spirit, the influence of the other two creatures would also help guide his way through life. She considered him blessed.

As he grew older, Kane realised that what others attributed to instinct or conscience, was actually their own animal spirit trying to find its way. They simply were unaware of it, and so heard it only at certain times, and always in the voice of man. His ears, the channels into his spiritual chambers, were always open. He saw early and from afar, he reacted swiftly and with cunning, struck deftly when it was required, and fortune so often favoured him after the animals had whispered their sage advice in their own tongue.

The discovery that the two men he was chasing now had a companion, was a revelation, but it did not get him any closer to finding out where they were now. However, it did compel him to pass that information along to his Irregulars.

People were often surprised to learn that Kane even read books, let alone the works of Sir Arthur Conan Doyle. He had particularly enjoyed episodes in which the Baker Street Irregulars were employed by the famous detective. These characters who lived in the shadows and beyond were an early form of Confidential Informant, and Kane made use of such men and women throughout modern-day New Mexico. It was one of these Irregulars who called him the night before and gave him a name and a pattern of behaviour associated with that name. That was enough for Kane. He did the rest himself.

He had driven to the saloon in Roswell early on Thursday morning, feeling the rush of the hunt spread throughout his body. He had no idea what was happening or where this diversion would lead, but his guides insisted he was getting closer all the while and that he must keep both heart and mind open to every possibility. He felt it deep inside the marrow of his bones, in the blood flowing through his veins, and in every single breath he took.

When he first entered the saloon, Kane's intention was to be direct. He would ask whoever was behind the bar for Al Chastain. This was the name he had been given, together with an interesting connection between Chastain and the men he sought. But as he closed the door behind him, something told him this was the wrong approach. That caution was required. He bought a large coffee and a Danish pastry, found a seat in the corner looking out on the other customers, from where he could also observe both the bar and the entrance. He decided the best way forward was to sit and drink and listen. The snake inside him was at peace with this.

It was a popular spot with the locals and tourists alike. This was the place he was meant to be, no matter how long he had to sit and dwell upon all the other possibilities.

Which turned out to be not long at all.

There was something immediately off to him about the two men who entered as he sipped his second coffee of the morning. Something that sent Kane's alert sensors soaring. It existed not only in the way they carried themselves, but also in their watchful and intelligent eyes. The taller of the two, with rough stubble on his face, glanced over at Kane and for a moment their eyes locked. He knew that there was only one thing to do that would not draw attention to himself. Looking away too quickly was not the solution. Neither was holding the man's eyes engaged in a staring contest. Instead, he lingered for a couple of heartbeats, and then looked back down at his mug of steaming hot coffee, which he drank from and savoured the taste of.

A couple of minutes later, Kane heard an English accent as the other man ordered two coffees. He managed to keep his head and his eyes perfectly still when a moment later the same man asked to speak with Al Chastain. From the corner of his eye, he saw the barman return to his post, pick up a counter phone and dial a number. He did this three more times in between fixing drinks. A while later he walked across to the table at which the two men were sitting. The barman's voice was low and this time Kane could hear nothing of what was said, but he did notice a look of concern pass across the face of the man with the stubble.

The two had come for Chastain.

Chastain was clearly not available.

But what did that mean?

As the two men rose from their seats, Kane had to make an instant decision: remain where he was in the hope that Chastain would appear, or follow these strangers. Joining the dots he imagined how the separate pieces slotted together. There were direct links here, from the men he had been seeking to Chastain, and now seemingly from Chastain to these two Englishmen. Perhaps those connections would eventually form a circle. He sent his mind in search of guidance, and before the bar door had even closed behind the two men, the snake whispered in his ear with its answer.

TWENTY

We walked back out of the Weather Balloon bar shortly after 9.30am. Terry and I had been in the United States for virtually sixty-five hours and still Vern Jackson was no closer to us than he had been when we stepped off the plane at LAX. That bothered me, and I knew it was bugging the shit out of Terry.

The evening before, I managed to persuade Van Dalen that she would be safer with us on the Lear than remaining in the hotel on her own. It was a simple matter of extrapolation and logic, I told her – if we could find her then so could the bad guys. And I doubted they would take her out for a meal and a drink once they tracked her down.

It did not take her long to reach a decision.

So the three of us spent the night on the plane, which remained tucked away inside the hangar alongside a Gulfstream, but refuelled and ready to go the moment we called for the pilot, who was staying in a nearby motel.

We spent time hashing things out, kicking the tyres on the story to see if it all held together. I got the distinct impression that Van Dalen was holding something back, though I could not work out why she would nor what it could possibly be. Clearly she trusted us – unless her entire story was a fabrication, which I didn't buy. She had also accepted our invitation to stay overnight at the airport. But there was something the young woman was choosing to keep to herself, and that made me feel uneasy. Usually when people elected to keep secrets, they were the things you most needed to hear.

We discussed our options. Other than locating Van Dalen, Terry and I agreed that things here were pretty much stalled. Our plan earlier in the day had been for him to head off up to Vegas while I stuck it out in and around Roswell. That remained a possibility, but less so now that we knew Vern had definitely been in New Mexico. The major problem remained in having no clue what had happened to either Vern or Bruce Kelper after they dumped the Kia.

Discussing that specific aspect reminded me of something. I asked Van Dalen if she knew anything about the vehicle Kelper had rented. She said the agreement was in amongst the stuff we had brought from the room the three of them had shared. I searched for it, discovered it tucked away inside a paper wallet with the car hire company logo emblazoned all across it. After checking out the details, I gave Drew a call.

'How's it going?' he asked me.

'We're getting somewhere. It's slow going, but it's progress. Vern was definitely here in New Mexico. We know where he was and when, and we know he drove the car down here. Also that he was not alone. In fact, your nephew was with two other people. We've located one of them, and we're talking to her now.'

'You keep saying he "was" there. Not that he still is.'

Drew's voice sounded strained, which was understandable. I had no idea how quickly he had expected us to wrap this up, but we were less than two full days in, and we had already come a lot further than his investigators had. Though we had benefited from the discovery of Vern's minivan, I thought we were doing okay.

'Vern dropped off the map again after dumping the car. But we're closer to him now than we were, Drew. We're catching up.'

'So who is the person you're speaking to?'

'Have you ever heard Vern talk about a friend by the name of Bruce Kelper?'

'Kelper?' He paused for thought before responding. 'Not that I'm aware of, no. That's who you have?'

'Actually, no. Vern and Kelper went off together. We have Kelper's girlfriend. And she's being extremely co-operative. Terry and I need to work her now to see what we can get out of her, see where it leads us next.'

'That's terrific. Thank you so much, Mike. I appreciate it. We all do.'

Now I heard some relief in his voice, and I was gratified by that.

'Well, we're still on the trail, but it did just get a little easier for us. We'll keep pushing at this end, Drew. But listen – I have a task for you. This Bruce Kelper that Vern took off with hired a car so that they could dump Vern's. We believe they are both with that vehicle now. I need you to locate somebody who can find out if it has an on-board GPS, and if so trace it for us. Can you get that done, Drew?'

He said he would give it his best shot and would get back to me. When he and I were done, I had a brief chat with Wendy, who was interested in where we had been and what we had done. I fed her the boring stuff and omitted the getting shot at and the fight out on the road beyond Roswell.

'Why are you doing this?' Van Dalen asked me, having listened to my side of the conversation with Drew. We had opened up a beer each and were trying to make the most of the evening. 'I thought it had to be for money, but that was your daughter you spoke to at the end there, right? Where do you fit in with all this?'

I explained about Donna and Drew. The telephone conversation that had sent me hurtling across the ocean.

'You must really love her,' she said.

'Wendy? Of course. She's my kid. My whole world.'

But the young women was shaking her head. 'No, I meant your ex-wife. You're out here risking your life to help someone you have never met; the nephew of the man your ex is now married to. You're certainly not doing this for either of them. You can only be here because the mother of your child needed you to be.'

Chelsea van Dalen might be young, tired, beautiful, and in a great deal of trouble, but she had a good head on those narrow shoulders. I shrugged mine.

'She needed help. It's only natural to give it if you can. Besides, I get to see my daughter.'

'Not out here you don't,' she pointed out.

I nodded. 'Right now I'm busy providing the help I offered. Me and Wendy will have time when all this is over.'

Van Dalen turned her gaze upon my friend. 'And how about you, Terry? Why are you here?'

'Mike asked me,' he said simply. He drank from his bottle as if ending his part in the conversation.

As the night closed in and the cabin lights reacted by dimming, the three of us put our heads together again to see if there was anything left to scrape together. That was when Terry threw out Chastain's name.

'What about him?' I asked.

'He could have more to offer. He may know more than he thinks he knows.'

'But he told us he never saw Vern. What more could there be?'

'I don't know for certain that there is. But everything Vern has done since he went to Vegas has centred around this UFO nonsense, from Area 51 to Corona to the crash site to Roswell. That's a definite link between the two of them. I don't know how it may be tied in, but it could be. Might be a good place to start.'

Overnight we had no better ideas, and by the time the three of us headed out of the airport in the Jeep nothing else had occurred, either. It was slim, but we decided that grabbing a cup of coffee and bending the old man's ear would take up only an hour at most of our valuable time. And we had nowhere else to be.

When the bar owner had told us that he had been unable to raise Chastain, he looked worried. He wore a deep frown on his tanned forehead. The kind of tan that had set in as a youngster and had yet to pale.

'Which is unusual at this time of day,' he said. 'Al likes his schedules and sticks to them almost religiously. I can't recall ever not being able to get a hold of him of a morning.'

Hearing that unnerved me. I had no idea what use Chastain might be to us, but learning that his pattern of behaviour had altered since we met him, gave me a bad feeling. I glanced at Terry, who shook his head once.

'You remember us from yesterday, right?' I said to the bar's owner.

The man nodded. 'Yep. You two and the young lady here from before.'

'So you know we spoke at length with Al and that we're no threat to him, right?'

'I don't know that. Not for a fact. But I'm guessing so.'

'Then I'd like you to give us his address. I know you won't want to. But believe me when I tell you that I think your friend may be in danger. If he is, me and my friend here are precisely the two people you want involved. I realise it goes against your nature, but you have to trust me. Us. I need to know where Chastain lives, and I need to know now.'

TWENTY-ONE

Al Chastain resided in a brick bungalow surrounded by a grey block wall, the gardens populated by a handful of naked trees so much younger than others in the street. It lay on a large plot close to Cahoon Park, in what looked to be a pretty decent neighbourhood. Terry was driving, I rode shotgun, and we cruised by the place one time without turning our heads to look. Though I had instructed Van Dalen to keep low down in the back seat, I had not told her why. She was elevated enough to notice that we were driving past the house Terry and I had been speaking about moments before.

'What's going on?' she asked 'Why aren't we stopping?'

'First time around is just to get a feel for the place. Also allows us to check for anything untoward.'

'Untoward? Such as?'

Terry hung a left at the end of the street, directly opposite the park. I turned my head to talk over my shoulder this time. 'Such as, on this occasion there was a black SUV parked halfway down the alleyway. It's a narrow thoroughfare, with no waiting or parking I would imagine. It means someone is in there now with Chastain.'

She put a hand to her mouth. 'Oh, my God! So what are you going to do? Are we calling the police?'

'That will only make matters worse,' Terry said. 'We need to contain this ourselves.' He powered on to the next junction and took a left. Left again at the next. Over the crossroad, left again at the next turn. At the bottom of that road we emerged by the park, but a block further along. Terry nosed the Jeep into a small visitors' car park and held his foot on the brake. He turned to face me.

'First thing I have to put out there is this is not what we're here for. Whoever is with Chastain right now is certainly not Vern Jackson. We could drive away and get on with our search.'

'We don't know if it's connected or not,' I said. 'If it is, do we want to miss this opportunity to find out more? We need another link in the chain right now, Terry.'

'That's true enough,' he admitted with a grudging hike of his shoulders.

'Then there's the fact that we both think the man is in danger right now. Are we really going to drive away from that?'

'No. I guess we're not. So, Chastain's place is a corner property. Between whoever is inside and the SUV driver in the alleyway to the rear they could have all ingress visually covered. This is the closest place to park without sitting out on the street, and with the driveways these properties have nobody seems to do that, so we'd stick out too much.'

'You're going in there?' she said, her voice loud with shock.

'I think we have to,' I said. 'I don't know if what's happening with Chastain has anything to do with Vern, but I do know the man is in trouble. We can't just leave him to it.'

'Mike is right,' Terry said. 'If we stick around and wait for them to come out we could be too late. My guess is right now they are asking him questions, so he's more useful to them alive. When they're done, when they get what they came for, they'll kill him. We don't have much time.'

'But how do you know any of this? He may just have visitors. They could be family or friends for all you know.'

'Family or friends park on the front drive, not blocking the back alley. Believe me, Chelsea, when it comes to shit like this, we just know.'

Terry had dug out his phone and had drawn up the location on Google maps. He leaned across so that we could all see the screen.

'We are here,' he said, pointing a thick index finger at a car park close to what looked like an open-air pool. 'Tree coverage looks good there, but not in winter. See here, though. We can cut directly across the road and make our way along the pavement. We really only leave ourselves exposed from the street corner. There's no way of sneaking up on the SUV driver, so we have to focus on the bungalow and expect the driver to react accordingly.'

'Driving over there puts us a little bit closer before they sense a threat, plus we get a few more yards of cover,' I suggested. 'Then we go in big and loud. Check the street view of the property.'

He did. What we saw was not exactly in our favour. 'Hardly any windows to speak of at the side. One door.'

He slid his thumb on the screen moving around to show us the front of the bungalow, where there was also only a single door at the end of the drive leading into the property, but also four windows. He flipped back around to the side.

'You know, these windows on this side are high and the door solid. I don't think we get seen coming that way.'

I stared at the screen for a long time. I thought back to what we had seen on our drive-by, put it together with the view from above and what I was looking at now. I worked the angles in my head and visualised how we might attack the property.

'Except we can't approach it directly without being spotted from anyone keeping watch at the front or sitting in the SUV down that alley.'

Terry nodded. 'You're right. We have to take it out,' he said.

I agreed. The question, as ever, was exactly how we were going to achieve that feat.

TWENTY-TWO

The jeep trundled over the uneven surface of the alley, whose mixture of gravel, slate, broken chips of brick and concrete required cautious driving. The vehicle continued bumping along until it was a couple of yards behind the black Dodge.

After a wait of no more than thirty seconds, Van Dalen climbed out from behind the wheel and, wearing the sexiest smile she could muster, with perhaps a little more exaggerated movement in her hips, walked towards the SUV. Its tailpipe coughed up fumes, but the tinted windows were down and the air-con not needed on such a mild morning.

'Excuse me,' she said to the driver, her smile switched to smoking hot. 'I thought I had room to get by you but now I'm afraid I might not. I can't reverse all the way back up the alley. Is there any chance you could pull out so's I can get through to the street?'

'You got room. Go by.' The voice was low and harsh.

Van Dalen turned the smile and smoulder up a notch or two. 'Oh, please. I don't want to risk scratching your car and I'd be in so much trouble from my father if I did anything to his Jeep. I'm just not used to driving it yet is all.'

The man sighed heavily. Maybe then he took her in more fully, and decided a show of valour at that moment might be worth something later. 'I don't want to move mine from this spot,' he said. 'But I'll get your Jeep by me. Deal?'

'Anything that gets me where I'm going. I'll be so grateful.'

That seemed to sweeten the deal. The driver climbed out and walked behind his vehicle. He might have been taken in by a beautiful damsel in distress, but even so he paused to size up the Jeep before he clambered in. He was alert, something clearly pinging his senses, but the beautiful smile had sucked him in.

The moment he closed the door, Terry reared up from the footwell behind the seat and stuck a gun in the back of his neck. I had followed the Jeep bent double all the way along the alley, shuffling around to the passenger side as Van Dalen got out to talk to the driver of the SUV. We had left the passenger side window down, and when Terry moved so did I. I fixed my Sig on the side of the driver's head, the width of the vehicle between us.

'How many inside?' Terry asked him.

'Fuck you,' the driver spat, his lips curling. 'And just so's you know, that bitch who suckered me is dead.'

'So you're not going to talk?'

The man said nothing.

'Then you're really not a lot of use to us, are you?'

Terry hooked his arm around the driver's neck and started pulling back and tensing his muscles to choke him out. The idea was to apply pressure to the carotid artery, causing syncope – a temporary loss of consciousness. I had seen Terry pull off this move a dozen or more times and had never failed to be impressed by it. The only occasion I ever tried it, I ended up cutting off the blood supply for too long. The Iraqi sniper I left lying on the roof of a building overlooking the harbour would have brain damage, if he had even survived. It had never sat well with me, which is why I had never attempted the hold again.

The moment the driver went limp, Terry and I scooped him out of the Jeep and carried him to the rear of his own SUV. Van Dalen opened up the back and we dumped the man face down inside. I cuffed his wrists and ankles with plastic ties. When he eventually came to, he wasn't going anywhere in a hurry.

Taking out the driver opened up the rear of the bungalow to us. But one quick glance told us there was too much glass and back garden to cover, leaving us far too exposed. Instead, I instructed Van Dalen to jump back into the Jeep, reverse back down the alleyway and drive around into the street, parking up a little shy of Chastain's property and holding off out of sight.

'Once you've done that, put it in park and climb into the back again,' I told her. 'Leave the engine running. When we come out of there we may be coming out hot. Whatever you see, whatever you hear, you stay in the car and keep your head down. If we're not out of there in ten minutes, you call the police. Understand?'

She was shaking, but nodded.

I smiled at her and rested a hand on her arm. 'Good. You did great, Chelsea. Really great. Just like a pro.' I forced the smile wider. 'And I mean a professional, not the other kind of pro.'

Van Dalen laughed a little at the remark. 'I do hope so. I can't believe what I did, Mike. You think that driver is a killer of some sort?'

I thought he probably was, but I shook my head. 'I doubt it. Usually those who are left behind the wheel are low level. He fell for the old damsel in distress with fluttering eyelashes trick, so he deserves everything he gets.'

'So, you won't hurt him?'

'No need. He's not going anywhere.'

'What would you have done if he'd just pulled out of the alley as I asked?'

I shrugged. 'I guess we'll never know.'

I felt better about the situation we were about to face. Provided we ducked down lower than the grey block wall that ran around the corner of the back garden, we had a better route to the house now from the side, completely unseen from within until we breached the door. By removing the SUV and its driver from the equation, the advantage had swung back around our way. I felt the adrenaline kick in.

'You good to go?' Terry asked, arming himself with weapons and spare rounds and adjusting his kit bag.

I nodded as I did the same. 'This is becoming a habit.'

He grinned through his salt-and-pepper stubble. 'Yeah. One we maybe need to break.'

TWENTY-THREE

Crozier had missed his breakfast and was both irritated and hungry because of it. It was a good seventeen hours since he'd stood in the Corona saloon pointing his shotgun at the bald Latino wearing snakeskin boots, with a whole bunch of other folk standing or sitting right there in the splatter zone, but his hands were still trembling more than he would have expected. Maybe it was the look in the Latino's eyes; the blank gaze of a man who did not give one flying fuck about either himself or anyone else. Perhaps it was the memory of two FBI agents standing too close for comfort. But he had an idea that the reason for the continuing shakes was the fear of having to one day pull that trigger and become a killer.

The single-storey sheriff's office and courthouse in Carrizozo was a plain, brick-built building with a canopy that looked like a long row of lower teeth supported by square concrete pillars. It was here that the sheriff had persuaded them all to come, having defused the situation at the bar – much to everyone's immense relief. The agents drove their own vehicle, while he put the other pair in the back of his cruiser, hands cuffed behind them despite their protestations of innocence. Crozier had taken a handgun off each man, plus Garcia had also been relieved of that nasty looking switchblade.

Garcia and Barclay were left to sweat for thirty minutes before being joined by Crozier and the two FBI agents. Once inside the largest of the sheriff's office interrogation rooms, Crozier turned on the two men still howling their declarations of virtue and purity of thought.

'Let me tell you what you are guilty of,' he snapped, leaning over the table to stare down at the two seated men. He pointed at Garcia. 'You, sir, are guilty of threatening an FBI agent with a switchblade. And now that I know who you are and have access to your record, you're also guilty of a whole lotta other crimes that earned you a seven stretch in the High Desert State Prison in Clark County, Nevada.'

'For which I did my time,' Garcia snarled contemptuously, staring down at his cuffed hands resting on the table.

'That may be so, but pulling a blade on a government agent could land you right back in there. Also, though I realise your Nevada concealed carry permits for the handguns are reciprocated here in New Mexico, they do not extend to my allowing you to carry them while you are here in my offices. So I don't want to hear no more about your innocence or whining about your firearm.

'As for you,' he said, turning to the wide bulk of Barclay, 'if we ignore your time in two correctional facilities, you are still guilty of pulling a loaded firearm on an agent of the FBI. So zip it, the pair of you, and let's shake the wrinkles out of this thing and see if we can all figure a way forward.'

'I want them charged,' Wilson demanded.

'You were coming at me, man,' Garcia said, narrowing his pinpoint gaze and zeroing in on the male agent. 'We had to defend ourselves. We didn't know who the hell you were.'

'Sure, because we were so brilliantly camouflaged behind our jackets with FB-fucking-I written all over them! Did you think we were attending a costume party, you fucking retard?'

'Hey-hey-hey!' Crozier slapped a hand on the table. 'No need for name calling. Take the higher ground, Agent Wilson. Now, let me make myself clear. This is my jurisdiction. No federal crime has been committed.'

'But we are federal officers,' Wilson reminded him.

'I know that. I can read the print on your jackets even if these two men can't. But I'm telling you that this is my case until I hear otherwise from my bosses. Now, I can walk away and leave you four to bitch and whine about it amongst yourselves, come back in an hour and we can move on. Or we can save ourselves time and get the job done right now.'

Wilson breathed out heavily. His partner, Agent Green, said nothing and appeared entirely at ease. With calm having been restored, he took them through the scene back in the saloon. It was Barclay who gave up their side of events, Garcia mutely fuming and not at all able to disguise it.

'Which leads us neatly back to ascertaining who you two were really looking for,' Crozier said. 'Because like our FBI agents here, I'm not buying into the tall and heavy-set black man story. Why not just come clean now and we'll see what we can do about it?'

'For one very simple reason.' Now Garcia was back into it. He seemed to have the shorter fuse. 'Who we are looking for is none of your fucking business, man. When these two assholes approached us it was none of their fucking business, either. They had no right to question us.'

'We had every right, dipshit,' Wilson shot back, throwing a dismissive hand into the air.

'And we had every right not to answer. Yet because I wanted to do my civic duty I did answer, but you weren't satisfied with what I had to say and so you pushed it. You stepped into my personal space. You caused my reaction. I was never gonna stick you, man, but you got in my face over nothing.'

'Fuck you, Garcia! I got you, *man*. I got you for threatening the life of an FBI agent with a knife. You're going down for that, *man*.'

Barclay put an arm across his partner's chest. Held it there a moment. He looked up at Crozier, who had been watching the exchange with interest.

'Sheriff, since you're the guy with the jurisdiction right now, let me lay this out as I see things. It's up to you to arrest us, if you decide that's the right way to go. You do that, we clam up and call for a lawyer. Our man is the best in the whole of Nevada, so I reckon that puts him top of the heap down here as well. He'll tell you what I'll tell you. My friend and I were provoked by two hostile FBI agents who refused to let us go about our law-abiding business. Other than the jackets they were wearing they offered no proof of identity. Under great strain and duress, my friend made a mistake, and that led to a chain reaction of sorts. No actual harm was done. Just a few feathers ruffled is all. My lawyer will demand bail and he'll get it. We'll be out of here, and with all the evil out there in the world, good luck to the agents in seeking a prosecution for something they started with no provocation from us.'

Crozier chuckled, smoothing down his moustache. 'You done this a time or two, that's for sure.'

'I have. And you know what I'm saying is true. So let me offer an alternative. One of the agents shows us a picture of the guy they are looking for. We tell you yes or no if it's the same man. But, before we do, know that we won't be telling you why we're looking for him, only that we mean him no harm.'

'Fuck that deal!' Wilson said, springing to his feet. His chair shot back two feet with a loud screech. 'We get jack shit and you get a walk. This time tomorrow you'll be in the wind. No-fucking-dice.'

Crozier turned to him. 'Agent Wilson, please either settle yourself down or leave the room. Things *could* go the way the man says. You want to talk, get this laid out on the table now, or do you want to wait for the justice system to cough and wheeze its way to a court date which will probably never even take place?'

Wilson put both hands on his hips and hung his head. His breathing was ragged through his nose, and a vein pulsed in his neck. His face was florid and looked as if it might burst.

'Fuck it,' he said. 'Get it over with.'

Less than thirty minutes later, Garcia and Barclay were being driven back to Corona by a volunteer deputy, having looked at a photo and denied that Vern Jackson was the man they were hunting down. At the table in the interrogation room, Crozier was chuckling.

'Well done,' he said to Wilson. 'For a moment there I thought your partner was playing it too cool and you were sliding over from bad agent to psychotic agent. But I think they fell for it.'

Sitting in the conference room now, pale morning sunlight spilling through the windows once again, Crozier thought back to those actions the previous evening. What neither Barclay nor Garcia appeared to have picked up on was the fact that, prior to the meeting between the five of them, the law enforcement trio had spent twenty minutes hatching a plan. They were in agreement that pursuing the weapons offence was pointless, but it was Green who suggested the con. She advocated getting the pair back out there as quickly as possible so that they could be tracked. Wilson and Crozier arranged for the green Chevy to have a GPS tracker hidden away underneath, so that the movements of Barclay and Garcia could be monitored. All they had to do was convince the witless duo that two FBI agents and the indignant county sheriff were at one another's throats.

It had been almost too easy.

Now Crozier sat watching the screen of a borrowed laptop. Last night he and the FBI duo had watched it trace the movements of Barclay and Garcia all the way back to Roswell. So far this morning it had not moved at all. He picked up his phone and dialled a number. Agent Green answered his call right away.

'They're still there at their motel,' he said. 'Have you got a link yet to the GPS?'

'It's running and searching now, sheriff. Hold on a… there it is! We have them.'

'You head back into my county and need any backup, you let me know.'

'Will do. And thank you. I'm not sure where these two will lead us, but I have a feeling it won't be too far away from Vern Jackson.'

'Happy to help.'

Crozier leaned back in his chair and gave a satisfied sigh.

And happier still not to have pulled that trigger yesterday.

TWENTY-FOUR

From his bag of tricks, Terry produced a couple of strip-shaped charges to use on the hinges of the side door. While I stood guard surveying the road and the homes around us, alert for vehicles and pedestrians, he moulded the charges into place, pulled back the covering film and set them to go. He stepped back a couple of paces and to the left, using the property wall as a shield. We exchanged nods. I was holding the grenade launcher, loaded with flash-bang stun projectiles, commonly used in hostage rescue situations by armed forces and police units across the world. I hefted it to my shoulder and with unhurried horizontal movements put a grenade through each of the three slit windows ranged along the side of the property. A moment later, Terry ignited the breach charges.

From outside the bungalow, the pop-pop-pop of the flash-bangs sounded no louder than old-fashioned cherry bombs before their potency was legally trimmed in the late seventies. The breach was a different matter entirely. The charges went up with a fearful *whump*, accompanied by brief but dazzling flame and a gout of smoke. The shockwave was minimal, the blast contained, but if you were unprepared you would feel it. We knew going in that we would have a few minutes only to eradicate our enemy, locate our hostage, and get out of there. The phone lines at the Roswell PD building were going to be red hot in the wake of the blasts.

Terry kicked aside the door now hanging lopsided on one sliver of hinge. He entered first, his M-16 automatic rifle supressed and swung around ready for business. I hooked the grenade launcher onto my belt, brought around my own M-16, and followed my friend through the door which now billowed thin trails of smoke resulting from the flash-bangs.

Terry had chosen the stun grenades as opposed to those with dense smoke because he wanted us to be able to see clearly without having to wear masks once inside the property. We had no idea how many men were waiting in there, nor how heavily armed they were, but our expectation was that the element of surprise, combined with explosives and bright light, would be enough to destabilise them sufficiently to allow us to rapidly take control of the situation.

We found ourselves in a hallway, one door to our left one to our right. Fortunately, both were open. Terry cut left, I went the other way. As I moved swiftly into a large living room with a carpeted floor, a tall figure stepped out from behind a bookcase which stood against the wall to my right. The figure was not Chastain. The man wore a dark suit and tie, pale blue shirt. His hand was reaching inside his jacket, where I caught sight of a crinkled brown leather holster and the pistol it was hugging. I had time to think of the man as brave but foolish as I put two rounds into his chest, followed by a third to the head as he was on his way down.

I felt a tap on my shoulder – a signal from Terry that he had cleared the other room and was now behind me and we could move forward with me on point.

Voices were coming from the next room. Yelling out, the words muffled and indecipherable. I moved ahead, my weapon raised, sighting down the barrel. I flicked the laser sight on, knowing that sometimes the red dot alone could freeze a man to the spot. At the doorframe leading into a room to our left I paused. I indicated with my fingers for Terry to move over to my right and cut across the living room to create a different perspective, where he could also see into what looked like an adjoining kitchen behind a wall that ran two-thirds of the way along the living area.

I nodded once. In a double movement lasting only a fraction of a second I peeked out into the next room and ducked back again. Same as I had done out in the desert behind the red monoliths. Not long enough to get shot – as the two rounds that came my way and embedded themselves harmlessly in the far exterior wall testified – but just the required time to build an image of the room and its inhabitants.

I glanced across at Terry. I held up two fingers, bent them back down, then raised one. Three men in total. One friendly. Two hostiles. The sound of explosives and gunfire echoed inside my head even though the actual sound had long since died away. I tried hard to listen, contemplating whether to attempt talking this through with whoever was inside that room next door. But time was wasting, and we could spare none of it for negotiation. If the police swooped down on us now, it would not matter why we were there, only that we were. And armed to the teeth.

I flashed up the mental image of the room. Chastain seated facing the open doorway. One hostile standing directly behind him, the other to their left. I did all this in a matter of seconds.

It was time to go.

I stepped into the opening and fired immediately at the spot where the lone figure had been standing. He must have moved at exactly the same time I had, because my bullets smacked into the wall instead, scant inches behind his retreating back. I heard a door being wrenched open and footsteps racing across a hardwood floor.

'One coming!' I called out to Terry. I did not turn. He would know what to do.

I moved my sight across to the left. The third hostile was panting. He had a gun pressed against Chastain's temple. I looked into the eyes of the gunman and shook my head. His weapon hand was quivering, the grip too firm. I eased back the finger on the trigger of my own weapon. This man was going to fold. All it would take was for him to see that I did not intend shooting him.

Only he didn't fold at all.

There was a gunshot, and the right side of Chastain's head exploded across the wall. Without hesitation I painted the far window overlooking the garden with the gunman's own blood, brains, and skull shrapnel. I had no time to feel anything about the man Terry and I had chatted with so amiably back at the Weather Balloon. He was gone, and nothing I did now could ever bring him back. Whoever our adversaries were they were now three down, if we included the driver of the SUV, but we had lost the man we had come to rescue. I turned as I heard firing coming from another part of the property. I dashed across to the kitchen area, saw Terry at the far end standing over the figure I had so narrowly missed. We looked at each other. I shook my head, and he sighed, shoulders slumping.

That's when we both heard the front door slam shut.

I swivelled, my body joining my head in facing the passage leading to where I knew the front door to be.

We had missed someone.

Without thinking beyond the obvious, I threw my weapon to the floor and shrugged off my kit and belts. 'I'll go,' I said. 'Clean up, get back to the car and trawl the streets for me.'

I did not want my weapons or kit to draw attention, but I still had a pistol tucked into the back of my cargo trousers. The shirt I wore was not tucked in and would conceal the weapon. I ran to the door, threw it open and sped out onto the front path. Another suited man was running hard in the direction of the pool close to where we had parked up earlier. I set off after him. I heard no sirens, but they would be coming fast. I knew I had no time, but I had to catch this man. He was now our only source of information.

I pounded along the pavement, cut across the car park and up a dusty rise of soil and out onto a manicured field of lush green grass. There were few people around, and fewer still looked my way. I was gaining on the fleeing figure, but there was still a decent gap between us. He glanced back over his shoulder, and I saw the panic written all over his face. He stuttered briefly in his run, looking around to get his bearings, and then he cut across to his left heading towards the pool. Until that point I was running at a pace designed for endurance, but I realised I could end the pursuit here because I was coming up closer on him with virtually every movement. We entered the pool area with perhaps five yards between us. Within a dozen more paces I was on him. I threw myself forward, head tilted to the side, and hit him with my best rugby tackle, arms wrapped around his upper thighs.

We hit the water together.

Momentarily disorientated and blinded, I clawed water from my eyes and felt my legs scrambling for purchase. As I turned my head a heavy fist smashed into my left cheekbone, and something detonated behind my eyes. We were in the shallow end of the pool, and my opponent had found his feet quickly, so had been able to pivot and hit me with his full weight behind the punch. My head spinning, instinct and experience told me to duck, shortly before his follow-up strike whistled over the top of my head. I sprang up and lurched towards him, but my equilibrium was still all over the place from the first blow, and I splashed back down into empty space in the water. After a moment, I looked up to see the man dragging his sopping-wet frame out of the pool using the ladder close to the corner.

As I started after him, he turned and pulled a gun from the inside of his jacket. I stood in the water looking up at him as he raised the pistol and aimed it at me. I knew then I was going to die. The man had heard us blow away his companions, and judging by the determined look on his face, he had no hesitation in returning the favour. I did not bother raising my hands. I was no more than a few yards away from him, and he was going to shoot me no matter what I said or did.

He couldn't miss.

I closed my eyes and waited to die.

But instead of the sound of a bullet being fired, I heard the snap of the firing mechanism followed by nothing.

Misfire.

The gun was still working, but the ammunition probably hadn't been watertight.

The man tried to fire again, but in his panic and confusion had forgotten to first eject the dud round. I decided I wasn't about to wait for him to clear the chamber. My thoughts still reeling, I heaved my body in the same direction, lunging in the water, knowing I'd made a real balls-up of the attack. By the time I dragged myself out of the pool, he had started running again and was further ahead of me than he had been at the start of the chase.

I had two options. Get back to the street and wait for Terry, or go after the fifth man.

I went with the latter.

We traced a path through a line of trees whose naked limbs looked weak and ugly, dense skeletal hedgerow shielding us from the street. Now I heard sirens, growing louder all the while. At least they couldn't see me if I couldn't see them. As I hammered after the suited figure, I wondered who and what these men were. Not military. Not cops. Nor were they private security contractors or government agents. They were armed, but not skilled. That made them hired muscle at best.

But for who?

And what had they wanted with Al Chastain?

As the chase moved out of the trees and out onto open land once more, we raced across a road on which there was thankfully no traffic. A waist-high railing bordered the next stretch of land. The man in the suit hurdled it but cried out and staggered a little upon landing. I made my leap clean and gained on him. Looking up I saw the black mouth of an underpass which ran beneath the highway ahead in the distance. I could tell the man in front of me was flagging. He was neither built for nor used to a foot chase of this duration. I put on a spurt as he seemed to be stumbling to a halt. He barely made it into the underpass, but once into the shadows he took a couple of final lumbering steps then stopped. He bent forward at a right angle, hands on his thighs, and vomited onto the floor.

I slowed and came up behind him softly. Waited for him to finish throwing up, and allowed him to catch his breath. He took it down in huge, greedy gulps, cheeks aflame, sweat pouring from his brow. His dripping suit and shirt clung to him like a second skin. He turned to look at me and shook his head.

'Just fucking do it, man,' he said between breaths. He used two extended fingers and a cocked thumb to indicate a gun. 'I'm gonna have a fucking heart attack anyway.'

'You talk to me and I'll let you live,' I told him. I sucked in some much-needed air myself.

'Yeah. Sure you will.'

'You have my word on it.'

Chest heaving, he looked up at me to check out my eyes. I don't know what he saw there, but it seemed to help him reach a decision.

'You can ask, man. I'll tell you what I know, but that ain't a hell of a lot.'

'Okay, begin by telling me what you wanted with Al Chastain.'

'All I know is that Chastain was supposed to have had something the boss of my boss wanted. I don't know what that thing was. Stuff like that gets compartmentalised. You can't tell what you don't know, right?'

I nodded. That was true enough, and a maxim Terry and I lived by.

'Did Chastain give it up?'

'No, man. We didn't have a lot of time to work him over before you guys crashed in. But if I had to guess, I'd say he had no clue what we were talking about.'

'So who is your boss?'

'Vincent Dorigo.'

'What does he do and who does he work for?'

'He fixes things. For several people. This time it was on the orders of Alexander Moore.'

'Neither of those names mean a thing to me. What does this Alexander Moore do?'

The man finally stood up straight, hands on hips, still taking down air as fast as his lungs could process it. He put back his head and gasped a couple of times before responding.

'He's a businessman. Whatever that means in Vegas. I don't know the guy, only *of* him. We don't move in the same kinda circles.'

Las Vegas again. This time the mention of it got me thinking. 'These businesses include a casino?' I asked.

'Uh-huh. At least one, maybe more. Has to be connected, right, despite what they say about Vegas having cleaned up its act.'

I breathed deeply, my clothes still wringing wet and sticking to me. There wasn't enough heat in the day to dry me out, although the cool breeze blowing through the tunnel was doing its best to get the job done. It just made me feel colder and wetter.

'What do you do now? When I let you go. I take it your boss, Mr Dorigo, wasn't with you on this mission.'

'He's far away, believe me. Compartmentalised, remember. I'll call him. He'll send someone for me. He'll want to know what went wrong. How many of you fuckers are there, by the way? Felt like a fucking army storming in there.'

I declined to answer.

'I don't suppose you're gonna tell me who you are and what you wanted with Chastain either, are you?'

I shook my head. 'The less you know, right?'

His lips thinned. Part smile, part grimace. 'What does it hurt, man? You ain't gonna leave me alive. I tried to shoot you.'

'I gave you my word. I have no reason to kill you. The driver of your SUV is tied up in the back of it, still breathing. Had no need to kill him, either. Sure, you can describe me, but that will help no one. You can't hurt me. At least, I hope you're not fool enough to try.'

'I'm no fool. I prefer breathing to not breathing.'

'The name Vern Jackson mean anything to you?' I asked, taking a gamble.

I noticed the change in his eyes immediately. He tried to hide it from me, but was a moment too late.

'Tell me what you know,' I said. 'And don't lie to me.'

He shook his head and gave a sigh of resignation. 'Track-IT. Triple four, double seven, two.'

'And that means what, exactly?'

'Tracking device. You go to the Track-IT website and enter that code you get a fix on a GPS position.'

'Of Jackson's vehicle?' Drew had not yet got back to me about the rental car, so this might be the opportunity we'd been waiting for.

'No. But someone else has been sniffing around. Looking for something. Same thing as us, probably. No idea who they are, but we're pretty sure they have Jackson and Kelper. We managed to get that tracker on their car yesterday. Last I heard it hadn't started reporting back yet, but it will.'

It wasn't exactly an address, but if that vehicle visited the place where Vern and Kelper were being held, we might be able locate them even if the vehicle had moved on elsewhere. All we had to do was check the tracking records to find the most out of the way place imaginable.

'Good. So here's how it goes now. You toss me your gun – and I know you didn't throw it away, so don't even try to conceal it. I take it with me when I leave. Oh, plus your mobile… your cell phone. The moment I'm out of this underpass you start counting off. You reach five hundred, you go your own way. You won't know when I leave the area entirely, so if I were you I would not attempt to go any sooner. Your weapon, your phone and less than a ten-minute head start in exchange for your life. That's a pretty good deal, I think.'

He shook his head, creases deepening across his forehead. 'Who the fuck are you, man?'

I looked at him and smiled. 'Your best friend if you do as I say. Your worst fucking nightmare if you don't.'

He did as I said.

TWENTY-FIVE

My phone was capable of withstanding a splashing, but not a drenching. It was ruined, so I could not call Terry. I broke it up into pieces and deposited it in the first bin I came across. The suited man's cell joined it. Steering clear of the scene we had left behind, I walked around knowing that Terry would find me.

Moving up a steep gradient where the road started to curve around towards the city, I glanced back over my shoulder a couple of times and saw the remnants of the commotion we had caused being played out in the distance. At least half a dozen police cars, two ambulances and a fire truck stood outside the bungalow, whilst more cars cruised the streets around the immediate vicinity. By now they would know the body count, and any sharp cop worth their salt would suspect a military presence from the breach charges and flash-bang debris. I wondered if it was enough for the Department of Homeland Security to be summoned. That would certainly raise the stakes.

The road was slightly elevated and exposed by the lack of buildings on either side so the breeze felt cold on my wet clothing. I was happy that so few people walk if they can ride, and the small number of vehicles that slid by me drove on without a second glance in my direction. I was glad of the time on my own, which I gave over to considering the situation I had unwittingly sucked people into.

I felt bad about Chastain. I was pretty sure that our first visit to the Weather Balloon had not led directly to the man's subsequent murder. I had a feeling that the chain of events leading to his death had begun unravelling long before we came on the scene. Nonetheless, we had breached the property in order to rescue the man, not because of the questions we wanted to ask after we had secured him. Terry and I had failed in our mission. More to the point, I had misjudged the situation by forgetting a cardinal rule: never trust the reactions of a non-professional. The suited hired gun had blown Chastain away in a moment of sheer panic rather than an act of bravery or fear.

The Jeep finally pulled into the kerb alongside me and I climbed in. By then I was six blocks away and on the other side of the freeway from Chastain's place.

'You stopped off for a shower?' Terry said, looking me up and down. His mouth was a thin slit, curving upwards.

'I fancied a swim. It was a nice enough day.'

'How'd you leave things?'

I liked the way he assumed I had controlled my part of the job. I often feel that if I had even fifty per cent of the confidence in myself that Terry has, I'd be fifty per cent better at what I do.

'I got a couple of names. But he knew very little about what was going on. They work in small cells. Less amateur than I'd imagined.'

'Names?'

'Two middleweights out of Vegas. Dorigo and Moore. The first is a fixer, who works for the latter, who owns a casino complex or two. Beyond that, nothing we can learn from.'

'We could use a stroke of luck by now,' Terry said.

I looked at him and grinned. 'I think we may have received it.'

I told him about the tracking device. 'It's not the rental,' I continued. 'But if Drew can't get hold of that information, then it's something. Maybe.'

While I was chasing the fifth man and Terry had scoured the neighbourhood searching for me, he had filled Chelsea in on what had gone down inside the property. She was visibly shaken up and quiet, and I wondered if she might be feeling responsible in some way. She had called upon Chastain prior to our visit, had shown him Vern's photo. She had involved him, and now he was dead. I looked back, saw the hard set of her jaw and a pain in the slits she had made of her eyes. I felt a wave of sympathy for her.

'Hey,' I said. 'Listen to me. What happened to Al Chastain had nothing whatsoever to do with you. For that matter, nothing to do with us, either. I get the impression that his murder had nothing to do with your visit to him, nor ours. Something else is going on here. Something we have yet to figure out. I can't see what it is yet, but I will. So don't beat yourself up. Okay?'

I wasn't entirely convinced by my own argument, but if it was a lie, it was a good one to tell.

Van Dalen nodded but made no reply. She barely glanced in my direction. I knew she must be terrified, having been caught up in something for which she was wholly unprepared. In removing her from what we considered to be a dangerous situation back at her hotel, it felt as if we had merely swept her up into a position in which her life was now made infinitely worse. The decisions Terry and I had made had cast the black taint of death on the young woman, and I knew from experience that it would her take a long time to recover from it.

I turned to look at my friend, who was nursing the Jeep back towards the airport. We agreed that our priority was to regroup, lay out everything we had, check the information I had been given, and move on to the next plan. The jet was our only base, perhaps the only place in the whole of New Mexico where we would still feel safe. Something about my recent train of thought nagged at me. I felt as if I had missed something vital, but it swam out of view.

'Does any of this feel right to you?' I asked Terry. I shook my head and smashed a clenched fist down on the armrest. 'This is not about Vern's so-called gambling debt – at least, a debt that might cause such a chain reaction of events. Those men we put down, they were looking for Vern and Kelper. I'm convinced of that. But why would they come to the conclusion that Chastain would know where the two of them were? I can't work any of this out. The only thing that does seem certain is that this all stems from Las Vegas, so there might yet be answers up there.'

He nodded. 'You got a couple of names out of the man you chased down. We may yet be able to track down a vehicle of interest because of what you were able to get out of him. We'll chew it over in the Lear, but I'm thinking it might still be best if I flew up there to find out more about them whilst you and Yoko here sift through the embers of whatever we've got going on in New Mexico.'

Despite our predicament, I chuckled. Referring to our current companion as 'Yoko' was so typical of his sense of humour, but I wasn't sure she deserved the title.

'We're missing a major piece of the puzzle. Maybe it's up there. But Vern could still be close by, so yes I do think I need to stick around. Quite what we do about Chelsea, I have no real idea.'

'Do I get a say in my future?' a voice queried from the back seat. It put me in mind of the troubles that had come my way over the previous summer, and another woman in desperate need of help without her even knowing it. Terry had described her and the child she took care of as our baggage, and now it seemed we had more to look after.

I nodded. Found her in the rear-view. 'Of course. You're not our prisoner, Chelsea. We brought you with us because we thought it would be safer for you. Looks like we were wrong.'

'We can't know that,' Terry said, his eyes busy on the road and in his mirrors. 'If these same people had found Chelsea at the hotel, it could be her lying dead right now.'

There was that.

This time I did twist in my seat. Van Dalen's glare was now a little hostile. I could hardly blame her. 'Terry's right. I didn't expect us to be driving you into a firefight, but my best guess is that these same men were after you three. Maybe they would not have located you at the Days Inn, but I suspect they would have eventually. I know you're scared and worried about what happened back there at Chastain's place, but on the whole I still think you're safer with us.'

I believed that to be the case, but I could not help but think about how safe people actually were around me these days. I had my daughter, which meant those who wished ill of me still had their hooks in my life if it suited them. My plan since walking away from sorry mess of the previous summer was to keep my distance from the security and intelligence services. Equally, I was aware that the unlicensed and disavowed darker divisions might one day decide to make an example of me.

Not on this trip though. This was a crazy situation whose complexities would make themselves known to us soon enough. Someone always held that final piece of the puzzle, even if they were not aware of it. It was our job to find them and squeeze it out of them.

The young woman regarded me with scepticism and fear. She had not directly witnessed any of what had taken place inside

Chastain's bungalow, but with the presence of the police and whatever sanitised version Terry had gone with when describing the scene, she knew lives had been lost and that we were responsible for some of them. There was nothing to be gained from pointing out that we had not done so by choice, and certainly with no malice or satisfaction. It went with the territory. Simple as that. You either walked away and managed the guilt, or you never saw the light of day again.

'Listen,' I said. 'Once we get back to the airport, you get some food and drink inside you, listen to what we have to say. If after that you want to go your own way, then that's what you do. Neither of us will try to stop you. You can take a cab, or I'll drop you off somewhere. Back at the Days Inn if you decide that's for the best. I would advise against it, but I'm not holding you against your will. In fact–'

Terry's phone rang. I held up a finger to postpone the chat with Van Dalen while my friend took out his mobile and checked the screen. He handed it across to me. It was Drew's number. As I thumbed the answer icon a couple of helicopters swooped overhead in the direction of the shitstorm we had left behind. The chase was hotting up. Having heavily armed men taking lives in your city tended to cause that level of reaction. I wondered if the man in the suit had also managed to secure his escape.

'It's Mike,' I said. 'I assume you tried contacting me first but got no joy. I had a slight… accident with my phone. I'll pick up another and text you the number. In the meantime, I hope you have some good news for me, Drew. We could use some right about now.'

'I had to go through another source,' Drew replied. 'But I'm afraid I have bad news. The vehicle's on-board GPS was deactivated. Someone beat us to the punch. The rental company are checking their records now, but it may be some time before they can tell me where the last signal was located.'

I cursed. It would have been too easy, but I felt our efforts deserved a break. I told him I had a tracker of our own to check out, fed him the details and asked him to call me back. I offered no further information of my own.

'Look for somewhere well out of the way,' I told him. 'Knowing where the vehicle is now will be something to get our teeth into, but if it has visited a remote location then that may be where we'll find Vern.'

We drove on in silence for several minutes before Drew called back. I still had hold of the phone. I listened, glanced over at Terry and gave him a thumbs-up. After Drew gave me the location I repeated the coordinates before speaking into the phone again.

'You said you had to go with someone else to try tracking down the rental. How come?' I asked, concerned that what we were doing might spread beyond the immediate few people who were directly aware of what was going on. 'And do you trust them not to talk?'

'I trust them. As for my other source, she won't pick up and refuses to return my messages.'

'I take it that's unusual.'

'She's a young, modern woman, Mike. She is always connected in one form or another. Though for now she seems to have chosen to take herself off the grid.'

I gave that some thought. Wondered about the coincidence. 'You don't think the two things are connected in any way, do you?' I asked him. 'I mean, did your hacker know Vern at all?'

'Not that I'm aware of. I told you, she was a freelancer who we had testing our software for gaps in security. She was damned good at it, too. But she worked off the books and never came to the office.'

'Yet she's been out of contact for a few days now, right? At least since you called her the first time to see if she could access the hotel records. Freelancers respond when there might be money in it for them. I think there's more to her continued silence than you might think.'

'That's right. I see what you mean now, Mike. Vern has dropped off the edge of the planet, and she now won't answer her phone. The truth is, I can't say for sure that they never met. I guess it has to be possible. After all, they're in a similar line of work.'

My heart started to beat a little faster. I heard the rush of it loud in my ears. In a much softer voice I said, 'Drew, does the name Chastain mean anything to you? Al Chastain.'

'Uh, sure. He's retired USAF. Way back in the day he debunked the whole Roswell UFO nonsense. That did not make him a popular man, considering he lived right there in the city.'

'Do you know what he did when he left the Air Force?'

'I do. He was one of the early pioneers of computing. A worker bee, but funnily enough he was also a programmer. A pretty good one by all accounts. He went on to work for the Gaming Commission, which is how I first came to hear of him.'

As he said those words I happened to be looking at Van Dalen in the mirror. The moment our eyes met I remembered what had bothered me earlier, and I suddenly knew what was going on.

'Drew, what's your contact's name?'

'I only ever knew her as Neuroses. That was her hacker name.'

'But you paid her for her services. Under what name?'

'Still not her real name. Neuroses Enterprises was the account name. She hid herself away, Mike. These people do.'

I ended the call promising I would get back to him the moment we had checked out the vehicle. By then, Terry had already entered the location into the GPS and programmed in the Sat-Nav. He had also turned away from the airport and we were headed back towards the desert. Drew's check of the Track-IT website revealed that since the device came online it had shown movement in and around Roswell, but also a single return visit to the kind of remote location we were looking for.

I shifted around once more. I looked hard at Chelsea van Dalen. She looked hard back at me.

'Hi, Neuroses,' I said. 'We have a bit of a ride ahead of us. It'll take a while. Time enough for you to come clean.'

TWENTY-SIX

We headed north-west out of Roswell, past Border Hill and into the desert on Route 246. It looked much like the road we had taken out to where Vern's vehicle had been dumped, or the road into Corona, or the road out of Corona towards the crash site for that matter. Mile after mile of nothing but flat desert soil, with the Capitan mountain range a purplish-grey jagged smudge ahead of us. We stopped off at a petrol station on the edge of Border Hill to fill up the Jeep and grab some fuel for ourselves as well. Fatty snacks and sugary drinks were ideal, given we had no way of knowing when we might next be in a position to eat. We also stopped off at a store where I bought a prepaid mobile phone. I set it up and texted the number to Drew. I did the same to Terry so that he would have the number in his phone. As the desert swallowed us up, I was no longer riding shotgun, having moved into the back alongside our passenger. Easier for us to talk that way. And I had a lot to say.

After the young woman admitted to being the hacker Drew Jackson knew as Neuroses, the rest of her confession emerged in a torrent of words amidst a flume of apologies.

'I'm so sorry. I know I should have told you the truth from the beginning, but I was too scared to. I needed help to find Vern, and when you two came along I was terrified that if you knew the truth you might not help me. I'm sorry. I really am.'

'And that truth is?' I refused to be harsh with her, my manner remaining considerate in spite of my fury. She had already been through so much, it did not feel right to berate her for lying to us. I'd also experienced this exact same situation before, and I knew that anger was not the best solution.

'As I can tell you've already figured out, it's Vern I am close with, not Bruce. I'm sorry I lied, but you were hunting for Vern and I didn't want you putting the two of us together that closely. That night in the bar at the pool table that I told you about happened pretty much the way I described, only it was the other way around. It was Vern I went there to meet. The drive up to Area 51, the Black Mailbox, being followed, the tyre slashing, all of that happened exactly how I said it did. But as you rightly mentioned earlier, there are some important things you don't know. Things I didn't tell you. And I apologise for that, because I chose to keep those things from you.'

I processed what she had told us, and said, 'Okay. I knew there was something iffy about your meeting with Chastain, and even when it was mentioned earlier I couldn't quite put my finger on it. But it clicked back there and fell into place. The only photo either you or Chastain mentioned was Vern's. But according to your version of events, Kelper was supposed to be your boyfriend, so why would you be showing Vern's photo to anybody?'

'I never even thought about that. I guess I didn't cover my ass as well as I thought I had. Chastain didn't know either me or Vern, but he knew Bruce. He told me Bruce had stopped by briefly, but that he was on his own. I showed him Vern's photo in case he'd been sitting in the background somewhere, but Chastain said he didn't recognise the face. I am sorry, and I know I've probably only hindered things so far. I couldn't help myself. I was just so frightened.'

'I understand. More than you perhaps realise. Did Chastain mention what it was Kelper wanted with him?'

'No. And I didn't ask. I got the impression he was nervous about it.'

I nodded. I believed her. 'As long as you're being truthful now and continue to be, then you can still help us find Vern. So start with why this whole gambling and UFO enthusiast rubbish got thrown our way. I know there's a connection to both, but I also know that neither are why this is really happening.'

Van Dalen took a breath. Tears glistened on her eyelashes. She looked pale and vulnerable beneath her dark beauty. A woman lost, in search of a direction.

'We were running. That's totally genuine. But not from some hired muscle looking to claw back a minor gambling debt. Though you were right – casinos are a part of this whole deal. As for the UFO stuff, that was pretty much all Bruce's idea. Vern is into that whole deal, don't get me wrong, but not like Bruce. He's a total conspiracy nut. Anyhow, we thought we'd follow the trail because we could lose ourselves down here.'

'The trail?' I frowned as I asked the question.

'Yeah. Area 51, the Extraterrestrial Highway, the crash site, Roswell. It's the trail UFO nuts follow. It's like some kind of pilgrimage for them, I guess.'

'Okay. So you and Vern went along with Bruce Kelper's fascination with all this, using it as a distraction and a way to get out of Las Vegas and to try and lose yourselves down here.'

'Yes. Exactly that. I talked it over with Vern and it seemed like a way to be on the run without feeling the pressure of it that way all the time. It felt like a good opportunity to get our minds off the trouble we were in. I guess it must sound lame to you, but I thought maybe we could get so wrapped up in all the UFO and crash site bullshit that we might not spend every minute of every day dwelling on all the trouble we were in. So yeah, we drove down from Vegas, we visited Corona, hit the crash site just like I said, and then we did all the Roswell Museum stuff as well. We thought we were in the clear after ditching those men at the crash site. And I think we could have been, if it weren't for Bruce.'

I squinted at her. 'What role did he have to play in this? And did he know, by the way? I mean, was he aware of what you and Vern were really running from?'

Van Dalen shook her head. 'No, Bruce had no idea. Which is part of the problem and I suppose why we are where we are now. To him it was all a great big adventure. Bruce is still very much a big kid. He was following the trail and loving every minute of it. I wish now that we'd told him, but we didn't. At the time it didn't feel right involving him. We couldn't have known how bad a decision that was at the time we made it. Anyhow, when we were back in Vegas, Vern said he wanted to go off the grid, so he stopped using social media. I never use it anyway, so there was nothing for me to quit. Vern knows Bruce as a friend he sees from time to time, but they're not best buds, so we didn't think there was any way people would tie us in with him. We thought it would be helpful having him along, in case we needed anything requiring a credit card. I have a couple of fakes I could risk in an emergency, but you never know when you might need some additional help.'

'So you used Bruce as a sort of buffer?' It was an observation rather than an accusation. The more I thought about it, the less it all seemed like a bad plan.

'I guess. Plus, his knowledge of all that UFO stuff made us seem all the more legit when we were around others who are into it all. But what neither Vern nor I knew until much later was that Bruce was using social media to lay breadcrumbs for his UFO buddies. By the time we found out it was too late.'

'Why, what happened?' I asked.

'He told me and Vern that all he wanted was for his like-minded friends to follow our journey, join the trail with us online. Vern and I thought we'd managed to go dark, when all the while Bruce was putting our movements out there for anyone to pick up on.'

'He sounds like a bit of an arsehole,' Terry observed drily.

Van Dalen hitched her shoulders and blew out a sigh. 'It was a game to him, a bit of fun. I don't think it was malicious or anything. I guess he never even considered the downside. He had no idea what Vern and I were running from, so he had no idea he was hurting us. But that's why I went to see Chastain myself. Because Bruce had decided to go see the guy on the day they disappeared.'

'So how did you find out about these breadcrumbs?' Terry asked. It was the first question he had put to the young woman since discovering her duplicity.

'He told us. Just blurted it out. We would never have known otherwise. Like I say, we were not connected to the grid. He happened to mention it, thinking it was hilarious, and Vern blew up on him. He came close to telling Bruce everything at that point, though I managed to pull him back. That was the point at which we decided Vern's minivan had to be dumped. Only, like I told you before, I've not heard from Vern since he and Bruce drove away from the hotel.'

I saw it all unravel inside my head, like a spool of film. The journey they had made, the UFO-related sideshow that allowed them to forget why they were being pursued, the lame social media game Bruce had been enjoying. It was the kind of shit young people did. All that was missing was why any of it needed to have happened at all.

'Okay,' I said, 'Now we know what you did after Vegas. What happened before that? What kick-started this whole sorry mess?'

She hung her head for a moment. Then she sniffed, wiped her eyes with the back of her hand and looked up at me with a determined expression lacking regret. 'Vern and I were ripping off a number of casinos. Before I get into all that, do you know what Drew Mason's business is?'

'I know it's an IT company. A successful one, if his home and private jet are anything to go by. That's all.'

'They design software. One of their contracts is to supply various items of software for casinos and hotels. Most of it controls their gaming machines, but their accountancy tools are also installed in quite a few of the complexes. A significant number use both. Vern is a programmer, but he also travels around installing and upgrading and providing health checks and training. He knew of me from the times I tested out Drew's products, and we also collaborated on one project. For some reason he and I hit it off when we were online, and we decided to meet for a drink when he came out to Vegas. That led to dinner, a few more dates, and that was us together. We got to talking about the work, and one night I happened to mention how a black hat hacker might run amok where so much money was flying around and trapped inside the ether.'

'So you're what's known as a white hat,' I said. 'You're on the side of good, not evil.'

'That's right. Or, at least it was.'

'You went rogue. Vern, too.'

Van Dalen nodded, biting her lower lip as if the pain might somehow cause all her problems to disappear.

'So what did you do, and whose idea was it?'

'Vern had the idea that we could quite easily skim off some of the money casinos brought in. The plan was that we'd take the finished products and recode them so that in between the take from machines and the accounting, a few dollars here and there were electronically siphoned off to a different account which we would set up ahead of time. Each individual transaction would be too small to notice immediately, but it would amount to a fair slice per casino. We would also code it from a hacker's perspective and that way if anyone ever suspected or it was discovered in some way, the investigators would believe the software was legit but that it had somehow been hacked. You can code it so that the string of code responsible changes the modification date every thirty days or so. It didn't mean the hack would never get discovered, only that it could never come back to bite us.'

'Only it did.'

'Only it did.'

'How?'

'That's just it. We don't know. Not exactly. I guess it happened because we got greedy. Actually, that's not it entirely. We felt we needed to spread the load more, so that each casino took less of a hit. So Vern involved other software engineers whose employers' products went into other casinos. People he knew from conventions, that sort of thing. People he thought he could trust, especially if they were making a shit-load of cash. And believe me, they would have. We agreed to run the scam for three months, and then we'd blow the US and set up a life for ourselves in the Caribbean someplace. But then that night in Vegas, before he went to the bar where we played pool, Vern barely got away from a couple of guys he said looked mean and tough and who told him he had fucked with the wrong man.'

I puffed out my cheeks. Money and greed. Somehow it often came down to one or both of those things. 'So another one of the reasons New Mexico felt right was because Drew's company don't have any casinos down here.'

Van Dalen nodded. 'Not even any connection with one via his friends. So far as we knew, anyhow. I guess we may never be sure about that, because greed engenders more greed. So that's why all this is happening. We still don't exactly know how the casino owners found out about it, nor how they became aware that Vern was involved. Our guess is that one of the friends, or maybe even a friend of a friend, got stupid, got discovered, and ended up giving us up.'

Only after being unmercifully tortured, I thought but did not say. When you question somebody you don't accept the first answer they give you – if they give up anything at all. Whoever the source was, they were dead now. Disposed of somewhere out in the desert was my guess.

I thought again about what had happened back in Roswell. 'You think Kelper might have gone to see Chastain because of his expertise with both programming and the Gaming Commission? Could be he thought the man might have been able to propose an easy way out.'

'Could be. Yeah, that sounds like something Bruce might do.'

'I don't want to interrupt you in full flow,' Terry said, 'but we're coming up fast on the location, and I don't want to approach it head-on.'

I checked my new phone, saw that it still had a signal. 'Okay. Pull over when you can. See if you can manage to get us out of sight somewhere. We'll run up Google maps and take a look at what's out there.'

'I don't like relying on that, Mike. It can be years out of date.'

'I know. It's just a guide. And we don't exactly have access these days to real-time satellite feeds.'

'Roger that.'

'We'll check the lay of the land. Get some food and drink down our necks. Make some plans.'

'Okay. There's something up ahead and to our left, Mike,' he called out. 'Looks either closed or abandoned. Might be the right place for us to pause.'

I looked back at Van Dalen, who appeared crestfallen and emotionally wrung out. I was livid with her for lying to us, but I also felt sorry for her. Young and stupid often went hand in hand, and I'd been both back in the day. I could not hold on to my anger.

'You got in out of your depth,' I told her softly. 'What's done is done. Now we're going to try and help you safely back to shore.'

TWENTY-SEVEN

After some persuasion bordering on what he thought came close to being full-blown nagging, Special Agent Eugene Wilson eventually agreed with his partner that they should take no chances where Barclay and Garcia were concerned. The tracker would not do them any good if, overnight, the pair figured out what was going on. Green painted an entire scenario for him whereby they remained sitting in their office watching the computer monitor, while the men they were tracking rented another vehicle and left Roswell behind in a cloud of dust. That was why, since shortly after their shift began, the two FBI agents had been sitting in a parking lot next door to an office complex watching the Mayo Lodge opposite.

They had brought coffee and toasted bagels with them, purchased from a nearby gas station on the short drive over from the FBI field office. Those were now long gone, and Wilson had become restless the more thirsty and hungry he got.

'I still worry they ducked out of there during the night,' he said, nodding towards the cheap motel across the road from where they sat.

'How many times are you going to say the same damn thing in a slightly different way, Eugene?' Green complained.

He looked at her in surprise. 'I can't believe you're not worried. It's not right. They ought to be out there by now looking for Vern Jackson. Instead they're what… having a lie-in?'

'In case you'd forgotten, it was my idea to sit on them. My idea that they might figure out what we did and decide to sneak away.'

'Okay, okay. But what do we do if we're already too late and they sneaked out of the back door or in another vehicle?'

'Hey, here's a thought: we could actually search for Vern Jackson ourselves, rather than waiting for these two jerkoffs to do our job for us.'

'We could, but they have an inside track and we don't. They work for a powerful group, with huge influence, who will clearly stop at nothing when it comes to finding Jackson.'

Green looked across at him. She tilted her head to one side. 'You did not just say that.'

Wilson shrugged, raising his hands at the same time. 'What?'

'Does what you just said describe anyone else, Eugene? Have you ever heard of the Federal Bureau of Investigation? Way I understand it, they're a pretty powerful group, with some high-clearance influence, whose very job it is to stop at nothing in attempting to locate this young man.'

'Heather, you wear me out,' Wilson said, shaking his head. 'Look, we agreed yesterday when we were sat in the sheriff's office that this was a decent plan. It was like having another couple of agents out there working on our behalf.'

'Yes. But not if we're sitting here alongside them. It only works that way if we're back at the office doing the best we can to find Jackson through other means. That way there's them doing their thing and us doing ours.'

'But you were the one who said we ought to be here watching them in case they slipped their leash!'

'I know that, Eugene. But that was only because there was no other plan for us to work with. I figured if we had to involve these two idiots, the least we ought to do was make sure they were still with their car and not a whole state away by now. And if they look as if they're on the move we can–'

Wilson frowned. He hated it when she spoke to him as if he were a child. 'What? You just thought of something?'

'No.' Green shook her head and pointed. 'Barclay and Garcia are on the move.'

The green Chevy reversed back out of its bay, turned and came towards the road. The moment they saw the left indicator come on, both agents ducked down in their seats because the vehicle was about to turn across the main street and complete its manoeuvre right by the parking lot they were sitting in.

When they sat up, the Chevy was gone. Green checked the laptop monitor, relieved to see the GPS hot-spot moving with the Chevy as it headed west out of Roswell. Wilson started their SUV and pulled out to follow at a safe distance.

'I hope they're not just going for breakfast,' he said.

'If they are, let's join them and be done with this charade. That bagel was delicious but it was also a long time ago and I'm starving.'

They continued along West Second Street, and where Route 70 turned north they kept driving west on the 380. A few blocks later, they too started heading north, only on the 141 instead.

'Border Hill is up ahead,' Green said. 'Wonder if that's where they're going.'

A few minutes later they realised that wasn't happening, the Chevy now several miles ahead of them breezing by the Border Hill turns. It wasn't long before the town gave way to scrub and then working farmland, which at this time of year was mostly barren and little more than desert dust. Green kept her eyes on the monitor of the tablet they were using.

'They're turning west again… no… hold on… make that north-west. They're on Route 246, Eugene.'

'Better make sure we don't get too close. I know we swapped out the SUV so they won't recognise this one, but where we're headed it's best we keep a good distance between us and them.'

'Yep. We could be headed back into Crozier's county.'

'I bet he's seen it. You want to call him or wait and see if he shows?'

'Oh, he'll show.' Agent Green nodded to herself. 'The sheriff has a taste for it now, you can count on that.'

*

Lincoln County covered a little under 5,000 square miles of New Mexico, yet only 20,000 people or so lived there. This left a whole lot of area for the sheriff's department to police, with manpower in ever-dwindling short supply. As he did every working day, Crozier had headed out of the building to cruise the roads and towns around his county. There were probably more cattle than people to tend to, but he still took his job seriously. Most of the time he found himself acting as more of a social worker or arbiter in minor disputes than a sheriff laying down the law, but that was the way he liked it. Even so, today he had made special preparations. Before he left the office he arranged with Mitzy Gray, the civilian who managed the administration staff, to monitor the GPS tracking device attached to the car driven by the two guys out of Fresno, and to contact him on his radio when there was any sign of movement.

Crozier had eaten breakfast as usual, and afterwards on a hunch set off in the general direction of Corona. He took a couple of unusual routes across country, coming at the area from a slightly different angle. It was good for him to change things up once in a while, he figured. Your eyes could get tired and your senses lazy if you took the same old roads every time.

He had to admit that when the radio crackled he felt a jolt of excitement. Over the past few days it had become clear to him that something was going on in and around his boundary lines. Something major. There were enough comings and goings to suggest that, even without the sour feeling that had sat in the deep pit of his gut ever since hearing about the confrontation between Joe Kane and the Barrow boys. To his mind, the only way people like that came together was when bad things were either happening or were about to.

Mitzy called out the directions each time the tracker made a turn. The moment Crozier heard her mention Route 141 he saw the little area of Border Hill in his mind and knew trouble was coming his way. It was like sensing a storm brewing in the distance beyond the horizon, or feeling the chill coming from a cold winter sun. Deep inside his bones there was an inkling of foreboding that demanded to be heard. Crozier swallowed hard and stood on the accelerator, determined to meet it head-on.

TWENTY-EIGHT

'You know we're being followed, right?' Terry said to me after we had pulled off the road.

I nodded. 'Yep. All the way from Roswell. When we pulled in here he drove right by a minute or so later. A small truck.'

'You think it's that sheriff we ran across in Corona? I had the feeling he didn't buy into our story. Could be he took an interest in us.'

'Where did you pick him up first?'

'Shortly after we left the Weather Balloon.'

My friend was good. I had not spotted our tail until we were driving away from the heavy police presence resulting from the mess we had helped create. 'Then no, it's not the sheriff. He would have stepped in the moment we entered Chastain's place. Besides, we're out of his jurisdiction.'

Terry grunted. 'Right. You're right. So then maybe the two retards we took out on the side of the road changed cars – Mr No Neck and Mr Snakeskin.'

'Barclay and Garcia,' I said.

He snapped his fingers. 'That's them.'

I thought about it. Shook my head. 'Whoever's behind us is pretty good. I mean, there were a couple of times when I asked myself if I was wrong about being followed. I don't see either Roadrunner or Coyote being that adept, do you?'

Terry laughed at my description. Then he shrugged. 'So someone new in the game.'

He was about to say more, but paused. I left him with it for a short while. Eventually he nodded to himself. 'The Indian back at the Weather Balloon. He caught my attention. I wondered about him when I saw him sat at the exact table I would have chosen had I been looking out for someone. He was smooth the way he broke our eye contact, but maybe too smooth now that I think about it more. It wasn't quite natural. Almost as if he gave it some thought first.'

'The Indian?' I said, fixing him with a narrow stare. 'Do you mean a gentleman from the Indian subcontinent, or a Native American?'

The look he gave me back was not one of amusement. 'You know what I mean. Either way, it's him. I know it.'

Van Dalen leaned forward to rest her elbows on the back of our seats. 'Are you two always like this?' she asked.

'Like what?' Terry and I said in unison.

'So laid-back. Relaxed as if we're out sightseeing. Someone is following you, you got into a shootout, men were killed, and you're about to drive into more of the same it seems to me. And still you chat like nothing is wrong. You didn't even bother to let me know we were being followed.'

'I didn't want to scare you needlessly,' Terry explained. 'And Mike and I have been in worse scrapes. One of the things you do ahead of a skirmish is to analyse the abilities of your opponents. From everything I've seen and heard so far, these men are pros, but professionals within their own sphere. I doubt they would ever have encountered people like me and Mike before. So, while I'm not being overconfident, let's just say I fancy our chances.'

'But you have no idea who they are.'

'True. But I know their type.'

'The men who probably have Vern and Bruce are just like those men who murdered Chastain, right? So they have no problem with killing. Vern could already be dead for all you know.'

I nodded. There was little point in denying it. 'Anything is possible at this stage, Chelsea,' I said. 'But with the vultures we seem to have circling, my hunch is Vern and Kelper are still alive.'

'That didn't help Chastain.'

Her words stung, but she was correct. I had no doubt that he would have been killed anyway, but I felt a huge amount of regret that we had not managed to rescue him.

'Our intention is to get in and get out without anyone ending up with so much as a scratch,' I told her. 'But conflicts don't always go the way you expect. Me and Terry are good at what we do, but men in fear can sometimes do the most unexpected things.'

'But you can't know for certain that they're not already dead. You just admitted that.'

'True. But looking at it dispassionately, they were brought all the way out here into the middle of nowhere for a reason. That suggests whoever has them wanted time and space to question your boyfriend and Kelper.'

'Oh, my God!' she cried. 'That means they're being tortured.' Tears gushed from her eyes, and her face creased in anguish.

I turned and put a hand on hers to calm her, but she shrugged it off. I tried again, and this time she let it rest there. 'Even if that's true,' I said, 'you have to hold on to that thought as a positive thing. Because if that's the case then it means they're still alive. Terry and I don't know what we're going to find out there, and the chances are it won't be pleasant. But if they are alive, then we'll keep them that way.'

Van Dalen sat back, her hand slipping away from mine. She stared at me for a moment before shaking her head, saying, 'You don't even know for sure that you can keep yourselves safe.'

'There's nothing certain in life, Chelsea. All I can promise you is that we intend to walk back out of this place we're going into, and that we won't be alone when we do.'

We had pulled over to check out the location on Google maps and put a plan together. From what we could tell from the terrain, there were some sweeping hills on three sides of a deserted crop of buildings. On the other side, a relatively flat, curving track ran from the main road right up to whatever the place was. I zoomed in as close as possible, and after looking at it for a few minutes, Terry and I agreed that the area had once been some kind of business, probably a mill, and had been abandoned for many years. The different types of buildings had different types of problems, but both the wooden structures and the brick one with what looked like a slate roof were carrying significant cavities, which told us they were no longer in use. One of the wooden structures was what looked to us like the mill itself, and its appearance was one of complete neglect.

We chugged our way through a large bottle of Coke and snacked on corn chips and Twix fingers. Terry and I were hungry, but mostly we wanted a sugar boost and to keep our fuel intake topped up. Van Dalen ate and drank about a quarter of what we did, but she seemed satisfied with that. While we took it in we also threw a decent makeshift plan together based entirely on what we had seen on the electronic map. Like all such plans, it was fluid and would evolve based on circumstances.

I thought about what Van Dalen had said about us, how we were laid-back and relaxed. The truth was very different. We did not act that way because we were fearless. We did so because we had fears to overcome. You did not overcome them by dwelling on the negatives.

The moment we were done snacking, we moved further on up the road, and half a mile away from the mill dropped off the blacktop altogether. We bumped our way across the open land, avoiding fallen rocks, boulders, and clutches of wild shrubs and plants. After easing our way around a gentle curve, we tucked ourselves behind a hillside where we could not be seen from either the route we had come in on or the buildings on the other side of the steep rise. Which is where we sat finalising our strategy.

'Our follower would have gone ahead on the road, probably intending to stop on the other side of the hill,' I suggested. 'Now, I suppose it depends on whether he's looking for us or looking for Vern and Kelper as to what he actually does next. He'll spot the mill, put it together with us peeling off the road, and will presumably lay up further ahead where he can't be seen. That said, I would expect to encounter him at some point.'

'I agree,' Terry said with a firm nod. He turned to Van Dalen. 'Now, listen up, because this is very important. Once again, I want you to leave the engine running while we're gone. This time I also want you in the driving seat. I'm leaving you a two-way radio. Ignore any chatter you may overhear between me and Mike. What you listen out for are a series of squawks.'

'Squawks? What the fuck?'

'Clicks. The radio will give a harsh, static sound. A rapid double click means you get the hell out of here, you find the nearest and safest place with a signal for your phone, and you call Drew Mason.'

'Can't you just use words? Tell me what you need me to do when you need me to do it.'

Back at the abandoned petrol station she had appeared to be lost in thought, but now Van Dalen was on the edge of her seat and fully alert.

'Under normal circumstances,' Terry said, nodding. 'But the clicks are a shorthand. I may not be able to speak out loud, but with the radio send and receive button I still have a means of communication. Please, just listen and do as I say. When you reach Drew, tell him we're blown, tell him exactly where we are, and then you drive further away and keep on driving. That's two clicks, remember. Three rapid clicks means head back to the road and meet us at the entrance to the mill on the other side of these hills. Got it?'

Van Dalen nodded. 'Two clicks, scram. Three clicks, come running. Why not a single click?'

'Because that could occur by accident.'

'And do not divert from either of those,' I told her. 'I mean it, Chelsea. Terry and I believe we're coming back and that the next you'll see of us we'll be walking over that hillside, hopefully with both Vern and Bruce by our side. Either that or at the side of the road by the entrance. But no conflict ever went according to every step of the plan. It rarely lasts longer than the first encounter. So be prepared for anything, but *be* prepared and listen out for the squawks. Our lives may depend on it.'

'What if that man following us finds me here on my own?'

Terry shook his head. 'He's either lying in wait for us further up the road, or his interests have now turned to the place on the other side of this ridge. I'm betting it's the latter, because I suspect he's following us because he thinks we will lead him to Vern.'

That was it. Terry and I grabbed our gear and left her there. Either she would be waiting for us when we came back or she would not. My bet was that she would tough it out. As young as she was, Van Dalen seemed pretty devoted to Vern, and whilst she was clearly frightened by the predicament she found herself in, I thought she appeared defiant enough to see it through.

TWENTY-NINE

I FOLLOWED TERRY WHO WAS walking briskly up the hill, the loose and dry soil not making life easy on either of us. We leaned into it, and despite my recent fitness regime I felt both calf muscles burn and spasm. Just before the crest we slowed and then got down on all fours, creeping our way to the point where we could see the lay of the land below us.

It was an impressive sight, and exactly how it had appeared on the map.

Scanning left to right, from the direction of the road, the first collection of old buildings looked as if they had been rickety from the moment they were built. The water tower did not look strong enough to support the enormous sealed tank that at one time must have held thousands of gallons of liquid. There were eight supportive legs, held firm by multiple crossbeams, but still it sagged uneasily to one side and looked as if it might topple over at any moment.

Another wooden building stood opposite, and seeing it from the rear it was hard to tell what it might have been. To me it looked like maybe a mess hall of some kind; a resting and dining area for the workers, sheltered from the elements. Beyond that was the mill itself, a vast, multi-layered construction that spread out in all directions in an architecturally haphazard sprawl. A long horizontal elevated runway was now broken off into three separate sections somehow still supported on rickety towers, but I could see that at one time the lumber had passed through the saw and been shifted along the runway to its destination point.

A vast storage area built in red brick squatted to one side of the mill, its windows and doors missing, much of its tiled roof also, leaving behind gaping wounds in the otherwise sound structure.

Towards the far end of the complex – our right – there were three smaller buildings cast from poured concrete. Though cracked and worn by time and varying extremes of weather, these appeared to be as solid as the day they were constructed. Strewn around the entire site were bundles of jagged timber, mounds of crushed ore, crumbling bricks, broken slates, and smashed, powdery stone.

I puffed out my cheeks when I spotted what I had been searching for.

Sitting behind the centre concrete building was a grey SUV. It was the one Bruce Kelper had rented.

I tapped Terry on the shoulder, pointed towards the vehicle and said, 'They're here. Or at least, they were. If that was you down there running the show, would you have parked that vehicle right next to where you were holding someone, or some distance away?'

'A good question. On the one hand I wouldn't want to draw attention to it, on the other I would want it close in case I needed a quick getaway.'

'A tough call, then. There's something missing, though.'

He nodded. 'The other vehicle. The one Drew tracked to this place.'

That left us with more questions to answer: like, was it coming back? If not, had they left Vern and Bruce alive? If it was returning, when? And how many men had they left behind? If any. We certainly hadn't spotted anyone so far.

I ran through the permutations with Terry. He gave it all a stir, eyes focussed on the entire area taken up by the sawmill site. As he did, I saw the first flakes appear around us. Few at first, and more floating than falling from the pale grey sky. They quickly increased in both volume and density, which meant they started hammering down upon us.

'Snow,' I said. 'How helpful.'

'We have to get this done quickly,' Terry said, ignoring my weather commentary. 'Assuming they left our targets alive, it's better all round if this is all over before they return.'

'Agreed. And you know, now that I think about it, if they've been here overnight at the very least, then where would they shelter at night? Somewhere warm. Somewhere sealed from the elements.'

'Unless they left their victims dumped in one of those derelict buildings and never came back for them.'

The possibility filled me with dread. But if they were still alive, Vern and Bruce were probably being guarded and maybe questioned during the day, perhaps left tied up somewhere within the mill by themselves overnight. I laid that out for Terry, and he nodded.

'All right,' he said. 'I think they have to be in one of those three concrete buildings. I think we have to assume they are currently being questioned. I think someone will eventually be coming to collect two, maybe three or even four men for the night. Given it just started snowing, it's possible they will come earlier than intended and that we have no more than thirty minutes.'

I rested my hand on his shoulder. It was time to move.

We scuttled around the hillside until we were on the far side of the basin, now directly overlooking the three formidable-looking concrete structures. The slopes had been tricky, and we caused one or two rock slides, but they were on our side of the ridge and created little noise. Every so often we stopped, edged our way up, and took a peek over the crest. Now that we were in position, we felt a lot better about our chances. If these men were of the quality we thought they were, then they would be focussing on either their captives or the dirt track leading in from the road. Perhaps even both. We were betting they would not be expecting any ingress from behind them.

As we started making our way down on a slippery surface of compressed loose rock and dirt that felt like a tide of shale underfoot, my eye was caught by an approaching vehicle. At the same moment, Terry, who had been taking point ahead of me, stopped and raised a hand with a clenched fist, telling me stop also.

'It's Roadrunner and Coyote,' I whispered, recognising the old Chevy with the sagging shocks.

We crouched in place. Terry said, 'There's no way they followed us as well. If they're here for the same reason we are, they're making a real mess of it.'

The green saloon bounced off the track and slid in behind a small ridge and a collection of rocks and boulders, where it came to a halt and the two thugs got out. From the rear seats of the Chevy they each claimed a rifle. As they moved away from their car and out into the open, both of them carried their weapon loosely in one hand.

Rank amateurs.

So bad I felt embarrassed for them.

They approached the sawmill with some caution, but seemed to be studying the ruins as if admiring the landmark rather than concentrating on the purpose for their presence there. In disbelief, I shook my head. These two deserved everything they got.

Snakeskin jerked around for a moment, looking back towards the road. A second later the sound of another vehicle approaching up on the asphalt reached my ears. Barclay and Garcia scampered across the debris-strewn dusty soil and took shelter inside the building I had thought might be a dining area but could now see had once been a store of some kind. Looking beyond them, I watched with grim fascination as a black SUV slowly wound its way towards us, eventually pulling up well short of the mill. It sat there with its engine running, its occupants no doubt sizing up what they were seeing.

'You think this is the bad guys returning, and maybe got spooked by something?' I asked Terry.

Before he could respond, a shot rang out. The report was loud and bounced back off the surrounding hills and rocks. It had originated from neither the trashed wooden building nor the newly-arrived SUV. Instead it had come from one of the single-storey concrete structures right in front of us. I guess that answered my question. I tapped Terry on his right shoulder, signalling that I was ready to carry on down the hill. It seemed to me the opportune moment to make our own strike, whilst whoever was inside the building was concentrating on Barclay, Garcia and whoever else was out there.

Terry moved without a word. The snow was still falling, only much harder now. The flakes were more like clumps, and rather than dissipate as they kissed the desert floor they adhered, coating the reddy-brown, tawny and khaki surfaces with a layer of pure white. This unexpected snowfall was not going to help with camouflage, but that would be the same for all parties. We clambered down the last few yards where the slope became more shallow, before finally finding flat soil a mere ten paces from the buildings.

By then, several more shots had reverberated around the mill, pinging off concrete or taking out a few chunks of wood. No one enjoyed being shot at, and they had predictably reacted in kind. From the top of the rise we had been able to survey the entire site, now we could see little but the three most modern buildings rising up before us. We moved forward as one this time, and crouched down again behind Bruce Kelper's rental.

'I think the first shots came from the building to our right,' Terry said, his mouth close to my ear. 'You distract everybody by spraying a few grenades left, right and centre. Drop them about halfway between us and the two tossers holed up in that wooden ruin. When you've done that, follow me into building one.' He indicated right again for confirmation.

Maintaining a low crouching jog, Terry moved across to the rear of the first building and crept alongside it, making sure he kept below the windows whose frames and glass were all removed. There was a rear door whose handle he tugged at. He turned his head to me and shook it.

Locked.

I wondered if he would try to pick it, or head around the side of the building instead. He did neither. I watched as he pulled out the same kind of strip shape charge that we had used back in Roswell. This time he pressed it into place around the lock and stepped back. His focus on me once again, Terry raised a hand and counted off with his fingers.

One-two-three.

While he had been doing his thing I was doing mine, preparing for my delegated task. On three I fired a rapid double volley of grenades over the top of the building and out towards the left-hand side of the sawmill's central yard. Before they had even detonated I sent two more into the centre. By the time I pumped the final two across to the right, the first volley had exploded, two crashing waves of sound followed by a shower of desert soil spattering back to earth.

At the very moment the second two went off, Terry blew the rear door of building number one. He entered through the resulting gap quickly filled by smoke and flame. With my friend swallowed up by the ugly concrete, I set off to join him.

THIRTY

Kane was fascinated by the two Englishmen. Throughout his life he had encountered many warriors, each of whom was different in the way they carried themselves, in the way they prepared for and fought their battles. He could only admire the way these two had gone about their business so far.

He had followed them from the Weather Balloon, observed from a distance the way they went about their business at the bungalow. Their single-minded determination was something to savour, and when they fled the area he bolted with them. His focus was on the Jeep, the two men and the young woman travelling inside it, and their ultimate destination. Because he felt certain that wherever it was, Vern Jackson was going to be found at the end of that journey.

At some point as they nudged their way through the steady flow of traffic, Kane got the impression that something had occurred during the drive. They had initially seemed to be making their way to the south of the city, but then suddenly the Jeep diverted towards the north. Kane's resolve was tested when he realised that they were going back into the desert. Through the streets of Roswell it was relatively easy to follow another vehicle at a safe distance while keeping two or three vehicles in between. But out on the desert roads, the traffic was minimal. He doubted he would be able to keep even a single car between him and the Jeep, and if the two men inside it were as good as he believed them to be, they would eventually realise he was tucked away behind them.

If they were not already aware of his presence.

After tossing it around for a few seconds, Kane decided to continue. These men had already shown their expertise and determination. They clearly had a goal in mind, which he was not a part of. If he let them be and allowed them to go about their business, they would do the same in regard to him. Their task in hand would be all that mattered to them, his presence behind them merely an irritant they would deal with only if it became necessary.

Kane followed them into the desert on a road familiar to him, yet one he had not driven in several years. Initially he wondered if they were going to cut off onto one of the many rough and pitted B-roads that spider-webbed the area, perhaps taking a less travelled route towards Corona that would keep them away from obvious traffic. Comfortable with the desert and the terrain he was approaching, Kane felt himself relax into the long drive. But several miles further on when they indicated left and pulled across the road into the lot of a derelict gas station and pulled around the back of the building with faded paint and boarded-up windows, it had forced him to swiftly re-evaluate.

He'd had no alternative but to drive on by – confronting them at this stage was not an option. The question he had to ask himself was, continue on to where? He tried to work out exactly where he was on the long stretch of road that would eventually wind around the foothills of the mountains, which were still vague, greyish-purplish peaks in the distance. Kane was barely beyond the next rise when he saw a sign at the beginning of a dirt track that wound off into the hillsides, and his mind started wrapping around the many possibilities.

The faded, sun-bleached and flaked wooden sign that traversed the entrance read SMITH & SON LUMBER AND MILL. Kane had heard all kinds of stories about the place. Some kids came all the way to the mill on a dare, intending to spend a night. Legend had it that none ever stayed right through to daybreak.

As he pushed on by, he knew he had to make a decision and not simply continue on towards Capitan.

The road curved left and took him beyond the view of anyone who might be trailing behind him. He thought again of the sawmill. And then back to the Jeep and its occupants. At first when they pulled off the road he thought they had grown weary of being followed and had decided to pause their journey to allow him to pass by. Yet if he was correct, it did not make sense for them to also duck behind the abandoned gas station. There was a clear purpose to that particular manoeuvre. Alternatively, if they intended on leaving the vehicle there and moving elsewhere on foot, there was only one logical destination.

His mind made up, Kane had thrown his truck to the left, driven onto the verge and continued up onto a small plateau some twenty feet above the road level. Shutting off the engine, he snatched up a pair of binoculars, jumped out of the cab and ran hard up the hillside, scrambling on shifting soil, loose and dry beneath his feet. Towards the peak he moved on all fours, his powerful arms assisting with the arduous climb. At the top he first crouched and then threw himself to the dirt. From there he could see the sawmill away to his left, the road curving to his right. More specifically, from this vantage point he would see the Jeep approaching his position from far enough away that he could either choose to remain where he was and allow it to continue along the road, or dash back down and jump into his truck and get ahead of it.

The mill and the curving hillsides sweeping around it appeared deserted. Beyond them, Kane could see the dried-up stream which snaked around the landscape, fed from the snow, ice-thaw and rain run-off flowing down from the Capitans throughout the spring. The man-made spur which had allowed the mountain loggers to send the fruits of their labour down the foothills to the mill had long been dammed, narrow tunnels dug through the hillsides filled back up and plugged with rocks and boulders. It left the mill looking out of place, as if a folly had been constructed on the whim of a man with more money than sense. Kane felt the history of it, though. It spoke to him in a thousand different voices.

As he'd studied the large site, he came to understand why those who spoke of it did so in hushed tones. It was like a ghost town, its ramshackle wooden structures leaning awkwardly, but remaining standing like wizened old men guarding the entrance to the past.

The sawmill comprised a dozen disparate buildings built at various stages over a hundred-year period, each in various stages of disrepair and decline having been abandoned at the turn of the millennium. Any metal, cable or mechanical item had long since been stripped out for scrap, leaving behind a ruin that somehow still seemed to reverberate to the sights and sounds of working lives. Kane could easily picture the men who had once laboured here, as vividly as if they were doing so right in front of his eyes. Gaunt, exhausted men, hard-muscled and mentally strong, burnished by the desert sun and wind. Now they were shivering from the cold and hurrying to shelter from the snow.

Kane felt at one with the visions of men he thought of as fellow travellers in time, each of them granted a certain number of breaths. The last of their allotted number had been drawn long ago, but as Kane had settled down to focus on the road once more, he questioned whether his own count had an expiry date far beyond any future he could see, or closer than he cared to imagine.

A dark spot shimmering on the road alerted him to an approaching vehicle. In the haze it was too indistinct for Kane to identify, but as it grew closer he recognised the shape and colour of the Jeep he had been following. The warriors had undoubtedly taken time out to plan and refuel their bodies, but had otherwise not lingered. Kane decided to wait and see what they did.

To Kane's surprise, instead of either coming further along the road and making the turn towards the mill, or driving on by, the Jeep slipped off the road ahead of the sweeping desert mounds shielding it from being observed from the abandoned buildings within the mill grounds.

Kane took a breath and nodded to himself. Of course. Great warriors would not confront their foe head-on while alternative methods existed. The sawmill was now confirmed as their destination after all, but their path towards it would be concealed. These two men were preparing for an assault.

He had not seen Chastain emerge from the first encounter, and had reasoned that what he believed to be a rescue attempt had failed back in Roswell. This was perhaps another, the hostage this time being Vern Jackson. Kane bowed his head in deference to the two Englishmen. While he feared no man, he would avoid contact with this duo if at all possible. Both were capable of wreaking havoc and causing great damage, and he had no desire to be in their way when that happened.

For quite some while, Kane barely lowered the binoculars as he scanned both the mill itself as well as its surrounding terrain. He projected his snake spirit and looked into the hearts and minds of the warriors. In checking out the old neglected buildings through the binoculars, Kane saw no vehicles, no movement, no people. For a moment he wondered if maybe the pair were the first to arrive and would initiate an ambush, although their cautious approach suggested otherwise. Kane considered his own next move, and opted to continue assessing the situation. He would wait to see how it might all unfold. Which was precisely what he was doing when the snow began to fall and, shortly afterwards, the green Chevy drove into the sawmill.

Soon after the Chevy had rolled up, an SUV appeared and followed the same track towards the mill. He was startled to see a man and a woman wearing FBI jackets emerge from the vehicle. Kane found himself silently bemused by their misguided direct approach. He would have expected them to demonstrate similar methods to those of the two warriors, taking a more oblique route. Perhaps the federal agents had become seduced by what they believed to be true, as opposed to taking the more sceptical, and therefore more circumspect, path.

The chaotic action that followed took place quickly and seemingly randomly at first. The dynamics of that changed the moment the warriors became involved. The grenades launched over the concrete building into the area devoid of structures were unexpected, but Kane guessed they were intended as a diversion aimed at drawing attention to the centre of the plot, whilst the men gained entry from the rear of the building. Shortly afterwards, the unmistakable sound of automatic gunfire and the sight of men running from the building left Kane in no doubt.

This changed things. He knew for certain now that the sawmill had to be the place in which Jackson was being held. Kane's respect for the two warriors did not allow him to contemplate the Englishmen not achieving their objective in rescuing the man. Though confident in his own abilities, Kane was devoid of ego. He believed that if the warriors emerged from the battle with their prize, then Jackson was lost to him.

Kane cursed into the gentle breeze, pulled out his cell and made a call he did not wish to make.

THIRTY-ONE

As I stepped across the threshold I heard rapid bursts of automatic gunfire. I knew that had to be Terry already engaging the enemy. I ducked my head left and right. Other than a now torn and shattered stud framework of wood and broken plasterboard at the far end to my left, the remainder of the building was a single, cavernous room.

A handful of prison-style bunk beds lay scattered across the dusty concrete floor, the olive-green spray job over the metal now chipped and pitted, sagging mattresses limp, torn, and patterned with little islands of stains. In the far corner to my right sat two figures. Both were hooded and wearing only boxer shorts, each sitting on their own wooden three-legged stool. Their hands and ankles were bound with thick cord, but the pair thrashed around on their seats, and in hearing their muffled cries of alarm and terror, I knew they had to be gagged beneath their hoods. Over on the far side of what I now realised had been a block of sleeping quarters, Terry was crouching over a prostrate figure wearing a leather jacket and blue denims.

I inched my way closer, all the while staring down the barrel of the M-16 and ready to go. Terry turned his head, raised a clenched hand once more. 'Four men,' he said. 'Two inside, two just outside. I put one down, the other got out but I think I winged him.'

I could still hear gunfire, so I assumed that the three remaining opponents were busy fending off an assault from the far end of the site as well. They were now caught between the proverbial rock and a hard place. I glanced back at the men sitting in the corner. The room we were in was huge, with only empty space where doors and windows used to be, but still it reeked with the acrid combined odour of fear, sweat, urine, vomit, and excrement. The only thing missing was the coppery stench of blood, which I took to be a positive thing.

'What about them?' I said to Terry.

'Cut them free. Tell them to head back over the ridge and find the Jeep. We'll catch them up. I want to snatch up at least one of those blokes outside and find out what the fuck is going on.'

'You don't want to cut and run?'

'No. We do that we free Vern for today, but we'll never know if or when he'll be safe in the future.'

I nodded. It was the right move, not that he needed my approval. Terry stood upright and headed towards the doorway. He fired off a couple of bursts as he moved. I ran across to the writhing figures in the corner.

'Take it easy,' I called out as I approached. 'We're here to help.'

I yanked off the hoods. The pair blinked hard at the intrusion of light into their dark world. I recognised Vern Jackson immediately.

'You Bruce Kelper?' I said to the other one, wrestling with his gag. He nodded as he spat and used his tongue to clear his mouth and moisten his lips.

After repeating my actions on Vern and cutting their bonds free of their hands and ankles, I took a knee right in front of them. As more gunfire announced itself outside the building, both men jerked and ducked instinctively.

'Listen to me,' I said, my voice flat and even. 'We came looking for you, Vern. We have you both now, and you are safe. Tell me, is your clothing anywhere nearby?'

Vern pointed to the tattered partition at the opposite end of the building. 'In there, I think. Close by the sleeping bags and other supplies they gave us.'

'Okay, good. Now, you both need to get down there, put on as much as you can as quickly as you can.' I pointed over at the back door through which Terry and I had entered. 'Then you head out that way. You go straight up the ridge and back down the other side. Move around the hillside back towards the road. Before you get to it you'll spot a silver Jeep. Vern, Chelsea is waiting for you inside. Go now. We won't be more than a couple of minutes behind you.'

The pair nodded as if one. Then Vern widened his eyes and said to me, 'Who are you? Who sent you?'

'Your uncle sent me. Now go, and wait for us where I told you to. Don't even think about running off. It's cold, it's snowing, and there's only mile after mile of desert waiting for you out there. Believe me, we're your only way out of here alive.'

I turned as they stood and started running across the concrete floor. I was cold, so I could only imagine how they must feel. Their pale bodies were almost blue in tone. I made my way across to the doorway to the front. It was all still going off outside. I peeked around the corner and saw Terry squatting behind a stack of rotten lumber. A couple of yards further out lay the motionless figure of a large man lying flat on his face. Blood bubbled from a jagged wound in his neck, pooling quickly around the head. I came low out of the doorway and hurried across to Terry's position. A single shot came my way but it slammed harmlessly against the concrete wall a couple of yards high and wide. As I scrambled for shelter I caught a glimpse of a man wearing a dark blue sweater clasping a pistol in front of his face. I stopped dead and got off a triple-tap, at least one of which found its target as the man first dropped his weapon and then, knees buckling, staggered backwards and stumbled to the ground.

'Don't know where the other one is,' Terry said as I joined him behind the protective barrier of dark old bricks of wood four inches thick. 'I'm not sure if anyone knows who or what they are shooting at out there, but I don't want to leave things as they are.'

From the corner of my eye I spotted a fleeting movement. It vanished swiftly behind the corner of the brick-built storage area. 'Cover me and wait for me,' I said. I did not stop to listen for a response.

I flew out from behind the lumber as fast as my legs would carry me. No one shot at me this time as I pounded my feet on the snow-covered soil and hurled myself into the red wall of the building. Pausing only to take a couple of breaths, I skirted along the side and peeked around the corner. About thirty yards away, a man in a dark suit was running towards the wide-open mouth of the mill. As I saw him I heard a shot, followed by another couple of rapid bursts. They sounded distant, and I got the impression none of them were aimed at either me or the figure I was chasing. I ran on in the ungainly manner resulting from carrying my automatic rifle in both hands across my chest.

It was not a pretty shuffle, but it was effective. Clumps of snow flew up in the wake of my boots as I scuttled forward, my eyes barely straying from my prey.

The suited man blew through an open doorway and disappeared into the darkness of the mill's wooden guts. Moments later I did the same. There was only one way to go and that was up a flight of wretched-looking stairs with several treads missing. It looked for all the world as if a sneeze might bring them down, but the man ahead of me must have used them so I did not stop to think twice.

I charged upwards and on the landing above stopped to recce my surroundings. Above the sound of my own heavy breathing I heard the clattering of fast, heavy footsteps racing over floorboards away to my left. The internal walls were inconsistent and many boards were missing, but through the gaps I could see the man fleeing ahead of me. I powered on after him, sucking air into my lungs, grateful for all the fitness training I had done back in Scotland.

I sped past an opening which led onto the long and broken dry log flume we had spotted earlier. I could still hear the thudding of leather shoes on wood, but I ducked my head out to peer along at the framework jutting out of the mill like a jagged finger pointing the way home. I pulled back inside and continued on the way I had been heading. Slamming through another opening where I presumed a door had once stood, I could see we had entered another part of the building. The floor sloped upwards in a long tunnel until another opening led me out onto a massive square platform which was enclosed only on two sides, with no roof whatsoever.

It was also empty.

Snow continued to fall hurriedly, which made the boards beneath my feet more perilous. About to head across to an opening on the far side, I caught a flash of something in my right peripheral vision. I glanced down and across, and there was the man I had been chasing. He had ducked beneath the platform and was now descending the external wall using the crossbeams to stand on as he levered himself down. I raced after him, but as I neared the centre of the floor I felt something shift beneath my weight and in a horrendously loud crack of snapping timber the boards gave way and I plunged straight through them.

The fall felt timeless, like Alice tumbling down her rabbit hole. In reality it lasted little more than a second, but I was conscious of an exhilarating weightlessness. It felt like flying rather than plummeting, as if I, rather than gravity, was in control of my descent. That notion was soon disproved when I hit the floorboards beneath the hole I had created with a heavy thump that forced the air from my lungs. My head bounced twice on a solid floorboard, which groaned and creaked and gave a little under my back. I was staring straight up as the snow cascaded down upon me, together with a spray of dust that had erupted like a mushroom cloud when I came to rest.

I gasped and sucked in some more air. My head swam, and for a few seconds I felt as if I had been drawn into one of those cartoons Terry and I had mentioned, stars fluttering around me like an ever-circling constellation. Sharp pain like the wound from a blade spread out across my shoulders and deep in the pit of my back. The floorboards on the ground floor were clearly more solid and sprung than those which had collapsed beneath my feet, and hitting them that hard was sending shockwaves through my entire nervous system and cramping my muscles in fierce spasms.

Only when my head cleared was I aware of a vague shape, tall and thin, seeming to emit an incandescent glow in the pale light that cast itself from the dull sky above and through the seams in the exterior walls around me. The indistinct figure moved towards me, soaking up the meagre daylight as it drew closer. I blinked away some double vision, and immediately wished I had not bothered.

The man I had been chasing stood over me. He looked down into my eyes for a moment, and then raised a gun and pointed it straight at my forehead. I saw his trigger finger twitch and start to stroke the metal. I flashed back to the moment in the swimming pool, and knew I could not get that lucky again.

When it came, the gunfire was shockingly loud. I stared up at the man, wondering if he had missed me deliberately or if he was simply the worst shot in the entire world. Something warm and wet dripped down on me. I felt it splash against my face. And then the narrow figure fell backwards, hit the floor with a rippling clatter, and was still.

'Goddamnit!' someone said in a harsh, guttural tone. I heard the anguish but did not recognise the voice. I raised myself up on my elbows and turned my head to look behind me. There in the shadows, blinking rapidly in the snowfall, tears spilling from his eyes, stood the county sheriff. Crozier removed his white Stetson hat, hung his head so far down that his chin touched his chest, and allowed the gun to slip from his grasp and fall to the floor where it bounced and skittered away on the dull wooden surface.

Pain pulling at me and threatening to cramp my muscles tighter still, I sat up all the way, managing to clamber unsteadily to my feet. I stepped across to the man I had chased and who had been about to kill me. I kicked his gun away, but did not need to check for a pulse. His wide-eyed, vacant expression, shredded hole above his left cheek, and the pool of blood spreading out from beneath his head, told its own story. I turned and looked at the sheriff. He was slapping his hat against his thigh and shaking his head back and forth, cursing beneath his breath.

'Nineteen years,' he muttered without looking up. 'Nineteen goddamned years. All for nothing.'

I had no idea what he was talking about. I had no idea how he had come to be there. I was just so happy to see him. 'Thank you,' I said, my chest heaving and my head still reeling a little. 'You saved my life.'

Right then I heard the scrape of a boot, and twisted my head to face the direction the sound had come from. Terry was making his way over to us, eyes surveying the scene before him. 'What happened here?' he asked.

I looked up at the gaping maw in what had been my floor but was now my ceiling. 'I came through there. The bloke I was chasing got the drop on me. Sheriff Crozier here dropped him instead.'

Terry nodded. His eyes met mine and I felt the relief flow between us. 'Sheriff,' he said, rifle slung carefully between his arms. 'Before we get into explaining all this, you need to know a few things. My friend and I have been tracking down a young man who went missing in Nevada. Turns out he was with two other people. We have them, all three. I can take you to them, but it's a bit of a steep climb up and over the ridge and then a fair walk around to where we're parked up. If you feel the need, you can come with us. I'll understand why. But we are not the bad guys here, and I'm happy to meet you back up on the road at the entrance to the mill. I have to tell you, though, other than this man you killed and several others who were holding the men we were looking for, there are five others unaccounted for. Two of them are thugs from Reno, two others arrived here in a black SUV – one of whom I think was a woman – and somewhere out there I think a Native American man is watching and waiting. I don't know their roles in this, but my guess is we're all after the same thing.'

Crozier took a few deep breaths, replaced his hat as if he considered it unworthy of his position to discuss lawful matters without wearing it, and looked between us for a couple of seconds. He took a step, stooped to pick up his pistol and holstered it with a look of both disgust and embarrassment on his face.

'I know all of them,' he said, his voice low and bitter. 'The two hoodlums are also hunting one of the men you apparently rescued here today, and that's Vern Jackson. The two in the SUV are FBI. Those four got involved in their own exchange of gunfire, though you probably know better than me what set all that off. As for the Native American, I know who he works for and I have a fair idea that he is also on the trail of Mr Jackson. I can't speak as to why. Now, I don't rightly know what triggered this whole hurricane of unlawfulness, but I aim to talk with Mr Jackson in order to find that out.'

'Sheriff,' I said, wincing as I stretched out the muscles in my back and shoulders. 'We came to New Mexico to find Vern. We found him. If he's done anything wrong, then what becomes of him, lawfully and legally, well that's your territory. We simply needed to locate him and make sure he was safe. He is now, and he will be when we hand him over to you.'

Crozier nodded. Hooked both hands into his belt. 'All right, then. I need to check on those two agents out there. Meet me up at the entrance.'

'Thank you for trusting us. But you need to be aware that we think friends of these men will be here shortly, looking to collect them and return them to Roswell for the evening.'

'Okay. You see them first, you'll stop them from driving down here?'

'We will.'

'Then if I reach the entrance first, I'll do the same.'

I nodded at Terry and we turned to leave. I could see the sheriff was in a mild state of shock, and although I wanted to express more of my gratitude to him for having saved my life, I knew time was trickling away for all of us here. Without another word we made our way back across the site, maintaining vigilance all the while. We had cleared our targets, and now we were aware that two of the unexpected arrivals were friendlies, but for all we knew both Barclay and Garcia, as well as our follower, were still out there somewhere. I had neither the time nor the inclination to detour in order to see who had lived and who had died, and as Terry marched ahead of me without mentioning anything, it was my guess that he was equally uninterested.

For the first time I caught sight of the some of the damage caused by the six grenades I had launched. The small craters they had produced were still smouldering, with a couple of small fires flickering nearby. But one of the first two blasts had caused a smaller wooden structure to catch light, and it was now blazing and crackling and spitting, belching thick black smoke, flames spearing out towards its closest neighbour. I worried that the whole place might go up. I felt bad that a local landmark might be razed to the ground by my actions.

As I rounded the central concrete building, Terry was waiting for me, and I saw that the grey SUV was still in place. On my way back it had briefly crossed my mind that Vern and Bruce, once they had found their clothes, might also have located the car keys and driven away whilst Terry and I were otherwise engaged. Either the keys had not been there, or the pair had simply done as they were told. Terry and I sped past the vehicle, and dug our heels in as we trudged back up the hillside. I was still feeling the effects of the fall through the floorboards, but I shook it off. Whatever aches and pains I was feeling right now were so much better than taking the bullet that had been coming my way.

We made our way across the spine of the ridge. I glanced down into the sawmill site as we came around above the battered old store and the shacks beyond. Outside one of the small wooden buildings, beside a confusion of tyre tracks, a male body wearing a navy blue FBI jacket lay sprawled out on the ground. There was a gruesome mess where one side of his head should be. I had no idea what had taken place here, but I knew I could not leave without first checking.

I tapped Terry on the shoulder. 'I'm going down there. He has to be dead, but I can't walk away without knowing for sure.'

He, of all people, would know what I meant. We were on the side of the good guys, and the FBI were included in that. I had no idea what their role in this had been, but that did not seem to matter with one of their own lying in a pool of his own blood and brain matter on the desert soil.

'You get back to the Jeep,' I told him. 'I'll be right behind you.'

Terry nodded once. 'Be careful. You don't know who or what else you'll find down there.'

I made it down the slope quickly enough. I made a rapid assessment of every window and door and roof of every structure, but saw nothing to alarm me. Easing around the side of the store I ducked my head inside a cavity which at one time held a window. Lying on the floor was the man we knew as Barclay. He had taken a large round directly beneath his left eye, most of the damage to his skull created as it exited his head. I listened hard, scoured the area again. I had the overwhelming sense that I was now alone down there.

I reached the fallen agent and checked his pulse despite knowing I would have been too late to save his life even if I had been standing right by his side when he was hit. You don't recover from a large calibre bullet wound that blasts through the brain and decimates the cranium in such a devastating manner.

As I made my way back up the hillside I wondered who had taken out who. But unless their bodies lay unexposed somewhere else – and judging by the lack of vehicles I doubted that was the case – then there was an FBI agent and the man in the snakeskin boots unaccounted for.

Not to mention our follower.

THIRTY-TWO

Upon reaching the jeep I discovered that Bruce Kelper was both unconscious and bleeding profusely. I had seen enough scalp lacerations before to know that this was what they did, even if the wounds were superficial. I was more dismayed by the fact that he was not conscious, because to my mind that was far worse than the cuts to his head. I looked across at Terry who was crouching down on the other side of Kelper, tending to his wounds.

'He slipped and fell,' Terry explained. 'Cracked his head on a rock.'

'Are we taking him to hospital?' Van Dalen asked.

'We are,' Terry replied before I had a chance to respond. 'We'll make sure the staff there get him on a gurney, then you two go with him and stay with him. On our way we'll figure out what you can and can't say about what happened here today. For obvious reasons, neither Mike nor I can be mentioned. As far as you're all concerned, we were never here.'

There was no resistance. I knew the young woman had to be beyond the limits of her endurance, given everything she had witnessed over the past few days. Jackson seemed to be looking inwardly, still suffering from shock in my estimation. He held on to his girlfriend's hand so tightly I could tell it would bruise her, but to her credit she made no complaint.

Terry had just taken his seat behind the wheel and fired up the Jeep when my replacement phone rang. Only two people had the number, and one of them was sitting alongside me. I accepted the call and put it on speakerphone.

'Drew,' I said, injecting as much good cheer as I could manage. 'I have good news for you. We–'

'Mike, whatever you're about to say or do, stop right there. Donna and Wendy are gone, Mike. They've been taken.'

A fist-sized weight wrapped around my insides and started to twist. 'Taken?! What do you mean? Taken where? By who?'

'I don't know. I got a text telling me to go home. When I got here there was a message waiting for me on the kitchen counter. It gave me a number to call – not the same as the one I got the text from. They didn't give me their name, they just said they had been watching the house in case they couldn't get their hands on Vern. I'm assuming things went south on them, so they snatched up the girls. Wendy was home on study leave. They're gone, Mike, and whoever has them means business.'

His voice had grown louder and more shrill, fear and adrenaline squeezing his throat muscles. I calmed him down and asked him to explain more about the call.

'I was told I'd made a big mistake hiring someone to find Vern, because his own man had been getting close, and if that had gone as planned then there would have been no need to take Donna and Wendy. With Vern about to be rescued, that put me and the rest of my family in play. I tried asking questions, but was told to be quiet and follow instructions. When the call was over, I called my sister and told her to leave home and find a place to crash. But they won't need her while they have Donna and Wendy.'

I took several deep breaths. Drew was not the only one I had to keep calm right now. Because everything Terry and I had endured in order to rescue Vern had directly led to Donna and Wendy being abducted.

'Okay, now listen to me,' I said. 'What do they want? They must have made some demands.'

'They did. But it didn't make a whole lot of sense to me, Mike. The man I spoke to told me the only way I would ever see Donna and Wendy alive again was to exchange them for what Vern had been hiding.'

I glanced over my shoulder at Vern Jackson. I knew from the look of horror in his eyes that he knew precisely what was being asked of him.

'Drew, Vern is safe and secure right now. Whatever it is they want we'll get it to them. What arrangements were made for the exchange?'

'None. I was told that when I had what they needed, I was to text the number first used to contact me. I would then receive a reply telling me which number to call next.'

'Did they tell you what it was they were after?'

'No. Only that Vern would know.'

'Okay. Was there anything you picked up on, Drew? Anything at all that might give us a clue as to who these people are?'

'Now that you mention it, there was. I don't know how much this helps, but the man I spoke to was definitely a Native American. I could tell by his accent and the way he strung his words together.'

Our follower.

Had to be.

Or whoever he was working for, perhaps. He was involved, though. He had seen everything, and in rescuing Vern we had set in motion the abduction of Donna and Wendy.

I thought about how this might now play out. It didn't look good. But it was hard for me to think straight, not with the knowledge of my daughter having been swept up in all this madness.

'Give me some time,' I said to Drew. 'I'll call you back after I've spoken with Vern and Terry and we have a handle on this.'

'Let me speak to him, please.'

'Not right now. Sorry, but I think this is a conversation only Terry and I need to have with him. I'll call you as soon as I know more.'

I cut the line before he had a chance to respond. I turned fully in my seat and looked hard at Vern.

'I admire you for resisting whatever those men did to you back at the sawmill. I really do. But this just escalated. Men died today, and now my daughter and ex-wife are in trouble, and you need to tell us everything you know. The root cause needs explaining, and I need to understand it. Chelsea told us all about the scam with the software, but I don't believe she gave up everything. You have a lot of people wanting your blood, but it seems to me they are after more than simply the money you stole.'

He breathed out slowly. A slight, ineffectual-looking man, Vern was what might be classed as a 'hipster'. His gaunt features hiding behind a straggly-looking beard that I reckoned had been neatly manicured before all this shit went down, spiked hair long short of product, eyes downcast as if afraid to meet our gaze. He didn't smell too fresh, and he remained bloodied and bruised. He had suffered, of that there was no doubt, but having twice taken part in the carnage today, I had little sympathy for the man who was in some way responsible.

'The people who abducted us wanted answers we couldn't give them,' he said eventually. 'The scam they knew about, so too how I'd gone about it. So yes, they wanted their money back, and I gave it to them right away. I swear I did. They sat me in front of a laptop and I put every dime back where it came from.'

'So what else did they need from you?'

'The software. Chelsea told you all about the scam, but what she didn't know a thing about was the other coding I put inside our product. I know you probably think we were dumb to take on powerful people like that, but the truth is I thought we would be in and out before they even realised, and that by the time they did the software would have reverted back to normal and the scam code removed. But I added another layer of protection to be sure. These casinos rip off money of their own, especially from the IRS, so my code found all the wrinkles and siphoned the information off onto a separate device. I told the guys doing the questioning that if anything happened to any of us, and by that I meant any permanent harm, the code was pre-triggered to send the details out to the FBI and news agencies around the country. Truth be told, I lied about that part, but I did have the data on an external hard disk. Plus a copy on another disk. Or at least, I did have.'

'What do you mean by that?'

'I buried them. While me and Bruce were out in the desert. Wrapped them in a freezer bag and sealed them first, then buried the bag. Those men were getting too close and I couldn't risk carrying it around with me any longer, and it's not as if I have anywhere safe to conceal it. I had to make sure we had an insurance policy if they caught up with us. Something to barter with. After Bruce and I were beaten black and blue and we realised our lives were in real danger, I finally gave it up.'

'So what was the problem?'

'The disks were gone. Only Bruce and I knew where I'd buried them. But the guys who were sent to look for it came back empty handed.'

'Where was this, close to where you dumped the Kia?'

He shook his head. 'They checked there as well, thinking we might have been lying to them even at that stage. That, or we were mistaken about the location. But no, I buried it in a place I figured it could not be found because nobody was allowed to search there anymore.'

I closed my eyes. Of course. 'The crash site. The bloody UFO crash site.'

He barked a quick, humourless laugh. 'Yeah. Since the new owners took over that land they'd banned all tourists and enthusiasts, made it a trespassing offence to even set foot on the property afterwards. I guess it pricked both my sense of humour and irony to bury something so valuable in a place like that. We did it before we dumped the car.'

'But now you're saying they couldn't find it. You think they just missed it somehow?'

'No. I was too specific about its location. They told us it was gone, and I believed them.'

As I believed him. Because I also knew who now had the disks. 'Where does Al Chastain fit into all this?'

'Chastain? I... I have no idea. Bruce went to meet with him. He wanted to ask him something about the overview the Gaming Commission has on casinos, who to deal with in terms of providing information. I think Bruce was looking to find a way to nail them if things went badly for us.'

'Chastain is dead,' I said bluntly.

Vern hung his head but said nothing more.

'Let's go,' I said to Terry.

He nodded and got the Jeep rolling. 'What about Drew?' he asked.

'I'll call him as soon as I have a plan.'

We were silent as Terry drove around the base of the hills and back towards the road, where he hung a right. A few moments later I felt a surge of relief at seeing the sheriff's SUV sitting by the entrance to the mill, facing our way. He'd made it out, and I was glad of that. I jumped out and dashed across to the cruiser as Terry came to a hard stop.

'Everything all right?' I asked.

The sheriff nodded. He had removed his hat, and I saw that his flattened hair was wispy and sparse on the crown of his head. He ran a hand through his moustache before he spoke. 'I just drove up the road a ways to call this mess in, came straight back here to wait for you fellahs. There are a lot of bodies back there to explain away. Including the man I had to kill.'

'I'm so sorry about that, sheriff. I mean that. I would never have wished that on you. But I'm also very grateful to you that you did, and in the days and maybe weeks to come, when the nightmares kick in, you will need to keep in mind that you took a life this day to save one. Now look, I know you will want us to stick around, but we have a problem.'

I told him about the rescue of Vern Jackson and Bruce Kelper, Kelper's subsequent injury, and the dead FBI agent. It turned out that he had seen the agent's body for himself, and had also checked for signs of life. When I moved on to the call from Drew, I neglected to mention what it was the caller wanted, but I told him about the escalation which appeared to stem from our follower, the man we believed to be the Native American from back at the Weather Balloon. The moment I mentioned him, Crozier became instantly concerned.

'Well, now ain't this a fine thing,' he said, shaking his head and squeezing his hat tight. 'I got blood on my hands myself today, and a small battle back there at the mill to try and figure out. I'm guessing your first thought is to get that young man to a hospital, and your second is to find this Native American fellah.'

I nodded, hoping he would not try to stop us. I did not want to confront the man who had saved my life, but now that my ex and daughter had been swept up by this avalanche, I knew I had to match its momentum. I could not allow him to slow us down. Before either of us could say more, we both looked up as a black SUV moved in towards us at speed from the east and pulled up behind the Jeep on sliding tyres spitting gravel. A woman exited the driver's side. She wore a navy blue jacket with FBI emblazoned upon it, but still she flashed her credentials as she approached. Her other hand she left on her unstrapped gun holster.

'Sheriff Crozier,' she said, noting the others sitting in the Jeep, her eyes holding mine for a moment. The show of ID was strictly for our benefit. 'Is everything okay here?'

'No, things are far from okay, Agent Green. But if you're asking if things are good between myself and these people here, then the answer is yes.'

'Good to know. Are you aware of what went down here? And who these people are?'

I heaved a sigh. 'We haven't got time to get into this,' I whispered to the county lawman. 'Kelper needs a hospital right now, and we have to get moving.'

He nodded and held up a hand, eyes only for the newcomer. 'Agent Green, I arrived at the mill in time to see a great deal of what went down. I know you just lost your partner, and I'm as sorry as I can be about that. I reckon it was those assholes from the bar in Corona.'

She nodded once. 'Yeah. They had us pinned down from the moment we arrived. Eugene covered my ass as I headed inside an old shack, but before I could do the same for him, one of those bastards shot him dead.'

I knew she understood well enough that death was a part of life, and that in being an FBI agent the suddenness of one becoming the other could be both shocking and brutal. But by now she would also be aware that nobody is ever prepared for that moment when it comes around. I had seen what remained of her partner's ruined face, and I knew that vision would remain with her for the rest of her life.

'I'm sorry for your loss,' I told her. She regarded me with deep suspicion, still uncertain as to our role in her ordeal.

Crozier took a step forward and put a hand on each of her arms. 'What happened to your fellow agent is tragic, but one of the reasons you were able to get away – I'm guessing to call in reinforcements – was because of these two gentlemen here. Now, I shot my weapon for the first time a short while ago and I killed a man, so today is far from a normal day in the life of Dwight Crozier, and I don't rightly know which way is up at the moment. I do realise what I *should* be doing, but somehow with all that's going on, I'm having a hard job figuring out the difference between what's best and what's right. So, listen up and let's try and make this work for the benefit of all concerned.'

As quickly and concisely as possible, the sheriff explained what he had seen, outlining the role Terry and I had played in how things had transpired, that we were now both desperate to get Kelper some treatment and then be on our way to try and secure the release of Donna and Wendy. When he was through explaining, he looked up into the agent's tight face full of sharp angles and grief.

'I'm guessing you'd like nothing more right now than to avenge your partner's murder, am I correct?'

She was in a highly agitated state, but she nodded and kept her focus. 'I have teams on their way here from the city, sheriff. I told them what happened, but they will need to speak to me as well. They will want to take me through it step by step, debrief me thoroughly.'

'All of which can wait. The job ain't over yet as far as I can tell. Right now, a young girl and her mother, both no doubt in fear for their lives, have been abducted. The men who shot your partner were in some way involved in how we all ended up here, and now someone else has two more innocent people and is holding them hostage. So rather than stand around here waiting for my people, Roswell PD, and your Bureau teams to swoop in and have us waste hours going over everything we saw, heard and did, I think we're duty bound to help these men try and rescue the two ladies being held against their will.'

It took her only a moment to decide. 'So what are you suggesting?'

Crozier stared down at his boots for a moment while he paused to take a breath. 'These men here believe a Native American is responsible for taking the mother and daughter. That struck a chord with me, given incidents that took place out in Corona a couple of days back. I believe a man by the name of Joe Kane is somehow involved, and if I'm right then I also think I know where these two ladies are going to be held. My plan is a very simple one, therefore: we get one young man to hospital and then we go and rescue this man's wife and kid.'

'Native American?' Agent Green said in alarm. 'Please tell me he's not going onto the res.'

'No, ma'am. Not if I'm right. If I am, then we gotta make our way to Ruidoso. We can stop by at the county medical centre and have someone take care of our injured man here, then continue on to where I think the ladies will eventually be held. My guess is that shortly after they were snatched up they were put on a plane or chopper and are currently being flown down here to

New Mexico. If they're not there when we arrive, then someone there will very likely know where they are being held.'

It sounded like a plan. A basic one, the finer details of our end game still to be worked out. But it was enough for me to know that both the sheriff and the agent wanted in on the action. Terry and I had to move on irrespective of what the two law enforcement officers wanted to do, but I would rather have them with us than against us.

'Sheriff,' I said. 'Would you please take Kelper, Vern and Chelsea with you to the hospital. If you can, please arrange to have a couple of deputies close by to guard them. Terry and I need to go and fetch what it is these people want.'

'Which is what exactly?' Agent Green asked.

'It's a long story, and I'd rather we all just got on the road.'

I could tell she did not like that answer, but she bit down on her irritation. 'So they are proposing some form of exchange?'

'Yes. And we could try doing that, except I've never known something like this to go well, have you, Agent Green? Too many imponderables. Too many ways for it all to turn to shit.'

'So why bother fetching it in the first place?'

I shrugged. 'It may come in handy. There's a chance we could use it as leverage. Either way, I'd feel better about it being with us when we go in there.'

Whatever we were about to do was better than hanging around for all kinds of law enforcement people to show up and start asking questions neither Terry nor I had good answers to.

It also might be the difference between Donna and Wendy living or dying.

THIRTY-THREE

Henry McCarty, whose formal alias was William H. Bonney, and who in later life became known far and wide as Billy the Kid, left his mark on New Mexico during his short life. A casino at the Ruidoso Downs racetrack bears the infamous moniker allegedly created by a Las Vegas newspaper. There was also a scenic byway of trails dedicated to the outlaw gunned down at the age of twenty-two by Sheriff Pat Garrett, a long stretch of which ran right alongside the perimeter of the Crow residence overlooking Paradise Canyon.

In amongst the fir, spruce, pine and juniper that spread like a rash across Crow's land, ran a tall PVC chain-link fence that surrounded the property itself at a distance of approximately one hundred yards in any compass point direction from the house. That much was obvious merely by studying it from a distance. Any external assessment of the quality and prolificacy of the security system relied pretty much on hearsay, but rumour had it that the Judge was better protected than the New Mexico state governor. Certainly he could afford the very best, and intelligence gathered over the years by both the sheriff's department and local

PD suggested the patrols around the grounds were well-manned and dogs were also in use.

All of this Crozier explained to the three of us as we sat in his cruiser going over our plans in alphabetical order. Terry being Terry favoured a pre-emptive strike as his Plan A, with no favour and no warning given. His American colleagues might describe it as shock-and-awe, but to my friend it was just another day at the office. As usual I admired his confidence, both in his own abilities and mine, but I also had to point out that we would be massively outgunned and potentially outmanoeuvred if the security rumours were even halfway accurate. Agent Green, who by this time had insisted we call her Heather, agreed with the sheriff's own plan to drive up to the gate and request entry.

'If this Judge character is the man you say he is, and if he has Donna and Wendy in there, he'll demand a warrant,' Terry insisted. 'Do you think you have enough to obtain one? Even if you're lucky enough to have a tame real judge onside?'

'I doubt it,' Crozier acknowledged with a sigh of regret. 'But the threat of one might make Crow react positively. At the very least he may squirrel the girls away somewhere and invite us in. He doesn't have to know about you two, as we'll do some squirrelling of our own with the pair of you in the back of my vehicle.'

'But what if he doesn't? At that point you have forewarned him, and you can never wrestle back the advantage a surprise assault will offer us.'

'I think you're forgetting one significant detail,' Heather said. She sat alongside Crozier in the front, the vehicle itself located high up in the hills on a dirt track that petered out to a small empty plot of land encircled by trees and vegetation. From there we could see one of the gabled parts of the roof to Crow's home, and its woodland surroundings. She waited until she had drawn our attention before continuing. 'The sheriff and I are law enforcement. We can't go in there all guns blazing without a legal imperative. We have to try official means at first. That's not even open to debate as far as I am concerned.'

'And risk having your own Ruby Ridge or Waco to deal with?'

'Sure, creating an armed stand-off is always a possibility. All I'm saying is we have badges, which means we have rules, so we cannot go in firing first and asking questions later.'

'Okay.' Terry nodded, thinking on that. 'So you and Sheriff Crozier try the front door approach, while Mike and I go via the back door. You don't need to tell anybody about this discussion, nor that you had any idea what we were going to attempt. For that matter, you don't even have to acknowledge that you even know us or spoke to us beforehand. Fact is, it'd be better for all four of us if that was how this played out. Mike and I really need to hit and run.'

'So you go in and snatch up the hostages and we have to sit there afterwards and lie to our own people?'

'Well, yes. Tell me, Heather, exactly how did you imagine this would go? Did you really think you could take revenge for the death of your partner and not have to lie about your motivations or actions afterwards?'

Agent Green was silent for a moment, her eyes wandering as if she were reading something written across the front of her mind. 'I suppose I didn't think that far ahead,' she admitted, offering a small shrug. 'But if this goes sideways, it could end my career. That won't be much of a homage to Eugene, will it?'

'You could always leave,' I said. 'Nobody knows you are here right now. We can drop you off at your own vehicle and then you can head back to the sawmill. Yes, if you don't want to blow any chance we have here then you will still have to lie to your bosses, but at least you won't be a part of this if it all ends up going pear-shaped. Which it undoubtedly will. That way, you say only what you need to, the job here gets done, and you are miles away when it all goes down. You can live with that, can't you?'

She shook her head. 'That's just it, I'm not sure if I can.'

'Which part? The driving away or the lies you have to tell?'

'The first. I go and that leaves you one person and one gun down. You're already outnumbered if what the sheriff says about Crow's security detail is accurate. Plus, if the sheriff here can get us onto the grounds and in to see Crow, then an FBI presence is crucial. My being there steps it up from a county to a federal matter.'

'Then you have to make up your mind,' Terry said in a low voice that I knew was the most soothing and understanding he was able to muster. 'Because whatever plan we agree upon, we need to do it right now.'

'Sheriff,' I said, leaning forward so as he would not have to turn all the way around to respond. 'Do you know if there is any point between the gates and the house where your vehicle would not be seen? Somewhere you could stop to let us out?'

Crozier gave that some time. He nodded as he thought about it. 'I visited him once to introduce myself. I felt he and I should meet, but I also wanted to get a feel for his property. There are plenty of places hidden from view of both the entrance and the house as you drive around, but it's the security cameras I can't be sure of. I doubt they are all monitored all of the time, but I'm guessing they are whenever someone they let through the gates drives in.'

'I tend to agree,' Terry said. 'We can't take that chance. The best approach me and Mike could take would be to use an overhanging tree branch to gain access beyond the fence to the rear of the house. In my kit bag I have a device that seeks out Wi-Fi and electromagnetic fields, so in a more stealthy approach it should give us plenty of advance warning in terms of cameras.

Human patrol guards will cause us no bother – if they are out there walking around some rich bloke's property then they are not going to be top notch, and I doubt they'll be brave enough to risk their lives, either. My biggest concern would be the dogs; they will sniff us out quicker and from further away than we will them.'

'Looks like we're all dressed up with no place to go,' Crozier said, stroking his moustache.

'And there is also the elephant in the room to talk about,' Heather said. 'It's all very well you two talking about carrying out an assault in there and rescuing the hostages, but you seem to think that's our only way to address this situation. You're forgetting that you now have what this man wants.'

She was right about that. The moment Vern told us he had buried the disks out in the desert and where, I knew who had them. I instantly recalled Everest's metal detector, and Vigo's bumper sticker. Had to be one of them. I called the number Vigo had given us. She took some persuading, but when I explained that her life could be in danger if she held on to them, and that the lives of my ex-wife and daughter were in danger right now, she admitted to having uncovered them. After that, convincing her to hand the disks over to us was easy.

To save time we arranged to meet halfway. She gave us a suitable location and hung up. We took her at her word. She would either turn up or she would not.

As things worked out, Vigo kept her word. She handed the disks over with obvious reluctance, and the moment she let go she asked me to tell her the truth.

'Delta,' I told her. 'You made the right decision. You'll never know what was on these disks, but believe me when I say you should be glad of that. Some very bad people would have done some very bad things to you just for having them. Make sure Dale knows that, too. If people come looking in days to come, say nothing about it. Oh, and one last thing. Over the next few days, a package will be delivered to your local post office. It will be in your name as well as Dale's. You digging up those disks may have saved a life or two, so you've earned yourselves a finder's fee. I'll see that you receive it.'

When we drove away from the edge of a town that was smaller than a one-horse and whose name I could not pronounce, the woman was standing by her truck staring at us. She would never know how close she had come to real danger, though my guess was that Dale Everest would never let her hear the last of it for having given up their treasure.

On our way to Ruidoso to meet up with the sheriff and FBI agent, I called Drew and then waited for him to do his part. When he called us back he told us the instructions were for one of us to drive out to the Alto Reservoir, where we'd be met and further instructions provided. We were to come alone and to bring the package with us.

'It's a set-up,' Terry said immediately.

I agreed.

I thought about this as Heather's words tumbled around inside my head. It was not something I could easily ignore. 'I've considered the option of simply handing over the package as instructed. Believe me, there is nothing I would like more than to resolve this peacefully. But let's get real. This man down in that house had someone out hunting for Vern, had people watching the house back in LA, and then thought nothing of abducting a woman and a kid and holding them for ransom. Do either of you genuinely believe he's the type of man to carry out a fair exchange and allow us just to drive away afterwards?'

Crozier took a long, deep breath. As he exhaled he shook his head and said, 'Mangas Crow has a reputation that I understand is well-earned. He's known to act swiftly, and often with a terrible degree of finality. I think he has your ladies, Mike. And I don't believe he intends letting them go.'

'Heather?' I said, forcing her to meet my steady gaze. Her eyes glistened still, the lids red and swollen. Though overflowing with sadness at the loss of her agent partner, they were nonetheless captivating.

'Okay. In all honesty, if it were me, there is no way I would walk into that meeting at the reservoir. The most likely result of that would be I'd end up dead and the package would be heading back to this Crow asshole.'

'Can you get your SWAT team down to the reservoir? Surround the place and take down whoever Crow sends to collect the package?'

Nodding, Heather said, 'In all honesty I should be calling in HRT right now as well. I'm out of my depth, and this is their speciality.'

'Mike and I are not out of our depth,' Terry said firmly. 'I don't want a Hostage Rescue Team handling this while we have to melt into the background.'

'You call them in, Heather,' I said, 'and it'll be over before they even arrive. That's my ex-wife and daughter in there. I'm not putting their lives in the hands of anyone else other myself and Terry.'

With great reluctance, the agent nodded.

'Good,' Terry said. 'Then that at least is settled. We have to get them out of there some other way. So we need to settle on a plan right now.'

The sheriff made no reply, his attention elsewhere at that moment. I followed his gaze and nudged Terry, nodding for him to do the same. As we looked down upon the Crow residence, black clouds of smoke plumed out from the land beyond the house, deep orange tongues of fiery flame at their core. Crozier had his window down, and we could hear the crackle and pop of sap and burning wood from our vantage point.

'Damnit! Looks like someone beat us to it,' I said.

I thought of finding only Barclay back at the sawmill and wondered how Garcia had fared. Had he escaped only to carry out an assault of his own on the Crow house? Then my mind shifted immediately to Donna and Wendy. The level of danger they faced had risen exponentially with this unexpected turn of events. Before this, I was concerned at how Crow might react the moment he realised he was under attack, but also that my girls could get caught up in the resulting inevitable crossfire. Now that crossfire was a three-way split, and we were not in control of how it would play out.

Terry nodded. He tapped Crozier urgently on the shoulder. 'Let's make the most of the distraction, sheriff,' he said. 'Get us down there.'

THIRTY-FOUR

As CROZIER SPED DOWN the pot-holed road towards the Crow residence, Terry and I geared up. As the SUV cruiser burst out onto a more even surface we saw the entrance to the property straight ahead. Its wrought-iron gates yawned open. The crackling sound of rapid gunfire came to us on the smoke-tainted breeze. My guess was that the gates had been opened up by fleeing security guards.

'Don't stop!' I called out. 'Get us in there, as close to the house as you can.'

I thought that if all kinds of mayhem were being let loose inside, our chances of a successful entry improved if we hit the place at speed and made our way as deep into the wooded land as possible before having to leap out of the vehicle. The way Terry regarded me, he did not disagree. I thought of my ex-wife and Wendy trapped inside the property, knowing it was under attack, fearing for their lives. It ate away at my insides like acid.

The sheriff clipped the gate on the left-hand side as we hammered through the gap, breaking off his door mirror in the process. The drive had a serpentine curve to it; right, left and then a final right, taking us up to a wide turning circle with a round pond surrounded by rocks and plants at it centre. Amazingly we took no fire at all as we made it all the way up to a fleet of vehicles parked up outside the house. Flames in the distance were all but concealed by dense, black smoke. If this had been high summer then the whole lot might have already gone up by now, but the recent moisture in the air and the thin layer of snow that had passed through meant the trees were taking their time to burn, and winds were light so the fire would not spread quickly. What it *had* done was cause mass confusion, and that would be our ally.

The four of us exited the SUV as one, weapons drawn. Terry's constant mantra to me in the heat of battle was to always expect the unexpected, and I was in the zone now where nothing would take me by surprise.

'Sheriff, Agent Green, you take the front door,' Terry commanded them, moving forward quickly. 'Mike and I will find another way in.'

'Crow will have his best men surrounding him,' Crozier said. 'What do we do when we all catch up with one another?'

'Show them your badges. Tell them that they're under attack and you're there to help get them out alive.'

The sheriff nodded his approval. Heather said nothing, but she matched him pace for pace as they headed towards the semi-circle of stone steps leading up to a wooden deck and two heavy oak doors set into a porchway. I followed Terry as he hustled around the side of the house which was built right into the hillside, its front elevation much larger than the rear, where there was also a triple garage leading to a deep lawn and the woodland beyond. As we edged our way around the side of the stone and wood-clad building, Terry suddenly crouched low behind a trio of different coloured wheelie bins and raised a single clenched fist. I hunkered down behind him, peering over his shoulder.

On this side of the house the smoke was less dense and I could see no flames. The breeze was blowing down the hillside, but nothing had yet reached this far. I assumed many of the remaining patrol guards had been lured up towards the fire, from which direction the shots were also coming. The exchanges were infrequent, but they were persistent. Ahead of us, Terry had spotted two men wearing loose dark clothing, both clutching two-way radios and holding on to DPMS TAC 2 semi-automatic carbines. The two were focussed on the rear of the property, drawn by whatever action was occurring further along to their right and beyond the house itself. The fact that they had both been drawn in the same direction without checking their backs told me everything about them.

Terry turned to me and nodded once. The look in his eyes told me what the nod meant. These two armed guards would not hesitate to kill us, so we had to be prepared to engage them with the same conviction and lack of emotion. That would come later. For now, we had a job to do and would not turn away. Violence sometimes met violence head-on, and those who were left standing were adjudged the victors and the writers of history.

As he stood upright, stepped around the bins and launched himself forward once more, Terry scraped his boot across the concrete pathway that ran around towards the garages. I knew he would not have wanted to shoot the men in the back, and so had deliberately alerted them to our presence. Our own weapons now held in firing positions, Terry and I snapped off two rounds each at the men turning our way, and all four bullets found their intended targets. As he stepped over the two fallen bodies, Terry put a further round in each of the victims' heads. The old-style double-tap has become a triple-tap because protective vests are now standard issue. That final shot – always to the head – is primarily used to put the target down.

As we approached the corner of the building, I noticed for the first time a side door close to the angle. My mind imagined an opening leading from a utility room, which itself led into the kitchen area. Either way, I was certain Terry would choose this entrance into the house. I now followed him whilst turned sideways on, so that I could see both behind us and to our left. For all we knew, the garages were concealing further guards, perhaps sheltering from the gunfire they could hear going off all around them. As we approached the door I saw Terry readjust his grip on his weapon, and then his right hand slipped out towards the handle. As it moved, so did the door, swinging fully open in one swift movement.

Terry took a step right and slammed himself up against the wall behind the open door. I raised my weapon and waited for whoever had decided to exit that way to move into my line of vision. My finger was resting on the trigger guard, ready to slip into place. No matter who was emerging from inside the house, and irrespective of how well-armed they might be, I would have the drop on them and if I chose to fire they would be dead.

It was that simple sometimes. Especially if you always expected the unexpected.

Instead of combatants, however, two flustered women appeared from behind the door. Both appeared to be Native American, one middle-aged, the other much older, their flesh heavy and thick with wrinkles. As they turned and saw me, both let out loud yelps of surprise and alarm. I held a finger to my lips and shook my head, lowering the carbine.

'Do you work here?' I asked, taking a chance. For all I knew they were relatives of Mangas Crow, but I had a hunch they might be his employees.

The two women jumped a second time when they caught sight of Terry, but by now he had also lowered his weapon to become a less threatening presence. Nonetheless, the women looked anxiously at each other, then back at me. Their eyes remained fearful and neither made any reply.

'Do you work here?' I punched the words this time. 'If you do, just tell me what's on the other side of that door and where we can find Crow. Then you can go.'

Again the exchange of looks. Something more than words passed between them as the elderly woman nodded. The other one turned to me and said, 'We do. My mother cooks, I clean.'

'Good,' I said, offering a smile. 'We're not here to hurt you. We just need to know the layout inside and where Crow is.'

The woman laid it out for us. My assumptions had been correct. Through the door we would find a utility and wash room. Beyond that the kitchen and open-plan dining area, which in turn led to the guts of the house. The woman told us that Crow could normally be found in the vast living room, but was now almost certainly upstairs in his office where he kept a floor-to-ceiling gun case.

'Have you seen a white woman and her daughter in there today?' I asked.

The two women glanced at each other but said nothing. I felt it was important to find out. That way I would know if I had to ensure we took at least one of Crow's henchmen alive. 'Please!' I said more urgently. 'The woman is my wife. The girl our daughter. Please tell me if you have seen them.'

Again it was the younger of the two who spoke. 'Yes. They came a short time ago. He has them.'

I thanked her and pointed towards the garages. 'Wait over there in the corner, keep down and stay together. Whoever is out there shooting won't fire at you if they see you squatting there, but if you make a run for it they almost certainly will.

When the shooting stops, then you leave as quickly and quietly as you can. Okay?'

They both nodded and scampered across to the garage driveway. As they moved, two figures came around the side of the building and made their way towards us. I kept my rifle pointing down.

'No shifting those two heavy doors at the front,' Crozier said. Heather was behind him, edging sideways and checking their flanks exactly as I had done moments earlier. 'We tried the windows, too. No luck.'

Terry stepped away from the wall behind the door. 'Mike and I are going inside,' he said. 'Can you cover us from here, make sure we have an exit to use?'

The sheriff nodded. 'I can. But as the man with the badge I really ought to be going in there with you.'

'Me too,' Heather said immediately.

'There's a probable combat and hostage rescue situation inside this house,' Terry said, no emotion in his voice. 'Even if you two are trained for that, I doubt you will have done it for real as many times as Mike and I have. There are only four of us, and two need to remain out here to help protect our exit strategy.'

'Yet you were okay with us gaining entry through the front door,' the sheriff said, eyeing Terry shrewdly.

My friend hiked his shoulders. 'I guessed they would be locked and dead-bolted and you'd have no chance of breaking past them.'

'You might have said something.'

'You would only have argued, sheriff.'

'Two of each, then,' Heather suggested. 'One of us comes with one of you.'

'No.' Terry shook his head and was firm about it. 'We do that then we'll have two pair who don't know the other's moves. Mike and I can't be thinking of other people when the bullets are flying.

Now, I'm not asking I'm telling. Mike and I are going in. You can come or stay as you think best, but if nobody remains here to protect our route out, we may find ourselves without one.'

I felt my chest swell. Terry was good at taking charge. It was easy to forget that, prior to last summer, he and I had not fought together for a number of years. But he was right; two unfamiliar pairings made us less effective as a whole.

I pulled my shotgun out of its sleeve attached to my Bergen, and handed it to Crozier. 'Take this,' I said. Heather was already carrying her own. 'You might need more stopping power than your hand gun.'

I felt Terry tap me on the shoulder. 'Gear up for flash-bangs and smoke,' he said.

It took me a few seconds to remove the gas mask from my pack and pull it on over my head. By the time I turned, Terry was already heading through the doorway. I looked at the sheriff and Agent Green. 'We'll be back with our hostages,' I assured them. 'Buy us time.'

I had no idea if they could understand me beneath the breathing apparatus, but I thought they would get the message. With that, I followed my friend into the unknown.

THIRTY-FIVE

Terry tossed flash-bangs and smoke grenades into every area we entered. There was no resistance until we were in the main hall at the foot of the stairs. There, we came under fire from a semi-automatic weapon. The rounds went high and wide, but they held us back momentarily. The gunman was clearly unused to the rifle, and emptied his magazine within seconds, providing us with a gap in which he would have to pause to reload. Terry and I rose up at the same time from our hiding places, our aims more deliberate, the result more effective. We entered the next area stepping over the tattered remains of the body we had put down.

As we stepped past a tall square pillar, two men were coughing and weeping as they waved their arms around uselessly to fan smoke away from their eyes, which they would find partially blinded for a while yet. With the men disorientated by the sound as well as the flash, it felt a bit like shooting fish in a barrel, but we had no choice other than to put them away. I felt sure they would have done the same to us given half a chance.

We cleared the ground floor quickly. Through the wall-sized folding glass doors in the vast living room I could see the fire in the wood more clearly now, and although the treeline stopped well short of the house, small pockets of vegetation were also catching light, the smoke thick and climbing high. Somewhere out there gunfire was still snapping through the trees, and there was some rapid movement. Given the spread of the fire and the choking smoke rolling through, I did not think it would be long before everyone in the woods had to retreat from their entrenched locations. I heard dogs barking in the distance, the odd shout or cry of alarm. Thankfully, it was all taking place outside the house. Beyond the immediate area I could hear distant sirens.

I tilted my head to look up at the ceiling. Donna and Wendy were up there. I knew it as much as I could know anything at that moment. What I did not get a sense of was whether I would find them alive or dead.

I shut the thought away in a steel trap. I could not take it with me into the next skirmish, or the distraction might mean it was my last. Not knowing what awaited us was both terrifying and exhilarating, but I had to keep thinking positively.

As we headed up the stairway, Terry and I continuously swapped positions at the front, covering the steady movements of the other in turn. As we reached the landing there was a short burst of fire, and wooden splinters from the bannister handrail flew into the air around us. A couple of balusters were shredded in the same way.

Terry shot back and fell to one knee. I did the same beside him, covering our flanks once more. Terry tossed two more flash-bangs in rapid succession and we followed them as they exploded ferociously, our eyes and ears protected from the worst effects. That was not the same for whoever had shot at us, and as Terry took lead once more he rattled off two more rounds.

This time I fired the third, not even bothering to glance at the devastating results.

The third room we attempted to clear was locked. Given the hostage situation we could not fire through the door without knowing the layout inside the room beyond. Instead, Terry gave the lock a thumping kick, then stood to one side behind the wall. He had expected shots to come back the other way, but there was only silence. He did it again, but the door refused to yield. It was a sturdy timber construction, and the lock looked solid and new. He stood aside and allowed me to slip a breach charge into place, opting for the hinges as he had done back in Roswell. Ten seconds later the door blew inwards, despite the charges being relatively small. I knew the detonation would cause confusion and panic inside, and hoped to take advantage of that.

But when we stepped inside, our weapons raised and ready to fire, we encountered our first genuine headache since entering the house. A large Native American man stood behind two young girls, one arm snaked around them as he pulled tight, the other hand holding a gun which moved from head to head in swift succession. The girls were little more than children, and wore only thin, shapeless nightgowns.

Another native stood close by holding on to Donna. She, too, was pinned by a muscular arm, the tip of a heavy hunting knife jammed against her exposed throat. Donna's eyes were wild and moist, filled with panic and fear. Still my heart leapt – she was alive, and I had to hang on to that.

Book-ending them all stood two more large Native American men, both holding handguns pointed in our direction. My gaze drifted beyond them to a chair on which Wendy sat. She was bound and gagged, and even though she squirmed horrendously, those movements flooded my senses with joy and relief because each of them meant she was still alive.

'Put your weapons down,' the man holding the two young girls said, his voice not at all unsteady. It was a tone and manner entirely used to being in charge. 'If you don't, the woman and the kid die first. But these two get it next.'

My eyes flitted between them all. I noticed the figure holding Donna glance sidelong at the man who had just spoken. I had not spotted the man back at the Weather Balloon, so I did not recognise him now, but I figured this was our follower looking askance at Crow. The sheriff had told us his name was Joe Kane, and what I saw in his eyes made me think. I wondered if Terry had also clocked it.

Whether he had or not, Terry's instinctive response to the threat was to triple-tap the gunman to his left. Less than a second later I did the same to the man standing farthest right. Both men were thrown backwards, dead before they hit the floor.

Behind her gag, Wendy gave a muffled cry of alarm. Her squirms reached the point of convulsions. Donna screamed, as did the two young girls.

'That was to show you we are serious,' Terry said, as the loud echoes of gunfire died away.

'And you think I'm not?!' roared the man I took to be Crow, yanking more firmly on the terrified young girls who both screamed louder still and wept uncontrollably. Their cries were piercing shrieks of terror. As he pulled them closer he also ducked down a little, leaving less of his frame exposed. Now the girls were not merely bartering material, they were human shields.

Terry casually swung his rifle across, aiming for the man's head.

'You want them to die?' the man cried out. 'You think I won't do it then you carry on standing there ignoring me in my own home. They are disposable. They mean nothing to me. I can replace them with a snap of my fingers when this is all over and you two are long gone. If you want them to live, put your weapons down. Now!'

I noticed the other man – who I was sure had to be Joe Kane – slip his blade back into its sheath with great deliberation, and instead draw out a handgun. Donna wriggled in his grasp, her eyes focussed on me, but made no bid to escape. She had already submitted to her fate. I kept my focus on the man I believed to be Kane. There was something about him, buried there in the contours of his face, and in the deepest recesses of his eyes. Something that told me he was not about to pull the trigger on my ex-wife. The man was hard to work out, but I sensed there was a battle raging inside his head to which only he was privy.

'If those girls fall, you'll be the next to go,' Terry said to Crow, ignoring everyone else in the room. 'But we are your enemies, not them. Be a man and take the fight to us. Don't stand behind girls for protection, you fucking coward.'

I knew he was goading the man. The second Crow's hand switched the gun's aim from the girls to either me or Terry, his head would disappear in a huge puff of blood and brain matter. But not until he moved that gun, because Terry would realise, as I did, that Crow's finger could convulse and squeeze his own trigger even as he died.

I thought we were at an impasse, and my mind scrambled for an answer. Then I saw Kane's hand move, the gun come up. I put some tension into my trigger finger, but all of my instincts screamed at me not to squeeze it yet. I watched in mute fascination as the man holding Donna raised his gun and fired a single shot.

The girls shrieked and broke away from the Judge as he pitched backwards and toppled like a mighty oak, and even before he hit the hardwood flooring inside the office, Terry had put two more rounds into him. Clearly Kane had not anticipated Mangas

Crow reflexively pulling his own trigger as he died, because he had shot him in the head anyway.

Kane released his grip on Donna and raised both hands, allowing his gun to tumble to the floor. He and I looked at each other as Donna staggered away and slumped to her knees beside our daughter, her legs having given way to the flood of adrenaline and the sapping effects of shock. I thought Kane realised that I could have shot him before he pulled the trigger, but that I had given him the benefit of the doubt. I could not be certain, but it seemed to me there was an element of gratitude in his eyes. Along with respect.

I then rushed forward to remove Wendy's bonds, hugging my girls and smothering them both with as much love, affection and relief as it was possible to summon up. Not only were they alive, they were also unharmed. I had a feeling Kane would have had something to do with that. From the corner of my eye I could see Terry attending to the two girls, who had both swapped screams for moans of incomprehension and shock, checking the pair over for injuries as he attempted to calm them.

'I always knew this was the wrong place for Crow to make his home,' Kane said. 'This could never have happened on the res. There he would have been protected by more than guns. He would have had the defence of an entire nation at his fingertips. His ego killed him as much as I did.'

'Why did you shoot him?' I asked, standing upright again to face him.

'Business is one thing,' the big Native American responded. 'But using two of his own people as shields, protecting himself with two children he also abused...' Kane shook his head. 'I could not allow that to happen.'

'We have to get out of here,' Terry said to me.

I nodded. 'Will you take care of the girls?' I asked Kane.

'I will.'

'And you have no reason to come looking for us, none of us, right?'

'Not any longer.'

'You worked hard to find your man. I assume you were the one who told your boss that we had rescued Vern. Are you really happy to know that he walks freely away with us?'

'The man who ordered me to track down Vern Jackson is dead. I did my job by calling him from the mill, without knowing what he would do next. I did not know of his plans until I joined him here and then the two female hostages were delivered to us. I then followed my conscience. Take my gun with you when you leave. No one need know what I did here.'

'It's time,' Terry said again, more urgently this time. The wail of sirens grew louder outside.

I extended my hand to Kane, who regarded it with suspicion for a moment before grasping it. 'Thank you,' I said. 'For what you did here, you deserve our respect. You fight with honour.'

Kane gave a single nod. 'As do you. You are both warriors.'

'There's a county sheriff and an FBI agent waiting outside. They have our backs, but you might want to avoid them for the time being.'

Another nod, this time accompanied by half a smile of gratitude.

'You're a man of few words, Mr Kane. You and my friend here should start a club.'

Terry was now standing, holding on to Wendy who still seemed to be lost deep in shock even after being freed from the chair. It was understandable after all she had endured. Donna stood by our daughter's side, softly caressing her arm, whispering soothing words. The two young girls clung to each other. I turned to leave, and as I did so I caught a vague blur of motion from the entrance to the office. I started to cry out a warning, but it was already too late.

Five shots cut through the air, none of which were muffled by suppression. Stunned by both the noise and ferocity of the unexpected attack, it took me a few moments to gather my wits. When I looked up through the doorway preparing to fire back, I saw a figure now lying on the floor. All but the lower legs were hidden from view, but as I stared down I saw a familiar pair of snakeskin boots, toes pointing up. They were perfectly still.

Then someone stepped across the doorway, staring down at the same pair of boots. It was Heather Green. The FBI agent continued to look down at Garcia for a few further seconds, before slowly turning to me. Her voice was soft as she spoke.

'I caught sight of him entering the house from the garden. I followed him as quickly as I could. Either he or his partner killed Eugene, so I'm glad it was me who put the bastard down. I'm sorry if I was too late.'

I realised immediately what she meant. I turned to my right. Terry appeared completely uninjured. As did Donna, and the two girls now shrieking once again behind her, hands to their mouths, eyes wide and round. Wendy had crumpled to the floor, but she was sobbing uncontrollably and there was no sign that she had come to any physical harm. I continued to swivel, and as I turned fully my gaze fell upon Joe Kane who now lay on the floor alongside Crow.

His eyes did not lock with mine, however.

There had been five gunshots, and not all of them had been fired by Agent Heather Green. One round from Snakeskin had hit Kane in the stomach, the second in the heart. Blood had erupted from his body, but it no longer pooled or bubbled. The second shot had killed him within a beat or two.

He had been standing alongside me. I was certain that his life had been ended by bullets intended for me.

'We'll have to bring the girls with us,' Terry said, his voice as calm and even as ever.

I nodded. 'Get everyone out of here. I won't be a moment.'

In the silence of the room I heard the rush of water for the first time, and assumed there had to be a stream and a waterfall outside in the grounds. It was a soothing sound, and seemed so out of place amongst all this death and destruction.

Before leaving, I crouched by the side of the fallen Native American, reached out a hand, and closed his eyes. I took two quarters from my pocket and sat them on his eyelids. Not to stop them from popping open again, but to prevent the intrusion of insects. He did not deserve that kind of indignity.

Joe Kane had been my enemy, but had died an ally.

And a true warrior.

THIRTY-SIX

We drove in stunned silence until we were about halfway between the small towns of Angus and Nogal, coming up on a rest stop set into a ridge in the steep hills to our right. To our left the Sierra Blancas rose in the distance, their daunting snow-tipped peaks looking cold, uninviting and treacherous. Although we had all eventually agreed to meet back at the sheriff's office in Carrizozo, I decided I had to pull over to take stock. I was still shaking, and I had to admit that the emotional response to what had taken place was affecting me.

By the time the six of us had emerged from inside Mangas Crow's home, the shooting was all over. My guess was that Garcia had initiated the entry having initially caused confusion by setting the fire and then shooting at anyone and anything that moved. With no further instructions or command from the man with the snakeskin boots, I was pretty sure those with him had funnelled back and left him to his fate. These men were gangsters – if that – and would have no stomach for a genuine firefight. Their head gone, such snakes would wither and die.

I caught up with the others. Both Donna and Wendy fell into my arms, hands to their faces, weeping like they would never stop. We hugged it out. I held them tight, not uttering a single word. There was nothing I could say to either of them that would break through the horror unravelling inside their heads. All I could do was be there for them.

Crozier was waiting for us on the other side of the utility room door. A prone figure lying in a pool of blood several yards away on the stone patio bore testimony to the fact that our exit had been protected as we had hoped. Heather confessed to having fired the fatal shot before spotting Garcia, and she wore the pain of that uneasily. Crozier revealed that he had taken charge of the incident. He had allowed the firefighters onto the upper slopes of the property to do their work, but had kept the local PD encamped outside the entrance, the two female employees having already been escorted towards them.

'I got no idea how to explain away any of this,' he told us. 'But I sure as hell don't aim to sit here in Ruidoso being grilled by detectives. I can't keep them cops at bay much longer, either. So we gotta end this right now.'

It took us no more than a minute to come up with the next part of the plan. Green would badge her way out together with Donna and Wendy, me and Terry concealed in the back of her vehicle, while Crozier took the two young girls and filled the locals in on some of what had taken place. The idea being that the events both on the Crow property and back at the sawmill were now part of a federal investigation, and while the police and the county sheriff's office would have their say in matters, it was Green who held all the cards. She would drop us off at our Jeep, after which we would all head to Carrizozo. There we would meet up in Crozier's office as soon as he could get away, at which point we would devise a single strategy upon which we could all agree.

All very well in theory, but I also knew that despite us having rescued Vern from the clutches of the men back at the sawmill, we were going to lose him to the justice system before having the opportunity to question him further. There were things I needed to know before that happened. When Heather dropped us off at our Jeep, I persuaded her to allow Donna and Wendy to ride with me, and for Terry to accompany her. She took some convincing, but I was honest enough to tell the agent that I wanted to call Vern and have him open up about the past few days and the events leading to them – something I felt I could not do in her presence. The three of us headed out of town with Heather and Terry close on our tail.

After settling my nerves and waiting for my heart to stop smacking against my ribcage, I called Chelsea on the mobile number she had given me. She was thankful to hear from us, pleased to learn that Donna and Wendy were safe, and that same relief was evident when she told me Kelper was out of danger and had come around. He had a bad concussion and a few stitches in his head wounds, but looked all set to be released after a further forty-eight-hour assessment.

'Chelsea,' I said. 'You hold tight. I don't know how much you are in the frame for all that went down today, so when the police arrive – and they will – you tell them they need to speak to Sheriff Crozier and then you say nothing more. The sheriff is going to arrange for you to be brought over to his office, but the locals will get to you first and they are likely to try some intimidation. Don't buy into anything they try to sell you. Ask for Crozier and make sure his deputies stick around. Okay?'

She told me she was, and sounded clear-minded about it. I then asked to speak with Vern.

'Listen to me closely,' I said, looking briefly over my shoulder at Donna and Wendy who sat wrapped in each other's arms. 'You are clearly intelligent enough to realise that you are not going home today and maybe not any day soon. Now, I can prepare a story for your uncle and your mother, but I want to know the truth.'

'What more do you need to know?' he asked me.

'When you told me you'd put the money back using the laptop they stuck in front of you, was that only for the people who were holding you, or did you mean all the money?'

'All of it. Every last dime. I swear.'

'So their only concerns afterwards were the financial records you stole, plus the software that allowed you to carry out the scam in the first place.'

'That's right.'

'Okay. When you tell your story later on,' I said. 'You don't mention any of that. You hear me? Nothing about the disks at all.'

'I do. But how come?'

'Never mind. Let's just say that if it does have to come out, then it's better it does so from a position of strength.'

'I… I don't know what you mean,' Vern stammered.

'You don't need to,' I told him. 'Only that Terry and I have the disks, and that you and I will talk again. Now, tell me anything else I may need to know, Vern. And then I'll tell you exactly what to say when they come for you.'

THIRTY-SEVEN

The journey from the rest stop and the subsequent flight had given us all time to catch our breath and start the recovery process. Physically, we were all fine. Neither my ex nor my daughter had been harmed since being snatched out of their home, although at the point of the abduction, Donna reacted as any mother would and had received a back-handed slap for her troubles.

Emotionally, we were all over the place. Wendy held me tighter than ever, her head buried in my chest. Occasionally she would let out a sob followed by a low moan, and I knew she had been hit by a vivid memory. That was what living through such a terrible ordeal did to you; the elation at being alive and unharmed, safe and secure, in collision with the awful replay of things you had seen and the knowledge of what might have been. The disparity between the two sensations was vast, something the human mind was often incapable of withstanding.

Donna was mostly silent. Having boarded the plane, she and I had hugged and held each other for a long time. So long in fact that Wendy came over to wedge herself between us. I understood a little of what Donna was feeling, that dreadful sense of inadequacy that she had not been able to prevent our daughter from being subjected to the horror of abduction nor the witnessing of violent death at such close quarters. She needed the touch of another human being, someone to hold and be held by. I was more than happy to be that person.

Terry did his best to cheer everyone up when the silence became too oppressive, but his was a losing battle this time. Being the ex-wife of a Royal Marine, Donna was familiar with the stories of firefights, had been personally affected by such events when I was wounded. But now she had witnessed in all of its gory detail the shooting and killing of four men, each of whom would have caused a draught to brush against her flesh as they fell lifeless to the floor. It gave her a fresh insight into why I had not wished to discuss such incidents in the past, but the haunting nature of her new reality would not be welcome.

As for Wendy, I could only imagine how she felt at seeing her father gun down a man. I was responsible for only one of the four bodies we left back either in or slightly outside that room, but even though on the way out Terry had shielded her eyes from having to look at the other men taken down during our storming of the property, my daughter not only knew they were there, but also that some of them had died by my hand.

None of us spoke about the spatter on our clothing, though each of us had visited the Lear's bathroom to wash away blood and tissue.

At one point during the flight back to LA, Donna seemed to realise with a jolt that their ordeal was not over.

'Our home is going to be filled with police and FBI again,' she said.

I nodded. I reached across the narrow divide between seats and took her hands in mine, Wendy shifting with me as I leaned forward. 'They'll come. But I'll speak with Drew, and he can bring in a lawyer to help manage the interviews. But yes, they will want to speak with you both.'

'And between you, Terry, the sheriff and that FBI agent, you decided the story could be told without anyone owning up to knowing who you two were. Is that right?'

In the end we had not all met up at the sheriff's office as planned. Terry and I had decided that it would not be a good idea for us to be trapped inside that building should the FBI put in an unexpected appearance. Instead, we pulled over in a rest stop area along the way. I left Donna and Wendy sitting in the Jeep while the four of us hammered out an arrangement we could all live with. It amounted to both the sheriff and FBI agent dismissing us in their reports as merely two more men intent on raiding Mangas Crow's home. There would be no mention of our presence at the sawmill. When we were done, we shook hands with Crozier, and Heather gave us a hug and wished us luck. I liked them both, and believed they had the necessary strength and determination to pull it all off.

I had earlier related some of the conversation that took place between the four of us in Agent Green's vehicle. I nodded now at Donna's question, and said, 'It makes life easier for everybody that way. Neither Crozier nor Heather need to admit that they worked with us, and no matter who else was around to see us, like the two young girls, we'll just be two men amongst so many others who broke into that property.'

'And us? Me and Wendy. We're supposed to lie, too?'

I shook my head this time. 'I'm not going to tell you what to do, Donna. I think we all need to sit down to discuss it, Drew included. If we think it best for you to tell the truth, then that's what you do. Terry and I will figure things out. I don't want to put any further undue stress on you or Wendy.'

'I won't tell them Dad and Terry were there,' Wendy said adamantly, sitting up straight. She looked between me and her mother. 'I'm not getting them into trouble. Mum, they came all the way over here because we asked them to. They found Vern and they saved him. Then they found us and saved us, too. I'm not sure I'll ever sleep again after what I saw today, but I couldn't live with myself if I helped hand Dad and Terry over to the police. I just couldn't.'

I loved my daughter's spirit and sense of justice at that moment, but I was pained by her admission of how the events back in Ruidoso had affected her. Every time she closed her eyes she would see it happening all over again.

I knew.

I had been there.

I felt the bump and drag of the Lear's wheels dropping down. We were coming into land. 'Look,' I said gently. 'Nobody needs to make a decision right now. There is such a mess left back in New Mexico that neither the police nor the FBI are going to come knocking on the door tonight. And between us I think we can hold them at bay for any number of reasons until we are all much calmer and can think straight. So let's just go eat, then we'll head back to your place and figure things out.'

We ate at the In-N-Out burger joint on Cahuenga Boulevard close to Universal City, home of the movie studios. I chose it because I thought it might be the same place used by one of my literary heroes, Detective Harry Bosch from the series written by the author Michael Connelly. I understood how insane that sounded, and the look I got from Terry when I explained my choice, spoke volumes. But the place was thirty minutes from Van Nuys airport, and Drew agreed to drive over to join us there rather than pick us up at the plane.

Figuring I would need a vehicle if I was going to hang around for a few weeks, I rented one from a company close to the airport. The four of us arrived at the burger bar first and claimed a large curved corner booth. Wendy slid in beside me and wrapped both arms around my chest, her head resting on my shoulder.

'I missed you, Dad. I missed you so much.'

'I'd only been gone a few days.' I hugged her back and rubbed my nose against hers, something I had done throughout her childhood.

'I know. But even though you were only here for a night, you were still here and it felt as if that was the way things were going to be.'

I pulled my daughter close. She smelled clean and fresh and still so very young. Over her shoulder I looked at Donna, who gave me a nod and a shrug. Had she flown to England to see me, Wendy would have stayed with me knowing she was a visitor, understanding she would return home after a couple of weeks or so. My going out there felt different to her somehow. A more permanent arrangement, although I had suggested nothing of the sort. I could only imagine how hurt she would be when it came time for me to leave. I would make good on my promise to spend time alone with her, but this was her home, not mine.

Drew came through the door a moment later. After he and Donna had embraced and handshakes and smiles were offered all around, he asked us what we wanted to eat and then went up to the counter to place the large order. The food was good and fresh and plentiful, and my two cheeseburgers went down well.

Although I had provided Drew with the basic story before leaving New Mexico, the rest of us now had the opportunity to fill in the blanks. Most of them, anyway. Those we wanted to talk about. Others would never come to light if we had anything to do with it.

Donna took Wendy across to an ice-cream parlour: none of us thought it a good idea for her to be there while the story was told.

'So Vern is really guilty of this casino scam?' Drew said when we were done, a deep sense of betrayal squeezing his voice. 'He confessed to you both?'

'I'm sorry,' I replied. 'Chelsea van Dalen admitted to it first, and Vern's story almost entirely matched her own. There's no doubt in my mind that they did it together, but I have to say that so far Vern has been gallant, and has tried hard to keep her out of it. Provided those two say nothing, then she won't be charged. As for Vern, well, siphoning off money to the tune of millions of dollars means he will go to prison if he is found guilty. Which reminds me, have you managed to speak with him yet?'

'No. Neither has his mother. But while you were travelling this way, the best criminal attorney we could find at short notice was going in the opposite direction. Vern was instructed to remain silent until he arrived.'

'If it's any consolation,' Terry said, 'your nephew is in good hands. We formed a bond with the county sheriff and the FBI agent whose capable hands we left Vern in, and they'll treat him respectfully. They'll make sure he's not placed in general population until after his arraignment. If he makes bail, well then you probably have him for a year or so given the pace at which the law seems to function out here.'

'Thank you. That does make me feel better, and Sheryl will be grateful for everything you two have done. Which we'll come back to shortly. In terms of defence, how do you think Vern will play it? Because, in effect, no money was stolen at all.'

'In effect,' I replied. 'But not in the eyes of the legal system, I'm afraid. Just because the money was returned does not negate the fact that it was stolen in the first place. If they can prove that, and prove he was behind it, then he's in trouble.'

'What about other charges?' Drew asked.

'By and large, mainly it was bad guys who were killed during the past few days, but the FBI will be looking for a reason why their agent was shot to death. Then there's also Al Chastain's murder, although the police will have found his killer right there beside his body. I honestly doubt whether any of those casino owners will volunteer to step forward and make allegations against Vern. But perhaps the biggest thing in Vern's favour right now is that there is not a trace of this software having existed. He told me it was designed in such a way that the moment the install file was run it disappeared, but equally if it wasn't run it couldn't be copied without an encryption key.'

Drew was clearly puzzled by this. 'So if the casinos got their money back and the software is no longer around, why were these men still holding my nephew, why did they then snatch Donna and Wendy after you two rescued Vern?'

I shrugged. 'Because like most people, Vern has an ego. He was proud of his work. So proud he could not let go of it completely.'

'He kept his own copy.'

'He did. Not only that, but he also kept financial records stolen from the casino servers that they would much rather were never revealed. To them he became more than a thief, Drew. He became a threat.'

'So how will that change? Surely he remains a threat provided that information still exists?'

'We have that covered,' Terry reassured him. 'In whatever statement Vern makes to the police or FBI, he will insist that no copy exists, that he lied about it in order to buy time during his abduction. Agent Green will release that information, or at least make sure it is released.'

Drew was shaking his head. 'I can't help wondering if that will be enough. Will these people take the chance, when all they have to do to fully protect themselves is make Vern disappear for good?'

'That is a risk he has brought upon himself,' I said. 'The thing is, Drew, these men have their money back. Their sole concern now if they don't believe what the FBI statement says, may still be that Vern somehow still has access to tax-related data which could ruin them if the IRS got hold of it. That puts Vern in their crosshairs. But equally, they will ask themselves why Vern would ever release that information. No good could ever come of it. The only thing such a move would achieve is to put a target on his back once again. I think they will also have another concern. That if they take Vern for a one-way trip out into the desert somewhere, his absence or death might trigger the very thing they are afraid of: the appearance of that data. Cool heads will prevail, I think. I'm not saying for sure that Vern will be entirely safe, only that I believe these people will arrive at the same conclusions Terry and I have.'

'That sounds right. Hopeful, at least. Thank you both again. Sincerely.'

I waved his gratitude away with a smile and a flippant hand gesture. 'You're welcome. Your nephew may just have got lucky this time.'

'He was lucky you and Terry were around to save him. And I was lucky that you were around to save Donna and Wendy.'

'We were all lucky there, Drew. We had some help along the way, but luck always plays a bigger role than you might expect.'

We fell into silence then, the knowledge of how bad things might have been suddenly overwhelming us.

THIRTY-EIGHT

Donna and Wendy rejoined us at the booth. Donna squeezed her husband's arm as she sat down. She smiled at me and Terry, a little defensively I thought.

'Wendy and I heard the men at the house talking about a major battle at the abandoned sawmill where Vern was being held,' she said, looking pale and drawn. 'It sounded terrifying.'

At the mere mention of the incident, Wendy pulled herself into me again. I grabbed her chin and tilted it upwards, staring into her beautiful eyes.

'Kiddo, you don't have to worry about me now. I'm here, those other men are not. I had training and experience on my side, plus your Uncle Terry in my corner. He's like the Hulk when he gets going. No way he would let anything bad happen to me. And I must be getting better at it, because last time I ended up wounded and this time barely a scratch. That's a good thing, right?'

I pictured two different gunmen aiming their weapons at me. I blinked them away.

Wendy nodded. 'But what about next time?' she asked me softly.

'Who says there has to be a next time?'

'Isn't this what you do now?'

That brought me up short. It was a question for which I was wholly unprepared, because it was something I had not even considered asking myself. Was this what I did now? If so, what the hell *was* it exactly? Drew would pay Terry for his time, though I would refuse payment if it was offered. I had done my ex-wife and her husband a favour. This was not a living. I had no plans to make it so. But then, I had no plans for the future at all.

Or could Wendy be right? Was this something I now did? It was how Terry made his way in the world, and had done now for many years. While I was in Scotland making myself feel better, I had not planned anything beyond the time and place in which I found myself. Since being here I had not looked further ahead, either. There had been little time to consider anything beyond the moment. But now, Wendy's observation felt as if it had an almost suffocating importance. Not only concerning the rest of my life, but my daughter's also.

While I was considering all this, Drew took a call from Vern's attorney. When he was through, he explained how co-operative the sheriff and FBI had been, but that bail was in doubt due to the death of the FBI agent. Whilst all concerned accepted the shooting had not been engineered by Vern, and that at the time he had clearly been a victim, the entire process may well have occurred because of him. Or at least, that was the charge they were putting together. The conversations were ongoing, and the lawyer had promised to get back to Drew as soon as he had the final word.

'It's such a shame for everyone involved,' Drew said, looking around the table. 'That young man had such a bright future ahead of him. Now all those people have lost their lives. And I must apologise to you both, Mike and Terry. I had no idea I was putting you in so much danger. I thought we were asking you to find a missing person, not put your lives on the line.'

I raised a hand. 'That's okay. Things spiral out of control sometimes.'

Terry nodded and jerked a thumb in my direction. 'What he said.'

'Well, thank you anyway. You'll both be compensated, naturally.'

This time I waved my hand. 'Let's discuss that later, shall we?'

'Of course. You must both be tired and looking forward to getting a decent night's sleep. So, Mike, if I've pieced it all together correctly, I take it you have the disks?'

'I do. I need to ask Vern what he wants done with them. If it were me it would be a toss-up. One part of me would want them destroyed. On the other hand, if anybody ever comes asking in the future, it would be good to still have something to trade with.'

'If you want, let me take care of them. I can lock them away in my safe.'

Terry shook his head and said, 'You might want to reconsider that offer, Drew. As Vern's employer and the boss of the company responsible for installing all that software, the FBI may yet serve a warrant on you to go through your house and business premises.'

'You're right,' he said. 'I hadn't considered that. Of course, that would be a likely move on their part. Perhaps you two should hold on to them for now.'

Right then was the moment the penny dropped. At first I assumed I had to be wrong, that I was being ridiculous. I thought back, replaying the conversation. I felt sure I was recalling it accurately. I had no idea what it meant, but I intended finding out.

'Drew,' I said. 'Do you mind if you and I have a private word about the compensation side of things?'

'Of course. I could do with a cigar, so shall we step outside for a few minutes?'

I agreed. I stood and said to Terry, 'Play nice with others while I'm gone.'

Wendy giggled. Donna laughed. Terry looked sidelong at me and flipped me two fingers.

Outside, Drew was already lighting up, smoke coiling upwards from the fat cigar he held in his hand. Traffic trundled by us in a nose-to-tail river of steaming metal and hot tyres. He nodded at me and said, 'Whatever you and Terry want, you only have to name your terms. You not only found Vern as we asked you to do, you saved the lives of three people who are precious to me. That is priceless, Mike. Priceless.'

'Good to hear. But before we get into that, do you mind answering a couple of questions for me?'

'Of course not. Fire away.'

'Thanks. So when was the last time you actually spoke with Vern?'

'The day before he left to go on vacation.'

I nodded. 'You didn't manage to speak to him earlier today, then? Or last night?'

'No. I thought I mentioned it before. They would only allow him to speak to a lawyer the moment they knew one was flying out there.'

'That's what I thought. And you did mention that earlier, yes. So in that case, Drew, do you also want to tell me how you knew about the disks?'

'What?'

He was good. The look of bemusement seemed almost genuine.

'Well, Vern told me the only person other than him who knew about the disks was his friend, Bruce. Not even Chelsea knew he had them or had buried them. You admit you haven't spoken to him, and listening to your side of the conversation with his lawyer, it wasn't discussed when they met, either. So, given Vern has been out of touch since he left to go on vacation, how could you possibly know about the disks?'

'I… you must have mentioned them. Earlier, you remember, when you told me about the copy.'

I shook my head. 'No. I distinctly remember telling you there was a copy, but I didn't say what it was stored on, nor how we had acquired it or from whom.'

'Well, then I suppose I just assumed it had been copied to a disk.'

'No, I don't think so, Drew. I'm far from a technical geek, but even I know that most people these days would assume the files had been copied to the cloud. Thing is, Vern knows the cloud is susceptible to hacking, so still relies on the old-fashioned method. He also wanted to ensure it was in one place and one place only, and that it required physical interaction in order to make use of it. He was pretty clear about that. Nobody mentioned a disk earlier other than you, Drew. Not only that, but Vern kept a backup of the copy, which meant he buried two disks. Plural. Which is precisely what you keep talking about. *Disks.* Care to explain that to me?'

It was hardly definitive, but the verbal slip had given me reason enough to question him about it. The rest relied on my ability to read him correctly. And having done so, I now knew I was right about him.

He looked at me for a few moments, studying my expression. Seeming to reach a decision, he tossed his cigar to the floor and stood with both hands on his hips, shaking his head.

'You're going out of your way to protect Chelsea from being prosecuted,' he said. 'I think that's because you realise how events conspired against her and Vern, and she wasn't entirely responsible. As you alluded to before, provided everybody sticks to the same story then she has nothing to worry about. I see no reason why the same should not go for me. Even if your suspicions about me are well-founded, Mike, do you really think it's in anyone's best interests for my supposed complicity to be made public? After all, other than a slip of the tongue, what evidence do you have of any wrongdoing on my part? And do you really want to put Donna and Wendy through the upheaval these so-called revelations of yours would cause?'

I drilled a hard look through the man. 'You're playing on the fact that I would not want to rock the boat for my ex-wife and my daughter. You sure that's a gamble you're willing to take, Drew?'

'I'm not a gambling man, Mike. Whatever you may think of me right now, I know you will see the sense in what I say. If I had a part to play in any of this, who benefits from that becoming known? Nobody is worse off as things stand, and that situation won't change.'

'How about Vern?' I argued. 'If you put this together and he's taking the fall, then I'd say he is worse off as a result.'

But Drew was shaking his head once more. 'Even if hypothetically speaking you are right about me, you're wrong about who put it all together. I would say you need to strongly consider the fact that Vern brought the whole thing to my attention, and I just gave it the nod. Again, hypothetically speaking. You follow me, Mike?'

I followed it right enough. It was all kinds of wrong, but he knew what he was talking about. If he had simply allowed Vern to go ahead, then he was culpable but no more so than Chelsea van Dalen, perhaps even less so as he had not contributed any of the scamming code or technical input. His was an act of pure greed, no more. Certainly there had been no malice intended. He was also correct in his assumption that I would recoil at the prospect of tossing a grenade this powerful into his marriage, given the aftershock would blow right through my own daughter's life. A life she clearly loved and did not deserve to lose.

'You had all that wealth,' I said. 'And you risked blowing it by taking a cut from a little bit more.'

'You can never have too much money, Mike. The only people who believe otherwise don't have any to begin with.'

'You'll owe me,' I said to Drew, thinking about the gangland boss back in England who also owed me a debt I had yet to call upon. 'I want nothing financial from you in return for what I did for you here, but Terry will need paying. Fifty thousand ought to do it. Pounds not dollars. Plus there are a couple of people in New Mexico who could use five grand each. Then there's an FBI widow who may need a decent care package in the near future.'

'And you?' he asked, nodding his agreement to my demands. 'What is your payment going to be if not money? You must want something, Mike. Everybody wants something.'

I thought about it for a moment. Although his smugness irritated the shit out of me, I could not deny that he was right.

'Partially that my daughter continues to live the good life, and my ex also gets to keep her marriage intact. Other than being a cheating, conniving thief, you're not a bad bloke, Drew.'

'Thank you.' He gave a weak smile. 'So what's the other part of the debt?'

'Your gratitude. Which I expect you to deliver on whenever I may need something from you at any time in the future.'

'And you will have it. Whatever it is, whenever you ask.'

I shrugged. 'I hope Vern's lawyer is good enough to dig him out of a hole. When all the dust settles on the events that took place out in New Mexico, it seems to me that provided Sheriff Crozier and Agent Green keep their word, there really won't be a great deal of evidence against your nephew. I think he could make a go of it with Chelsea. I also see for myself now that Donna and Wendy are happy here, so you already have that covered. I'm not quite sure about my own future right now, but it'll be good to know that I have someone with money and influence to call upon if I need help.'

'You can count on it.' Drew held out his hand.

I stared down at it, left it hanging there. 'We're good right now,' I told him. 'But not that good.'

He withdrew his hand and spread them both. 'So what now, Mike?'

'Now? Now I enjoy the rest of the evening with my daughter, spend some time with her as a guest of her stepfather, take a trip with her and have some quality time with only the two of us to worry about. After that… well, as usual, I haven't thought that far ahead.'

ACKNOWLEDGEMENT

To my family and friends and everyone else who has championed me, please know that I will be forever appreciative. The same can be said for my fellow authors who have demonstrated kindness and friendship over the past few years.

There are too many bloggers and readers to thank individually, so I hope you will all accept one massive group hug. Your generosity and devotion to the written word is truly humbling.

This was a book I had no choice but to write. At the conclusion of *Scream Blue Murder* I simply had to take one more ride with Mike and Terry. I don't yet know if it will be the final journey with them, but never say never – I have a third story, all I have to do is find the time to write it.

Cheers all.

Tony – March 2021

You can sign up for my newsletter at:

tonyjforder.com

Printed in Great Britain
by Amazon